The
Black Book
of
Gyffe
(The Fribbling Squit)

Rupert Owen

For Katy, William, Rupert, Cesar, Xavier
and my Papa.

AUTHOR NOTE:

Much has changed since the dolmens went up. The machine we so readily prepared ourselves for is well underway and I fear I cannot see it through to the end. Looking back, those centuries were frivolous in comparison despite the brutishness and the odd stench. It is useful that you have this account but do not let it temper your investigation of the underlaying mechanisms at work. My old master used to say, "If you want to know a person's mind, ask them to remove their hat." I never quite understood what he meant but there may be something in that.

I hope I have not underplayed my role in the great event. I have sought to be wise where wisdom is due, be frank where truth be told and most of all be matter of fact where fact mattered. To be honest, I have tried my best. It now lies with you to take it from here. I have watched, listened and thought from my armchair for many years but have had little hwyl to go back there again, although, I know this world and the other world is synergising. It is only a matter of time.

In any case, bear with me as I leave you my last thoughts. I know it's not much, pennies even, but there may be something in it. Your legs are springy, your mind is keen, perhaps I am missing something?

Much love.

G

Cardiff 1978

CHAPTER ONE

It was on the 3rd day before ides, 1409.

The sky cast a gloomy shadow, and bruised clouds soared across the horizon's visage as if fanned by the wings of a snared dragon; a fettered beast making one last ditch effort to break free of its gyves and escape to the heavens.

'Long live the King,' shouted a voice.

'Get some sleep,' shouted another.

Footprints forged in the dust, from tumbling round shots which had shattered the great walls, began to splatter away with the oncoming squall. Streaks of blood, cut upon the blades of grass, drizzled into the muddy soil. The wind still carried the faint lingering scent of sweat and excrement, sated only by the top note of evening primrose, an afterthought to the sanguinary carnage that laid bare the carcass of a gutted castle.

'Long live the ...'

'One more peep out of you and I'll ...'

However, despite the spent temperament of the day's foray, someone was moving swiftly through the exhausted encampment as night descended, as if, by false prophecy, a rufous squirrel, foretold of hazel dieback, went nuts. The fraying twine from a tethered rope squealed from the urgency of a sharpened dirk. The nickering of a released steed was hushed enough to equal the general nuance of the night's uneasy recline.

'Long live … '

'I'm warning you.'

It was not a sigh or the heavy laden clop from a horse's hoof that stirred one shackled prisoner, but the fierce rumbling of a needy stomach louder than a cornered badger's snarl. This sonorous hunger pang caused the prisoner to haul himself up and crawl to the flaps of the tent. Peering uneasily between the heavily drenched folds, he just made out the silhouette of an old crone lifting herself up onto the profile of a horse. The shadowed form bucked and then vanished into the veil of rain. The extremity of the departing vision, only an extended arm raising a two-fingered salute to all and sundry of the sodden campsite.

'Long - '

Thump.

Six years later …

Tucked away at the top of a wooded hill, above a deep rivered gorge, at the end of a disused drover's road, was a sign. Etched on it was the time-worn name, The Knucker's Knest. It swayed from a breeze that wended its way through the branches of the surrounding trees. In addition to the words was a faded illustration of a dragoyle. Its outstretched wings seemed to flap as the sign rocked and with the occasional creak, it appeared to wail into the night.

'Hoo-hoo-hoo-hoo,' cooed an owl before fluttering to the ground and transforming into a cloaked figure.

The domicile attached to the sign was assembled from roughly piled sandstone, an attempt at orderly masonry, formed in the vernacular of a small tavern. The greying-straw thatched roof, like a crudely cut tonsure with a chimney shaped wart on top, was concealed amongst a dense thicket of hawthorn and hazel.

The cloaked figure made its way to the tavern door. It knocked three times. A postal hatch opened, and a voice called through it.

'Password?'

'Capital aitch, five, lower case gee, double-u, bee, nine ... asterisk.'

'I'm afraid I can't let you in, incorrect password.'

The cloaked figure grasped its hips and turned its back on the framed pair of lips.

'Embarrassing, I've got a brain blank.' The cloaked figure spun around. 'Is it upper case gee, lower case aitch, double-u, bee, nine, five ... asterisk?'

'Um, not quite,' said the mouth, 'need a hint?'

'That would be helpful, go on.'

'Could be the twenty-seventh letter of the alphabet, perhaps.'

'Ah, capital aitch, five, lower case gee, double-u, bee, nine ... and is it ampersand?'

'That's it,' said the voice.

The cloaked figure sighed with relief.

'Now, what's the memorable word?'

'Oh, for crying out loud,' the cloaked figure mumbled scratching its head, 'it is … it is … nope, it's gone now.'

'Close enough, it's lethologica, don't forget that the memorable word is forgotten at midnight, so for next time you might want to, make a note of it.' Then, the voice behind the door quivered in a magisterial timbre. 'Come, shelter yourself from cold and wind, take comfort in camaraderie found within. Seek knowledge and wisdom from friends and foes but most of all … please be courteous to the neighbouring wildlife and keep the noise level to a minimal gone the witching hour. You may now enter.'

The door unlatched, and the cloaked figure slipped inside. The modest interior featured a large hearth at the end of a single room, exposed beams stretched along the ceiling and decorative bracing held each corner. There was a small pot-bellied stove to one side which had upon it a cast iron cauldron containing a gently simmering rich green liquid of rich green. The grassy odour wafting from its contents likely signified that tonight's special was borage soup. At one corner of the room, a rough-hewn oak counter jutted out. The equally misshapen shelves behind it were stocked with tinted glass jars and bulbous terracotta pots containing various substances for the use of potions and spells. These were aligned in no particular order and had labels, written by a somewhat shaky or careless hand. Labels denoting such contents as Shrew Sniffles, Vetch Winkles, Unpredictable Pickles, Yawning Zest, and Cobbled Trots to name but a few of the less odd sounding ones.

'Hoy, you there!' The cloaked figure leered at the youth behind the counter who was arranging herb bouquets in alphabetical order according to toxicity. 'Is you not Spindle Tarcrust? Squittling Frib to the elemental mage Grinwort?'

The youth finished tying up the bundle of bittersweet and hemlock before placing it on the herb shelf under "D" for deadly; particularly for pythonesses and hypothesisers.

'No, that's not I, I'm Gyffe, a squit, fribbling mainly. What can I do for you?'

An audible harrumph grunted from the cloak. 'Well, in that case then, I'll have a hedgerow pie and a tumbler of mead.'

The order was fetched and placed before the cloaked figure who took a deft swig of mead. 'Getting prepared for the pilgrimage then?'

Gyffe did his best nonchalant wipe down of the counter before answering. 'We'll see.'

'Fence sitter then?' The cloaked figure laughed, took the tart and mead, and located a vacant table amongst the hubbub of cabalism.

The room was brimming with gentlemen and womenfolk of the Independent Order of Magi. Passwords were uttered, the door rattled, someone would enter, a draft followed, someone would leave, a gust of warm air at their heels. Nods were exchanged, chairs scraped, muffled murmurs and sneering chuckles resonated throughout, steam and smoke rose from soup bowls and pipe chambers, eyes flitted in suspicion and alliance, and at intervals a snore would join the cacophony when a magi, whose belly was brimming with wine, dozed off. So went the ebb and flow of the establishment. These were the comings and goings of the dewin, magic folk who had travelled the length and breadth of time across the four continents to trade their secrets, swap recipes, try new brews and indulge in idle gossip.

'Fence sitter indeed.' Gyffe scoffed, 'what does he know about squits and fences.'

Here, but to name a few, were the swynwyr, wyzen, shamans, healers, onmyŏji, conjurers, rheibwyr, witches, common mages, seiðr, sorcerers, enchanters, wand bearers, and least but not foremost, fribbling squits; who attended their masters and mistresses needs, mostly by keeping out of the way.

'Parapets on the other hand.' Gyffe was trying to look engaged in what he was supposed to be doing while attempting to notice everything else going on around him. 'Parapets are another matter entirely, we like sitting on Parapets. We often fish off them.'

Gyffe was particularly attentive to one corner of the room where a meeting was taking place, although the interaction between the two involved betrayed a complete lack of consequence, the meeting was actually of great significance.

'Haws,' grated a dishevelled old warlock.

'I beg your pardon?' said Gyffe unplugging his focus from the meeting.

'Two mugs,' grunted the warlock slapping down several precious gems.

Gyffe fetched the hawthorn berry wine, 'here, have the bottle.'

'Thanks kindly.' The warlock snatched the bottle and hobbled back to his table.

Gyffe returned his focus to the corner of the room where sat a mage opposite a bent figure whose shadow, against the light of the hearth, cast a repellent profile. The mage's purpose that evening was to affect a profound change to the known world forever. However, by all appearances, he looked more befitting a candidate capable only of changing, at the very most, his socks. He wore a weathered hat with a tip drooping disappointingly in the wrong direction. From its brim wept tousled locks, whence two knobbly ears poked out prominently either side. A patchwork cape, fastened around his shoulders with a brass clasp, draped to the floor. The seam of the cape soiled and frayed by countless years brushing across the ground and caught under foot. However, other matters were now far more pressing, and despite the dire condition of his apparel, the socks would wait.

Ought to find a more advantageous spot. Gyffe seized the opportunity and idly began collecting tankards and soup bowls. He floated from table to table until he found himself near to where the mage sat. At an adjoining table he hovered before Asphodel the Blind, who took an unprecedented time to lift his spoon from the bowl to his mouth. Gyffe noted that there were at least four more mouthfuls to be had and therefore at least twenty minutes before needing to collect the dish. He hovered in anticipation and was all ears.

'Haven't finished yet, squit,' said Asphodel with a gulp.

'No hurry,' said Gyffe, 'take your time.'

Behind Gyffe, the mage sat contemplatively at the table attempting to pluck a cluster of cleavers from his trailing grey beard. He glared expectantly at his companion, a haggish woman wearing a thick hooded cloak.

The mage finally spoke. 'The Rainmaker, if you please?'

She produced a whetstone from a small leather bag tied to her waist. The stone, if dipped in pansy oil, was used for sharpening a black bull's horn. Once stropped, the horn, raised like a beacon, lured the lunar cow into prompting the clouds to direct a downpour. At least, that was the explanation given for the mysterious properties of the stone.

'Very well, you shall have it.' The woman duly handed it over. As she slid it across the table, it rasped against the grainy wood causing a faint smack of thunder to be heard in the distance.

The mage took a cursory glance towards the sound. 'Careful,' he said.

'It has been a faithful ally.'

The mage mindfully pocketed the stone. 'Indeed, and as a result, you have given the wet weather a nationality all of its own.'

'Aye, the English call it Welsh weather.'

'And the cloak,' said the mage.

'Can I not keep it until I have found refuge?'

The mage wiggled his fingers in expectation. 'The garment served its purpose when you were seen not to be seen, now if you are not to be seen, you must be seen not to be.'

Both sat in silence for a few minutes, chewing over the mage's words.

'Still, I would like to hold onto it for a little while longer. In the art of concealment it is indeed powerful magic.'

'Technically it's a meta-material using negative refraction,' said the mage under his breath, 'however, for now there are still plenty of trees to hide behind and I expect that along the way there will be some aid in assisting you to find refuge despite the revolt being quashed.'

'In any case, cannot I not just hang onto it for a wee few more days?'

The mage let out a heavy sigh. 'The return of these gifts will reward you more than the gifts themselves could ever do.'

'But ...' began the woman.

'To be honest,' said the mage, 'I'm surprised you've managed to hold onto it thus far. It is not unusual for a person to remove such a cloak, only to be at a loss to where they put it, a drawback of its *magical* property.'

The woman hauled the cloak from her back revealing an affected hunch, which was achieved by a pillow tied to her back with coarse twine.

'If you please, the cloak?'

She hesitated. The mage reached out and made a grab for it. As soon as he touched it, it vanished.

Gyffe, who was still standing patiently by a hovering spoon awaiting a landing between Asphodel's lips, twisted slightly to see what all the fuss was about. All he could make out was the mage and the old hag appearing to be having a slight tug-o-war with thin air.

The mage suddenly jolted backwards as the woman let go, and then with an absurd flurry of his hands, he appeared to fold and roll the thin air before stuffing it into a basket by his side. He paused, reached back into the nothingness, then produced a besmirched rag.

'Ah, my handkerchief,' said the woman taking it and giving her nose a quick dust.

'One should always check the pockets,' the mage said, also passing over a Nine Men's Morris counter, a chewed ball of sap, and several coins.

Once the cloak had been removed, her more ill-favoured features came to light. The mage swallowed his revulsion politely and took a moment to adjust to the sight. 'You may keep the pillow though. I'm sure it has other uses such as the conjuring up of sleep. Something I imagine you have much to catch up on.'

'Sleep is for the dead,' said the woman obscenely curling a lock of her hair around a thick knuckled finger.

'Well, it is of no use to me, send it to the fire. I will cast some magic upon its downs to grant you safe flight upon your departure.'

The woman untied the pillow and with a toss managed to hurl it into the flames. The mage closed his eyes and muttered a spell as the feathers crackled. The sudden roar of the fire invited some attention, but it was mostly the noxious smell that stimulated most to cuss and cough simultaneously.

'What a stink,' cringed Asphodel, 'some silly goose forgot to pluck the grouse again, did they? Unfortunately, being blind, I am unable to have a gander at the culprit.' Asphodel chuckled to himself.

Gyffe reached for Asphodel's bowl.

'Haven't finished yet.' The final spoonful quivered before his mouth. Gyffe watched the spoon tilt and its contents drain between two wobbling lips.

'Finished?'

Asphodel picked up the bowl and let a pliant tongue run its course around the interior. 'Am now.'

Gyffe took the bowl but before he could hurry away, he felt Asphodel's steely grip on his arm.

'Tell chef,' Asphodel growled, 'that was one of the worst soups I've ever had here.'

'She won't be pleased,' said Gyffe, 'it's one of Ma Gwrach's recipes.'

'Oh,' said Asphodel releasing his grip, 'in that case, tell chef, that was the worst soup I've ever had here.'

Gyffe groaned in affirmation and scurried back to the counter. He turned his attention to organising an odd assortment of bottled compounds and powders, granules and flakes. He resumed his observance of the meeting, noting that the sight of the two sitting together exposed a somewhat unsettling courtship, although the mage, Grimoire, his master, was confident all magic must be relinquished for now. Gyffe had a niggle, and squits took niggles very seriously, that by doing so, other branches of knowledge would cause a far greater detriment. At the distance he stood, Gyffe struggled to follow their words. It dawned on him that he was holding a pot of preserved lugworms. Lugworms when mixed with the dried resin of seashells, and cast upon in the appropriate way, created a substance when put into the earhole could pick up sounds from great distances. Gyffe quickly performed the task and stuffed the mixture into his ears. At first he couldn't hear a thing and accidentally served an enchanter, corpse brine, instead gorse wine. Eventually, his ears were able to hone in on the smallest detail of sound around the room.

'Anything else?' said the mage glancing away to allow the old hag thought for the most prized of the last remaining magical artefacts. For a moment Grimoire caught Gyffe's watchful gaze. The firelight thrust itself from the rounds casting a diversion of shadows. Gyffe bowed his head ever so slightly but kept his ears pricked.

The woman reached for her face. 'Only this ...'

Grimoire watched patiently as the woman raised her hands to her head, they hesitated and trembled ever so slightly, with all fingers cast about her countenance they pressed hard against the skin. The hands then moved away carrying the haggard features with them as if holding a face beyond a face. The facade was delicately passed over to the mage.

'An improvement,' said the mage who took the mask as if it had been no more than a borrowed quill.

It was at this point clear that the woman was not some hideous hag but a brawny male with a combat weary glint in his eye. The mage plonked the expressionless mask in the basket. The man opposite now seemed to consider his predicament afresh. His eyes were resolute, his cheekbones high, the bristles on his face, still apparent, but more pronounced. He gave his cheeks a good scratch. 'Gets itchy anyway.'

Gyffe recognised that the man sitting opposite was Owain Glyndwr, the gentleman rebel who had led the revolt against the English.

The exile now regained the posture of kingly eminence. 'What now? The uprising has failed, my men in hiding or hanging from a rope. I am either wanted or repelled, and each desire only leads to death. '

'The uprising was necessary,' said Grimoire, 'to preserve in secret the order of magic until it needs to be summoned again and stabilise the ancient realm of Annwyn.'

'Ah, I have heard of it,' said Owain, 'it is the stuff of legends.'

'Well, it's actually an unreal interpretation of universal wave function,' said the mage under his breath, 'this is just one part of your journey, as with Arthur, you must rejoin your fellows as the essence of their spirit ... their limitations and abstractions must become yours, as your vision of unity became theirs, so too must theirs become yours.'

Both sat in silence for a few minutes, chewing over the mage's words.

'I fear that, during my absence, the King shall exact revenge on my people.'

'The King would be unwise to cut off his levy to spite his tax, so therefore the revenge he seeks lies solely with you. As a representative of your people, it will be vengeance enough.'

'What if he obtains your magic and uses it for his own gain?' said Owain.

'That is doubtful,' dismissed Grimoire, 'they are reworking the ideas of magic, through the sciences. My kind of magic will become a principle of the past. It will be the apparition in the apparatus.'

'So all that is magic, is finished?'

Grimoire cast a look around the tavern's muddled magical assemblage. 'Every person, every animal has a seed of magic within them. Some will germinate, others not. Spiritualists will carry on the magic of their gods, scientists, the magic of the cosmos. People who favour the idea of a reality to the point of all exclusion will still turn to the magic of illusion.'

Owain hung his head for a moment as if allowing the burden of the mage's words to drain away. 'On that note,' said Owain suddenly, 'I will leave you to your rumination and bid you farewell.' Owain stood before the mage and extended his hand. 'I will be forever in your debt.'

Gyffe watched the rebel make his way through the crowd. Before Owain could reach the exit, a dark sorcerer intercepted. The sorcerer glared with eyes so dimly pallid that Owain retreated, but he soon steadied himself, avoiding showing an affront to the threatening figure. The sorcerer's fingers, mere wisps, clawed at the air with curled yellowing spirals. He leaned in close to Owain, his mouth a solid knot of ageing cells encasing a cluster of serrated teeth.

'Can I help you?' Owain held his ground.

The sorcerer snarled. 'So, wolf, before you return to the pack there is something I must ask of you.' The sorcerer widened his eyes for a moment seeming to drink in Owain's full visage.

Gyffe wondered if Owain's legacy might end sooner rather than later. He heard the man chant something with a brythonic lilt under his breath.

The sorcerer dimmed his thickly pasted eyebrows and whispered into Owain's ear with a tongue lapping at the shoreline of its mouth. 'That evil eye stuff doesn't work with me for my eyesight is so poor that any vexatious curse I desired would be about as effective as a banshee auditioning for a male voice choir.'

Owain started to move past the sorcerer but that hideous hand halted him in defiance.

'Look, what do you want?' said Owain.

The sorcerer handed over a parchment along with a stick of charcoal. 'Would you mind giving a wee scribble on this parchment? I collect them.'

'What's this? Some sort of trickery.' Owain pushed the parchment away.

'He does you know,' interrupted a nearby sorceress, 'it's a right pain, can't take him anywhere. Anyone even close to infamy gets served the stick and scroll.'

'They'll be worth something one day,' The sorcerer sounded almost hurt.

Owain took the parchment, and the sorcerer leaned back with a satisfied grin, his hands locked together in the courtship of achievement.

'Dim problem,' said Owain as he scribbled his signature. He handed it back and pushed past the sorcerer. In response to the brusqueness, the sorcerer attempted a shrug but instead did a sort of jump, in his saggy skin, without leaving the spot.

'Thanking you,' said the sorcerer tucking away the scroll.

Mostly, the kabbalistic throng ignored Owain's parting. There was a sense of exigency and consternation consuming the room. Gyffe could feel the fixity of purpose as he watched Owain slip out the door, taking one last look at the rabble of magic folk, before disappearing into the night air. Gyffe returned to his duties. He had by now sorted and re-sorted the same amount of powders over and over again while observing the occurrence. Grimoire appeared at the counter and landed his basket down on it.

'Put these away will you,' he mumbled.

Gyffe cupped his ears. 'Ow, no need to shout, I've got lugworms in my ears.' Gyffe grabbed the basket and hid it beneath the counter and then shook his head side to side to remove the substance.

'You really are quite a nosey squit,' said the mage not unkindly.

'I'm sorry Grimoire, the occasion was too momentous not to behold.'

'And so you did. I might add however, rather that you should have been holding your attention to my groundings and granulates. You've spectacularly managed to muddle them all up.'

'Oh dear, how careless of me,' Gyffe said.

'Oh dear Indeed, you've muddled columbine talcum with horseradish snuff and put puffball paste with fermented medlar. It's a complete mess. You really must pay more attention to what you are doing at this moment, rather than watching history go by.'

'I will try.'

'Yes, well, we'll settle for that shall we? That's the trouble with you squits, too curious for your own good. It will no doubt get the better of us one day.'

'Us?'

Grimoire attempted his best irksome face before hobbling off to a seat by the fire. Gyffe for a moment watched the mage take out a pipe, light it and thoughtfully gaze into the hearth. Heeding Grimoire's words, Gyffe returned his attention to the botched mix of ingredients. He was indeed a curious kind of fellow. Consequently, it wasn't all that unusual that he found himself, by intentional clumsiness, overhearing a conversation between the sorcerer who had intercepted Owain and the same gloomy sorceress.

'That's another one on the list dealt with. The order thinks it can get away with damming serious spell crafters for the sake of pettifogging divinations and pompous prophecies.'

'What of the mage? He ought to be dealt with,' said the sorceress.

'His time will come. I will make sure of it.'

Gyffe swept up the last remaining fragments of crock dropped within earshot of the sorcerer. He then returned to the counter where a wrinkly witch was impatiently raking her blackened chewed fingernails on the wood.

'Tarts,' screeched the witch.

'I beg your pardon?' said Gyffe.

CHAPTER TWO

Just about all fribbling squits had pokey nosey attitudes towards life. In one sense it was of benefit because it meant they observed a great deal, whereas, others in their more woolly ways were liable miss as they went about their day to day. However, it did have its downside. This prolific preoccupation as to the unknown meant that the known quickly became redundant. So, it was to pass, that Gyffe having only just overheard the worrisome exchange a few hours ago in the Knucker's Knest, completely forgot to tell Grimoire when they arrived home. Hours had passed since Owain's visit to The Knucker's Knest. Grimoire had not mentioned anything more about it and, instead, busied himself with packing. Gyffe's oversight was exacerbated by an indescribable object he caught himself fondling without any deduction as to what it might be exactly.

'This looks interesting,' said Gyffe examining the oddly shaped item made from an unfamiliar material.

'Ah now that is interesting,' said Grimoire looking closely at the object, 'I've never figured it out. I found it amongst the odds and ends in a box of whatnots, it's called a Perplexity and I believe that its sole function is to bewilder the possessor as to exactly what it is.'

Gyffe put down the whatnot only to pick it back up again. 'This looks interesting,' he said examining the object once more.

'And it does that kind of thing. Cursed of course. The further you try to ascertain its purpose, the more uncertain you will become. Put it away.' Grimoire snatched the whatnot and tossed it into his bag.

'What's this?' Gyffe held up a small plain blue box.

'That's a Forget-Me-Not Box,' said Grimoire taking it and putting it into his bag, 'whatever it is you have lost, open the box and you will find it there.'

'What if you lose the box?'

'I have two,' said Grimoire holding up a second small blue box, 'one will find the other.'

Gyffe was gracile with a rather large head that rested on a long neck like a poppy on its stem. He wore the customary fribbled tunic, dyed dark moss green, the stitching in the brocade fashion, patterned with high buckled kobicha boots over tight black leggings. On his head was the signature squit hat cut from a single piece of canvass which rose to a sharp thin point at the top with floppy flaps coming down to the neck at both sides. His eyes were a peridot green and on his chin poked out a tufted goatee the squits called a wagger.

'And this?' Gyffe passed over a black band with an adjustable buckle.

'This,' said Grimoire in demonstration as he tightened it around his head, 'is a Wit-bit. It monitors brain activity, providing the wearer with accurate information on brain activity, measuring the shrewdness of ideas, counting epiphanies and intrusive thoughts, interpreting dreams.

That sort of thing.'

'Is that what it's doing now?'

'No,' said Grimoire, 'it's broken. Imitation Myddfai tat, only used it once during a rather prolonged cerebrated soak. Claimed to be waterproof, wasn't.'

Gyffe was a typical fribbling squit. Squits were lesser magic folk who would often serve as apprentices to wizards, mages and sorcerers. The reason for this is because amongst themselves, squits considered each other to be equally unequal. It meant that if one squit was seen to be serving another squit, it was the squit being served who was subservient to the one doing the service, and vice versa. Furthermore, this resulted in no squits being able to either work for, or indeed even help, each other. So alternatively, relationships were sought after with races whose clear definitions on hierarchy satisfied the equivocal pecking order of the squit.

'You'll notice, Gyffe.' Grimoire bound desiccated lavender and camomile in a silken cloth with a night sky pattern. 'Everything has its place. And you are no different from this soporific posy, which if placed at the feet, would bring me no more rest than a boot fitted to the head provides the invigoration of a brisk jaunt.'

Gyffe, without putting effort into their meaning, took a moment to let Grimoire's words discharge from his mind. He looked about their well lived-in dwelling. Over the years, he had imagined he might grow old and wise here, well at least, in theory the former might beget the latter. The living quarter was snug enough, it had a door to the left leading to a circular library and Grimoire's study. Beyond that was a kitchen. Cast iron troughs for preparing vegetables, a table carved from a single slab of stone, a spacious larder and a ceiling overcrowded with pendulous baskets, full of dried herbs and spices, dangling from hooks screwed into a weave of bendy beams.

Gyffe handed Grimoire a box of engraved toothpicks. As he did so, he held back the desire to sulk at being left behind. 'How long should I wait?'

'Nothing has been set in stone, until those chosen have been set to be set, in stone.'

Once again Gyffe offered the opportunity for Grimoire's words to make an exit before even beginning to consider considering them. 'And your work? The Sworn Book of …?'

'All up here,' said Grimoire tapping at his head, 'and were I to lose my head, no matter. I intend to leave all my notes with you. In time, you may decipher their meaning and it will be up to you to ah, cultivate the knowledge.'

Gyffe was well aware of Grimoire's notes. He recalled many a late hour of writing, bringing the mage mugs of piping hot oyster mushroom soup. He'd stood before the great stacks upon the desk. He'd heard the furious scoring of nib against paper, or else, Grimoire scratching himself.

He'd even roused the mage with smelling salts after finding him slumped over his desk, his nose gently bobbing in the ink well. The study was wedged in-between the living quarter and kitchen hearths. This placed it between the backs of two rising chimneys which through the gentle emission of heat helped to preserve the many books and scrolls from dampness. It was a modest repository for such a learned mage, with only just enough room to swing the most comprehensive catalogue of conjuration.

'What if you are chosen?' said Gyffe.

'For the equinox? I cannot be chosen. For one, I am beyond my years. Us more antique mages don't preserve so well. We tend to ferment after a while.'

This was certainly true. Grimoire at times effused that slightly fusty odour familiar to mages of a great age. Physically, Grimoire was hardy, but he was anything but spry. Gyffe remembered all the times he'd heaved Grimoire up the willow ladder that led from the study to the upper architrave which acted as a narrow ambling walkway around the second level of the abode. The walkway led to Grimoire's private quarter, bathroom, observatory and spell chamber.

'And it must be four elemental magi, either sorcerers or wizards. Each of the magi must represent the order of the dewin. I am a mage, I do not belong to any order, I belong only to magic.'

'In that case, why not leave everything as it is?' said Gyffe.

Grimoire hesitated, he seemed to be deciding whether or not to pack the palm of an antler. 'Although, I may not return for quite some time.' The antler was put aside.

'That's to be expected. You'll have to get to the cabal in the first place. There'll no doubt be a lot of pomp and ceremony. After ritual drinks? Then there will be the goodbyes and the usual machinations. All preceding the wearisome journey home.' Gyffe sighed as he expectantly awaited concurrence to the itinerary he had just laid out before Grimoire.

'No,' said Grimoire bluntly, 'by that I mean for some time I may never return.' Grimoire picked up the bone remnant again and, with some degree of awkwardness, stuffed it into the bag. 'You must prepare yourself for that non-eventuality. You must relocate all our worldly goods to the abode below, and with them, yourself also.'

Gyffe had been listening quite clearly to what Grimoire was saying, but for all intents and purposes, he had neglected to hear what Grimoire had just said. 'Do what?'

'All this, all this … stuff,' Grimoire said waving his hands about the general vicinity of everything he possessed, 'it must be moved. It must be hidden.'

'Below?'

'Yes, beneath this dwelling, to the enveloped remains of Crach Ffinnant's abode, sunken by saltpetre, now dormant in its crypt.'

'Alone?' Gyffe shuddered at Grimoire's last choice of word, crypt.

'Not completely, as you'll have Patch, whose company is as warming as a ray of sunshine through the cavum of an endless cloud.'

Gyffe looked at the solemn dollop of Patch, a grizzled hognome, cradling a walking cane as he snoozed in a rocking chair beside the fire. Every now and then Gyffe observed that Patch would chuckle to himself, as if dreaming of being imposing and towering instead of titchy and squat. The chuckle would degenerate into a snigger, presumably signifying the downfall of an imaginary adversary.

'And don't forget, you'll have the esteemed companionship of Crinkum also.'

Gyffe looked up at the hunched dragoyle. It was squatting on its brass perch, which was suspended by tufted ropes fastened to a high beam. Crinkum held a half eaten rodent in its claws. It was trying to grill the remains with regular but gentle spittles of fire. The dragoyle paused to acknowledge its audience before popping the gobbet into its jaws and with bared teeth, gnashed the splintering bones and slurped up the stringy entrails.

Gyffe winced at the sight while Grimoire turned his back on the display with a harrumph.

'Possibly, a passing wizard or two might drop by, although, few rarely use the underground river anymore.'

'Are you sure you want to leave Crinkum behind?' said Gyffe.

Crinkum was a dark purplish dragoyle, a metamorphic reptile

transformed from shale and Grimoire's familiar spirit. Gyffe watched in disgust as Crinkum sucked at the pulp like a hardboiled sweet and then spat the remnants of the demolished carcass into the fire.

'Sadly it has to be so …'

Gyffe noted, with a subtle frown, the addition of the word 'sadly'. He considered the favouritism inordinately unbalanced.

Grimoire continued. 'He is my eyes and ears to this world and indeed the underworld. He, too, must stay here to continue to fulfil that purpose and with you, of course, as my … er … hands and feet.'

Worryingly so, but not without an attempt by Gyffe to block the thought, appeared the image of Grimoire's gnarly chaffed feet. These were feet replete with random shags of hair that clung to them like lichen, and the occasional cluster of sulphur tuft fungi that found enough humus between the toes from which to sprout. Grimoire resumed busying himself by poking objects into his carry bag, as best a fit as he could squeeze, without popping the seams.

'Why can't you just leave Patch here with Crinkum? He is your retainer after all.'

Grimoire buckled himself upright placing his hands on his hips. He bent backwards in the shape of a bow which made him look like an aged weeping willow. Gyffe heard a succession of pops making their way down the bendy spine.

'Yes, yes, but look at him, Patch has been beyond the age of retainment for nearly fifty years now. When that became apparent, I didn't know what to do with him. It was either send him back to his kin or keep him on as a sort of symbolic retainer. If I sent him back, they'd only send him back again. Damaged goods you see.'

'But what makes you think we will be safe? I know only a smattering of magic, Patch can hardly hear nor see and Crinkum, although quite capable in conflict, does not always think first.'

Grimoire gave Gyffe a stern look. 'Trust me when I say that Owain has made it safer here in Wales. Anywhere else, and you would find yourself on the pyre.'

Gyffe understood that the Marches of Deheubarth, Gwent, Glamorgan, Gwynedd and Powys would hold the lore of magic and covert its practice with the least degree of persecution. Even though the newly anointed King showed a disposition towards the Church and had proclaimed his victory over Owain as the work of God, it did not necessarily mean he would take a stance against the rites of the magi. In any case, Owain had achieved just the right amount of self-governance to offer reliable refuge. But yet, Gyffe still felt a false sense of security, especially as Grimoire had packed his favourite porridge pot.

'But will it remain so?'

Grimoire shuffled over to a cabinet. He pulled a chain, and the front dropped open. He reached for a bottle of whortleberry wine, popped the cork with his finger and poured three goblets full.

'Dear Gyffe,' said Grimoire as if about to compose a letter, 'tell me what is it that concerns you most? That I shall be gone or that you shall be alone without me?'

He passed one of the goblets over to Gyffe who cradled it with his delicate fingers. He tapped the pottery gently with one of his long tough nails. It made a dull clink.

'I am worried,' said Gyffe taking a sip of the wine, 'that despite all our best efforts we'll suffer the same fate as ...'

'Best efforts?' Grimoire growled.

'... As the Nine Witches from Gloucester,' said Gyffe shielding his impudence once more with the goblet by taking a pronounced sip.

'They had it coming,' said Grimoire taking the third goblet over to a heavily rugged couch where slept a youth. 'Something for when our unexpected guest awakes.' He placed the goblet beside the sleeping figure and returned to the last remaining goblet which he lifted to his lips.

'Lechyd da.' Grimoire drained the contents.

Gyffe looked uneasily at their houseguest and wondered why Grimoire so readily took in strays. There was too much to be done without the added burden of an interloper. The library would have to be sorted, and only Grimoire could reason with the many documents and books requiring classification before going into storage. Gyffe, therefore, decided he would make himself useful in the area he was most familiar with, the kitchen.

'I'll be taking only the necessary tomes …' said Grimoire creeping away into his study. Before disappearing through the door, he popped his head out towards Gyffe who was still standing cradling his goblet. 'The rest will be boxed up securely. You may, of course, keep the light reading material and comics.'

The door to the study closed with a particularly satisfying thud. Gyffe heard Grimoire sighing with all the relish of someone slipping into a warm bath or sliding into a cosy bed.

Inside the library, Grimoire scanned over his vast collection. On his desk was a piece of writing. 'Ymddiddan Myrddin a Taliesin, recounted as best I remember at what he said at the time. Must send this off for inclusion before I leave.' Grimoire rolled the parchment and tied it with a thin strip of leather.

The many shelves housed books that Grimoire had collected over the centuries, Herbaceous Alchemy, Don't get Mad, Get Cursing, The Already Red Book of Soothsayers, Make Charms, Not Arms, Gerallt Scire's Spells On-the-Go, The Craft of Wand & Staff Making, Ars Notoria, Liber Juratus, The Complete Cauldron Cookbook, The Bound Book of Spellbinding, The Pocket Edition of Potions, Abramelin's notebook, Monchyn-y-nant, and the magic book of Cwrtycadno. These were some of the more notable codices in his collection.

'How to Spell? Not a title I am not familiar with.' Grimoire flicked through the pages. 'Oh, it's one of Gyffe's orthographical groat dreadfuls. Strange that it should find its way here.'

Grimoire began the slow process of removing each book selectively with a gentle dust down as he did so. He stacked them neatly inside a row of chests all fixed with a sturdy lock. 'Ah, Picatrix,' he stroked the astronomic talisman embedded in its cover, 'the enlightened's raison d'être, not one for Gyffe, yet.'

In truth, he wasn't worried about Gyffe advancing his magical abilities. His main concern was that if Gyffe's curiosity got the better of him, he might end up on the wrong side of a spell. 'Might cast himself into a hairy shield bug and be trod on by Patch.'

He picked up a rather tatty notebook bound in the hide from a boar. 'The Sworn Book of Grimoire Clapfart, one of which I have yet to complete due my ongoing services to magic, and one I should think hard about entrusting Gyffe with. For the time being,' he said tucking it under his belt, 'it shall remain on my person.'

Grimoire had taken the precaution of making sure his most prized collection of books were locked safely away. He felt confident that Gyffe could equally sate his thirst for knowledge reading such volumes as Lesser Charms for the Magically Challenged, Idle Incantations, and The illusionists Handbook. A book of which he was unsure actually existed, although in every respect was always seemingly present among the others. He'd also allow Gyffe access to The Voynich Manuscript, minus

Grimoire's translation.

'Domesticus Magica: Timesaving Sorcery for the Busy Wizard or Witch, that one goes in the Gyffe pile.'

Along with these, Grimoire had included some other reading material suitable for Gyffe to pass the time but not alter it. There were many letters and scrolls of a personal and professional disposition which would also be kept under lock and key. The chests would be too weighty for Gyffe to haul down to the derelict building below and so Grimoire would have to summon them down using a reasonably functional transportation charm from the modern Latin school of magic, *subcinctus consequentia.*

The kitchen was a right old mess and Gyffe had been spending an extraordinary amount of time trying to pair Grimoire's collection of love spoons according to compatibility. He also found himself brushing up shards from a damaged window inconveniently used as an exit by Crinkum and was about to unify a set of stacking caldrons when he heard a crash from the other room. A gust of cold air brushed across his skin. He went to investigate. The front door was wide open, and on the floor were broken pieces of a goblet with a stain of whortleberry wine streaked across the rug.

'Took off … just like that,' said Patch gently rocking on his chair as if in perpetual pursuit, his bristly eyes mimicking that of two startled hairy caterpillars. 'Gave chase, no good, boy too quick,' he added.

Patch wriggled earnestly beneath the knitted throw across his legs. It appeared he had not shifted from his chair at all. It then occurred to Gyffe that Patch might have indeed intended to pursue the boy, but by the time he thought it, the quick-footed boy had already legged it leaving Patch still simmering with intention.

'At least you tried.' Gyffe closed the door. 'And to be honest, his presence was making me feel uneasy.'

Left behind on the couch was a tightly bound scroll. Gyffe examined it and saw that the seal on it was the mark of Henry V. Gyffe's hands began to wobble, not because the seal was royal, but because he was a fribbling squit and squits were indeed curious creatures.

'Let me see,' said Patch authoritatively.

'Nothing to see.' Gyffe turned his back on the hognome.

Anything hidden, sealed, coveted or locked away was fair game for a fribbling squit, and Gyffe was no different from any of his other kind. He rubbed his thumb thoughtfully over the wax imagining it wearing thin and the scroll uncoiling in his hands. What could he do then? He'd have to take a look. He squeezed his legs together and gritted his teeth. Suddenly, the scroll was no longer in his grasp.

'I'll take that,' said Patch, grasping the parchment.

Gyffe was at once startled and annoyed at how quickly Patch had managed to catapult from his chair.

'I wasn't going to break the seal, I was just imagining what might happen if it did break.'

'Can't trust squits … with seals.'

'I'm afraid you will find that that is a fallacy. Despite the attribution of the phrase "dying to know" to the inordinately high percentage of squit fatalities, it is a little known fact that most squits follow a strict exercise regime in strengthening the will.'

'Call it what you like,' said Patch with a grumble, 'can't trust squits … with seals.'

'Let me take it to Grimoire.' Gyffe casually snatched at the air in the hope that his hand and the scroll might meet.

Patch stepped away hugging it tightly. 'I give to Grimoire.'

'Very well, we'll both take it to Grimoire,' Gyffe said, 'each of us holding one end.'

'I'll take it to Grimoire,' said Grimoire snatching the scroll.

Grimoire's sudden appearance elucidated less of a surprise on the faces of Gyffe and Patch than the smug satisfaction that neither would deliver the scroll. The mage snapped off the seal and unravelled the parchment.

'*Rex omnibus, ad quos et cetera, salutem …*' began Grimoire reading aloud before falling silent within the print.

'And?' piped up Patch who knew full well that he was doing Gyffe the favour of asking the question.

'Well, a knight' began Grimoire, 'who goes by the name of Gilbert, has been deputised to communicate and negotiate with Owain of Wales … et cetera et cetera.'

'Gilbert? Not much of a name for a knight is it?' said Gyffe.

'I think young squit that his knightly title far exceeds any opinion one may have in respect to his forename.' Grimoire returned his attention to the parchment.

' … *De et super certis materiis* … and so on … to offer themselves to our obedience and grace, and, in our name, to admit and receive all things, each and every deed and action which may be necessary to the matter … and so forth … *promittententes nos ratum, gratum, et firmum habituros* and whatnot … witnessed by the king at the royal castle et al.'

'Sounds like typical regal rhetoric,' was all Gyffe had to say.

'That is beside the point,' said Grimoire, 'this is a treaty. Whether in earnest or not; I cannot say. What I can say, is that the intended recipient has long gone, as too the courier of its pardon.' Grimoire motioned to Crinkum who all the while had been as motionless as a statue. Dragoyles tend to be this way when resting. Crinkum lifted one eye and without so much as a fluttering of its wings soared down to perch upon Grimoire's shoulder.

'Please try not to scorch this, as it cannot resist fire.' Having stated the obvious, of which dragoyles frequently require, Grimoire rolled up the scroll tightly and handed it to Crinkum who took it carefully in one of its claws. Crinkum sniffed at the scroll inquisitively.

'You must deliver this personally to Owain Glyndwr who is likely to be lying low somewhere.'

'Without the pillow on his back he may even be almost unrecognisable,' added Gyffe unhelpfully.

'That is a chance we have to take,' said Grimoire.

Gyffe felt quite proud of his observation, and Grimoire's sarcasm was wasted. The banter had bypassed Crinkum altogether who was thinking of the result a smattering of flame might have upon the parchment.

'Can I help?' asked Patch whose height often left him out of conversations between people who were taller than him.

'Yes, you can open that door, save us another pane in the glass caused by Crinkum's uncouthly departures. A habit that reflects the same inability birds have at not recognising that translucent matter may possess an unexpected solid quality .'

Patch hobbled towards the door. Gyffe, noting Crinkum preparing to launch, had gotten there first. The door was swung open to circumvent yet another evening spent picking shards and splinters of glass off the floor. Crinkum took to the night, his form barely visible against the darkened sky as he flew into the distance.

'I shall need to guide Crinkum on his way. Patch be a good fellow and pop outside to fetch me a few bits and bobs for an augmented sight spell.'

Grimoire turned to Gyffe. 'Now Gyffe I shall need you to prepare a place for me at the table. I have noted the steps you will need to take on this piece of paper.'

Gyffe took the folded instructions. 'Part of the spell?'

'Err, let's just say it's an essential component to the manifestation.' Grimoire hastily brushed past Gyffe and headed towards his study chamber. 'Don't forget, a spell is only as effective as the person casting it.'

Gyffe stroked his waggle in order to elucidate a look of contemplation at Grimoire's wisdom and to disguise the bafflement he was experiencing within.

Upon reaching the door, Grimoire had to wait until the chests, now bearing many tiny feet, made their way out of the room and down the hallway. One chest was lagging behind, its feet palmated like a duck causing it to hobble with an unsteady wobble. Grimoire folded his arms impatiently until it had passed. 'I'll get that charm right one day.' He entered the chamber, slammed the door shut and bolted it.

Gyffe turned to Patch. The hognome, basket in hand, was already half way out the door. 'Make haste little friend,' Gyffe said, 'for if Owain does not get the treaty, much travesty shall ensue.'

Patch glared, turned up his nose, and slammed the door behind him.

'I meant old chap,' called out Gyffe, 'no, I meant stout fellow, oh, never mind …' Gyffe about turned and disappeared into the kitchen.

CHAPTER THREE

Inside the chamber, Grimoire scanned round the room and noted the shelves had all been cleared and only one chest remained. It was the chest of books Grimoire had reserved for Gyffe. He slammed down the lid and proceeded to climb the ladder that rose past the shelves. Once at the top, he was able to scramble onto the narrow gallery leading around the entirety of the loft. He hurried along to the observatory tower. When he came to the door, he gently placed his hand on the wood and softly announced …

'ᐱᐯ◊ᚱ'

It unbolted from the inside. Grimoire stooped to enter. He sat down on a swivelling stool fashioned from the pelvic bone of a cockatrice. In front of him was a cast iron yoke and sticking out from a slit in the tower roof was a brass cylinder with two refracted glass eyepieces. Just as he had settled himself on the stool, hand on the yoke and eyes pressed against the eyepiece, there was a cough at the door.

'Ah, Patch, you are just in time.'

Patch crept into the crouched space with a basket containing all the necessary items to cast an augmented sight spell. Feather of screech owl, mucus of leopard slug, a posy of night phlox and a handful of gwyllgi droppings.

'Ahem,' said Grimoire fluttering his fingers in expectation, 'the truffle?'

One truffle was reluctantly handed over, these being a favourite snack of hognomes. Patch retreated quietly clipping the door behind him and pocketed the other truffle before scampering down the gallery.

Grimoire dropped the ingredients down a tube which was connected to a potbelly boiler crisscrossed with a scrambled connection of wire. He placed his feet on the foot pads below. He adjusted his face to the eyepiece.

The boiler sputtered and wheezed, wobbling and groaning as Grimoire began pedalling. Between huffs and puffs, he cast the enchantment.

'✓✔◣⅄'

Through the eyepiece, the dull twinkle of stars became apparent in a swill of foggy cloud. He now could see what the dragoyle saw. Crinkum's eyes glowed an azure blue, entranced by Grimoire's witchery, as it flew through the night sky.

'Dive, dive, dive,' cried Grimoire thumping down on the foot pads.

Crinkum darted low through a webbed shadow of branches. A white owl dashed across Grimoire's field of vision.

'An omen? Is Owain close at hand?' Grimoire shunted the yoke forward.

The Dragoyle took a nosedive down a narrow gorge where the crags glistened in the moonlight. Ducking and weaving through collapsed boles subsided by the measured erosion of the earth. Twisting and turning, it sped along a river until reaching a shallow estuary where it took a sharp turn across stretches of blotted marsh.

'Just a little bit further ... easy, easy ...' muttered Grimoire wiggling the yoke.

At last, Grimoire spied a speck of fire in the distance. An anthropoid shadow flickered against the shielding cliff face. The dragoyle was still too far away for Grimoire to be certain.

The mage felt a tickling in his ears. 'Could this be Owain?' He pressed hard down on the yoke.

Crinkum thrashed its wings and shot through the air like a black comet. Grimoire swivelled the yoke and Crinkum started swooping above what was now clearly a disturbed figure scrambling in the underbrush.

The man looked up, pulled out a sword and swung it loftily above his head. 'What devilry is this?' he barked.

Grimoire yanked back the yoke. Crinkum swerved to avoid the swing.

As it did so, an unfortunate nightjar, going about its business of foraging mealy grubs, collided with Crinkum. The poor bird veered off its trajectory, bloodily wounded and its appetite forgot.

'Curses, a knock-back from a nightjar, just a nick though, it should recover. Ought to try and talk some sense into the man,' Grimoire positioned a hollowed ram's horn to his mouth. 'Listen to me Owain, put down your sword.'

Crinkum, who was still spinning from the collision, managed to eventually steady itself by fanning its wings. It then proceeded to yowl a yowl as some sort of plea for the man to stop. But the man only recoiled at the sound and swung the sword with even more brute force.

'Translation decoder is on the blink again.' Grimoire blew hard into the ram's horn releasing a dust cloud. Pressing the tip of the horn to his lips, he spoke again, 'we mean no harm.'

'Waah-eek ... we ... mean ... waah-eek ... we ... harm ... waah-eek,' Crinkum bawled.

Grimoire began pedalling backwards. Crinkum tried to halt midair, but the sword hit its leg sending sparks into the darkness and the scroll was dropped.

'Blast,' said Grimoire joggling the yoke.

Crinkum cussed a smokey spittle of fire as it clawed hopelessly at the air. The wildly slashing blade making it impossible to descend any further. Grimoire watched in despair as the scroll fell towards the campfire. It danced momentarily above the fire before a flame tickled it

43

alight. A sudden gust of wind carried the flickering treaty towards the outstretched estuary beyond the marshes. Grimoire, pulling the yoke back, pedalled forwards again and Crinkum shot back up into the murkiness of the night sky.

'Down but not out,' Grimoire gritted his teeth and hastened to mumble a restorative particle spell, but it was too late. 'It's over.'

Pressing his eyes once again to the glass, he saw the narrowing vision of the figure kicking dirt onto the fire and ducking behind some gorse. Crinkum retreated to a nearby crevice. Grimoire yanked the funnelled horn to his ear. He heard the sound of marching footsteps. Then he heard voices. They were coming from Owain's makeshift camp.

'The coals are still hot.'

'He can't be far.'

'Look what I've found.'

'Not another one of your clues. The last time we followed one of them we marched for three days around in a circle until we found ourselves back at the clue again.'

'Part of a royal license I would say.'

'I guess by the condition of it, he's turned it down.'

'Or drowned.'

'What makes you say that?'

'Spots of blood leading out across the marsh.'

The men laughed at their various digs and jokes as they marched the other way.

'I wonder,' said Grimoire with eyes still pressed to the glass, 'is he planning on meeting up with his son? Such a meeting would present a great danger to them both. The only other option is to go to his daughter where he could at least find refuge.'

Grimoire released the augmented sight spell by pedalling backwards and chanting the spell in reverse. The potbelly boiler shuddered to a standstill. 'Best see how Gyffe has been getting on.'

In the kitchen, Gyffe had been following Grimoire's instruction to the letter. He had placed on the table a pendulum board branded with a kabbalistic cross. At each tip he had placed savory flowers and crumbs of peridot stone. Etched over the cross was a drawn constellation pointing to the fixed star of Vega. Apparent within the constellation was an image made up of; a downturned crescent moon; an upturned semi-circle with a centre line; thrice a three-pointed forked prong on each tip. Gyffe put a candle in the middle of the board and lit it.

'There, that should do it,' he said admiring his aptitude for following Grimoire's instructions to the letter.

He then retrieved Grimoire's special porringer with its mystical inscriptions and placed one of the spell spoons beside it. He built a small pyramid of kindling beneath the cauldron on the hearth and lit it. Then he read aloud the incantation at the end of Grimoire's instructions.

As the cauldron began to bubble Gyffe saw that, as if from nowhere, the mage appeared upon the seat at the table with impressed rosy rings around his eyes.

'Ah, I see I'm just in time, such magic makes me hungry indeed,' Grimoire rubbed his hands together, as his nose twitched, catching a whiff of the stew. 'Well, don't just stand there. Why don't you fetch yourself a bowl and join me? The deed has been done, albeit, not according to plan.'

It was at that moment that Gyffe realised what he'd been fooled into doing. Thinking he was assisting Grimoire with his manifestation spell, he'd actually only been preparing Grimoire's dinner. Gyffe groaned with a self-conscious flush of the mopes. Lazily, he ladled each bowl with a slosh of stew, and sat down to stare at it. He was suddenly feeling a distinct loss of appetite. Grimoire, however, was keen to get on with the eating and left Gyffe sulk in silence. Eventually, the spirit of inquiry gave Gyffe the impetus to speak.

'So what happened?'

'The treaty was gobbled up by the flames,' said Grimoire after allowing his throat to pass through a gloop of barley.

Gyffe haughtily crossed his arms and legs simultaneously. 'See, I suspected the temptation would be too great for Crinkum. Remember last time when you asked him to sit on the Book of Thoth to prevent a draft sweeping away the papyrus?'

'Indeed,' said Grimoire tilling the contents of his stew, 'it is with all too great sorrow that I recollect that memory. Bearing in mind that if I knew Crinkum was allergic to the feather of my quill, I would have never had him sit on it. No, this time it was not our stony winged friend who bore the brunt of the botch, it was Owain too hasty with his sword.'

Gyffe thought, that if Grimoire had let him assist, he might have foreseen and averted the whole situation. He decided not to voice this opinion as Grimoire had clearly wanted him out of the way. Instead, Gyffe toyed with his stew contemplating a more constructive statement to contribute to the conversation.

'On the other hand, if Crinkum hadn't of shown up, Owain might have been captured by the King's men,' said Gyffe.

'I suppose it was written in the stars,' murmured Grimoire slurping up a spoonful of broth.

'It is now,' said Gyffe, 'don't suppose we can un-write it?'

'We can't *un*-write it but we can rewrite it.'

Gyffe was about to let Grimoire's words follow the steam of the stew which was rapidly dissipating as it cooled, when he decided against it. 'How do you propose we do that?'

'If we can't get back the message we must get back the messenger,' Grimoire said between champs of chewy gristle, 'don't think that what I asked you to prepare for me was in vain. Much the opposite, I instructed you to arrange for a manifestation, and that you did. My supper was an afterthought.' Grimoire licked the contents of the porringer clean and filled the empty pot with water. With a beard now flecked with fragments of barley and beef, Grimoire retrieved one of the bones Gyffe had stripped for the stew. With the bone, he stirred the stew water with a calculated rhythm.

'The arrangement you have made is an oracle. It will apprise us of the whereabouts of the messenger and under what circumstances we will find him,' said Grimoire peering into the bowl.

Gyffe watched on with fascination. 'Well, well, well.'

'This bone is the scapula from the ox, it is particularly useful in intensifying the potency of hydromancy. This is a little known fact amongst common diviners, one of which I discovered purely by chance.'

The swirls of the water began to take on slithering shapes, moving out of sync with the stirring motion. Ripples oscillated from the rim to the centre of the pot. Grey clouds swilled beneath the surface and sparks of electrical currents whizzed erratically around the water. The candle extinguished and the oracle spoke. Grimoire stopped stirring, and both he and Gyffe leaned in close to pay heed to its message.

CHAPTER FOUR

The oracle had shown how the Plantagenet legacy was well in place. A young Lancastrian of Welsh birth sat on the throne as the King of England and Prince of Wales. However, the King's lineage evinced little empathy towards a sovereign bordering country, despite his subjects in that land being outnumbered predominantly by sheep. The oracle also revealed that it wasn't just by chance that Henry had overcome the so-called Welsh revolt, a revolt which lasted nigh on ten years. It warned that the Tripartite Indenture, a pact signed by Owain Glyndwr, the Earl of Northumberland and Edmund Mortimer, had become something of an indication that Owain was reaching further beyond the stars. That the dividing of the greater part of Cambria and Anglia between the three would be one step too far. The oracle, in its symbolic idiolect, also went so far to convey that a revolutionist, ultimately, evolves into an institutionalist. It suggested, that it would not surprise anybody, that six years ago on the fateful day at Harlech, Henry's application of God's will and Owain's corollary of Sod's law were, in fact, an indirect consequence of Grimoire's misguided meddling. At this point Grimoire had started humming loudly to himself. He eventually stopped when the oracle expressed the location and the fate that awaited the messenger, its misty tenor carrying them far beyond Gwent and the Welsh Marches ... and strangely enough into a welter of clucks and plumage.

Having studied the bedraggled passenger long enough, a cock-eyed row of chickens twisted their necks as if to affirm what they had just witnessed with the other eye. This had gone on for several days, and the passenger began mimicking them to pass the time. One roosted on the passenger's head, another two on either shoulder, two on each leg and the surrounding flock fixed themselves to every available space and shelf within. Occasionally, the driver would stop and pass a bowl of water and a chunk of bread through a hatch on the side of the cart. The bread was devoured hastily as no longer had it been handed over, a brood of beaks would begin to peck. Cold wind cut through the slits of the cart sides and the only advantage of being hemmed in among the straw and feathers was the warmth it provided.

Finally, the cart approached Portchester castle, the imposing stronghold positioned on the harbour of Portsmouth. It sat on the promontory like an enormous stone dais to the southern seas. The cart came to a halt just outside the gates. The cart driver wiggled his bottom in the earnestness of being sat for too long. The chickens murmured in bewilderment at the sudden jolting stop. The passenger spat out a feather.

'Got a fother of hens for His Majesty's kitchens,' shouted the driver.

A heavyset guard wearing an ill-fitting kettle helmet and a wry smirk on his face approached the gate and peered through the bars.

'You are in luck then, the King is in a foul mood today,' said the guard.

'I don't see how that helps me,' said the driver, 'I need full price for these birds. What with all the buzzard strikes and fox killings I've had of late.'

'Don't let it ruffle your feathers old man.' The guard chortled adjusting his helmet to see better through the bars. 'The King always fancies a bowl of chicken broth when he's brooding.' At this last remark, several of the other guards who had been looking over the gatehouse parapet let out grunts of laughter.

The cart driver sighed. He had clearly weathered these routines for as long as becoming a poultryman. Possibly, he may have even weathered them through his father, had the livelihood been passed down to him. His underwhelmed expression hung down his face until the guards had exhausted their merriment.

'I require entry and quick sale. What ailment troubles the King so much that tender meat is allowed to grow older and tougher by the minute?' said the cart driver sternly.

The smile on the guard's face vanished as he gritted his teeth behind the bars. 'If you must know, there would be those who wish to plot against him, we have therefore stepped up security on all matters including contributions to the Royal larder.'

'I am also carrying boy in back.'

'Is he fit for plucking or able to lay an egg? Otherwise send him thither and yon.' The guard snarled.

51

'A messenger no less, known to the King, at least by sight, but not a pretty one at the minute.'

'Show him to me and let me speak with him on the matter.'

The cart driver dismounted and disappeared behind the back of the cart. There was for a few seconds a disturbance of vigorous flapping accompanied by flabbergasted clucks as the messenger alighted. The guard pressed his face further against the bars of the gate to get a better look.

'Come closer boy.'

The messenger went up to the gate moulting feathers as he did so. The guard reached for his nose and stuck out his tongue in disgust.

'Not too close, as you do stink a bit.'

Unfortunately, the chickens offloaded a great deal of strikingly astringent waste throughout the journey. The messenger wiped as much off as possible but only managed to smear it into a thick unwelcome paste. The guard's eyes suddenly flashed with recognition.

'Well, if it isn't scrawny Caredig sent across to Cambria with a treaty for Owen Glendower.'

'If the King will attend to me, I have much information I must pass onto him.'

'I think you ought to seek council with some soap boy, before seeking the same with the King. Come with me, but follow at arm's length as I've just downed my lunch and wish to keep it that way.'

The guard gave a shout and the massive gates rattled in ascension. The cart driver shuffled up to the guard and tapped him persistently on the shoulder.

'Oi, what about me and these birds then?'

With a scowl, the guard flicked the hand away. 'Deliver your stock, collect what's owing to you and don't hang about lest you want to hang about with an audience.'

The cart driver climbed back onto the seat and, as a fine mizzle of rain descended, followed the guard and Caredig. The gates crawled down again with all the creaking and grinding of huge iron teeth. The outer ward was considerably quiet. The recent events concerning the plot to overthrow the throne had dampened the usual weekend festivities. The few market stalls that were allowed to trade were manned by somewhat dour vendors who pushed and plied their wares.

'Offal, sweetbreads, brawn, come see what we got inside,' shouted one shabby vendor wiping squidgy glops onto his apron.

'Get your blades whetted and stropped 'ere! We do daggers, halberds, caltrops, billhooks, pikes, anything with a pointy tip or a cut-throat edge. Keen enough to shear the fleece from a Welshman's jowls or put a smile from ear-to-ear on his face.'

'Hairs plucked, warts removed, teeth pulled … don't risk it yourself, your groat back if it grows back. Come take advantage of our special arm and a leg discount for any external body parts that might be bothering ya.'

Caredig passed one tent, where outside sat a young lad wearing a filthy leather apron and covered in black splotches. The boy looked up at Caredig and smiled. Caredig smiled back and was about to greet the lad when the boy jumped up and shouted, 'shoe, shoe, shoe!' Caredig, startled, scuttled back to the guard who was meandering all the while.

'Don't fret about him, he's the cobbler's son,' the guard mused while crunching a stick of chard he'd snatched from a grocer's stall. 'There's a spot to wash behind the back of the church,' he pointed.

The guard took the messenger to the far end of the grounds. They walked through God's acre past the berths of the dead to where the church was located. Encountering a friar on their way, the guard requested that the messenger got scrubbed and given fresh dressings. The friar took Caredig by the arm and provided escort to the back of the church where there was a round wooden tub.

'I can scrub myself,' said Caredig.

The presence of horses nearby suggested that this tub was also used as a trough. The friar raised his hand to indicate that the messenger wait. Caredig sat down on the bath's edge. Soon enough the tub was filled to the brim with piping hot water and soap flakes were sprinkled across its surface. The friar extended an arm and held out his palm.

'My clothes?' said Caredig, 'I was going to wash them as I bathed.'

The friar shook his head.

'You have fresh raiments for me?'

The friar nodded with a friendly smile.

With some accordance of modesty but mostly because the friar's smile had dipped into an uncomfortable leer, Caredig turned before peeling off the feculent clothing before sinking into the soapy water. The friar collected the garments, his smile wincing into a proper grimace, as he cupped his mouth and nose. Holding the offending garbs at arm's length, he hurried over to a furnace. With a satisfying gasp of breath, the friar tossed them into the flames. He soon returned carrying fresh clothes which he placed in a canopied basket to prevent them from becoming damp. The friar looked at the water, a silent smile beckoning on his face with a sort of dumb generosity of service.

'It's perfectly warm, thank you, you may now leave me to my soak,' said Caredig in a slightly vexed manner.

The friar didn't budge, instead, he repeated the hand gesture, palm up, waiting expectantly for something.

'This?' Caredig reached out and clutched a small leather pouch bobbing on the surface. The pouch was tethered to Caredig's neck, and the messenger now held it in a firm grasp.

The friar once again nodded as the smile grew between his bristly cheeks.

'No, not this, this is for the King.'

The friar hesitated but eventually backed away to leave Caredig immersed in a pool of mulishness. The slight rain cooled Caredig's shoulders. The messenger leaned back and poked two steaming feet out the end of the tub. The travel weary toes wriggled. Caredig stared up at the sky. The clouds blushed an overindulgent green, flushed out in fullness, they sagged in situ. With the noise of the market sellers growing dim, Caredig's eyelids slowly drew to a close. Without warning, a snapping sting in the neck caused the messenger to hurl about like a submerged feline. A heavy cough accompanied by a growl made Caredig spin around to see the friar, the usual smile, so readily given previously, now gone. The friar stood next to a rough-looking guard who held the dangling pouch as if toying with a kitten.

'This be for the King aye? What is gifted to the King is gifted to the King, not played about as a bath toy!'

Caredig made an attempt to swipe at the pouch but the tub was slippery and the pouch was swiftly hidden behind the guard's back. With a leer that was almost brutish, he scolded, 'now, now, better your fragile neck lost a pouch than gains a noose.'

The guard turned and marched away. The friar stepped a little closer and as he did so, he ran his finger across his neck and made a noise that sounded like 'squit, squit'.

CHAPTER FIVE

Caredig knew that audiences with kings, are not attained by hollering at the window of the King's garderobe shouting, "Oi, Your Majesty, you done?". A subject must either make an appointment or be summoned. It was the latter of which demanded that Caredig be led over the drawbridge to the inner bailey where an offer to wait on a bench was given, along with a number stamped on a wooden plaque. It was also the latter which meant no longer did Caredig request council with the King, but the King now sought council with Caredig. The reversal, ominously polarised the favourableness of the predicament.

'When your number is called, please make your way to the great hall,' said the man who had escorted Caredig.

Caredig looked at the number and sighed, 'eighty-four.'

A cloister which led to His Highness stretched alongside a pleasant well kept grass lawn with the occasional lady's smock and buttercup breaking through the greenery. Caredig had only attended court once before when ordered to pursue Owain Glyndwr. By all accounts, that mission didn't go to plan, however, Caredig had seen things. Things that ought to be reported to the King. Soon enough the padded footsteps of a royal servant trod down the long corridor.

'Eighty-one?' called the servant.

Caredig looked about him, no one else was present. The servant repeated the number again before disappearing down the cloister. After some time, the servant returned.

'Eighty-two?' he said without acknowledging the only person seated there.

'I have eighty-four.' Caredig held up the plaque.

'Eighty-four then,' said the servant still casting his gaze about as if addressing an invisible queue.

'I'm eighty-four,' said Caredig waving the plaque towards the servant.

The servant took the plaque, 'you don't look it.' He began to chuckle but swallowed the laugh before it reached completion.

Immediately, Caredig was on the heels of the royal servant who seemed to be fleeing the scene of his quip. It was if the servant had reserved this line for many years, and once the occasion of discharge arrived, it was best not to hang around to accompany its lingering residue. Two large doors opened and Caredig was shoved through them. The messenger stumbled inside the grand hall with its high ceilings and plated arched windows. Tapestries draped from the walls depicting heraldry and battles. An enormous hearth crackled down the far end but was obscured by a mass of villagers, gentry and courtiers, all huddling together and murmuring in sometimes raised tones. Occasionally, someone would burble a discontent or disgruntle with a clamour followed by stern chastisements from all sides.

'I can't move for taxes on my property. It'll be the dandelions they'll tax next no doubt.'

'What's gonna be done 'bout our village then? Overrun with witches it is. Even caught one at the end of me bed the other night, nibbling at me toes it was. The sensation wasn't unpleasant but still …'

Under a finely quilted canopy, at the far end of the hall, King Henry slouched on his throne. He was in conference with a mother and child on some matter. The child happened to be picking its nose, and with each pluck of the hole the mother would turn to it and offer the offending hand a stern slap. Eventually, Henry summoned one of his courtiers. There was a brief discussion in which Caredig saw the courtier's face wring itself like a wet rag. The courtier inched away from the King, then reluctantly knelt before the boy. Caredig gaped in disgust as the courtier stuck a finger up the boy's nose and twisted it several times to the left and right. Finally, the offending item must have been dislodged as the courtier produced a rather large cloth from his waistcoat and wiped the finger clean before returning to the side of the King. The conversation between the King and the boy's mother resumed only to have the boy continue his nasal investigation, but this time, the opposite nostril. Caredig turned his attention back to the crowd leaving the King's problems at hand. He spied the cart driver who had kindly delivered him to Portchester. The driver was nervously chewing his fingernails until he saw Caredig approach.

'Ah lad, you can be my witness,'

'Witness to what?' said Caredig.

'That my flock was worth more than what's been paid.'

'Me?'

'Yes, lad, as you can attest to their er … feathery finery … as you were in back with 'em mile for mile.'

'Indeed, I was but I can't confess to have gotten well acquainted. I am very grateful for the ride you kindly provided. I am, sadly, no expert on your trade, sir. Hence, I am unable to help.' Caredig turned his attention away from the driver.

It seemed this kind of dispute epitomised the King's afternoon problem solving. Disputes between husbands and wives, feuding families, underpaid tradesmen, disgruntled servants, unneighbourly neighbours, concerned gentry, tattletales and do-gooders. No wonder the King sought, so often, sanctuary on the battlefield. A berserk Saxon swinging a double-sided axe, a mere picnic perhaps, compared to the division of goods and chattels after a dispute concerning an extramarital affair?

'Besides,' said Caredig turning back to the driver, 'I have my own matter to address.' The driver didn't hang about to catch these last words and Caredig was left standing alone.

Eventually, the time came when the King was handed the contentious pouch. A man whispered into the King's ear and peered over the throng of nattering heads until catching the eye of the messenger. Caredig acknowledged the cue and nudged through the mass until reaching the throne's ascent.

'Kneel before His Majesty,' said a courtier who had suddenly appeared at Caredig's side.

The courtier put his hand on Caredig's shoulder applying enough pressure to cause a drop to the knee. King Henry bent forward, his almond eyes glowered above a steely jaw which appeared to be held to his face by being hooked around perfectly carved ears, a long ridge of a nose pointed to small pressed lips that barely moved as he spoke.

'And which errand boy are you then?'

It had only been less than a minute and already Caredig's knee began to tingle with numbness on the hard surface.

'My name is Caredig, Your Majesty.'

'Ah yes, I sent you not long ago to dispatch a treaty intended for the outlaw Glendower.'

'That you did, Your Majesty,' replied Caredig.

King Henry adjusted his robe and edged a little closer. He peered down his nose affixing his eyes on the messenger like a close-range bullseye.

'And?'

'There was a setback, Your Majesty.' The numbing becoming quite a welcomed distraction from the terrible confession of failure Caredig had just admitted to.

'Hmmm, your answer displeases me greatly.' The displeasure absorbed into King Henry's face in no other way than a deadpan glare, 'I wish to speak with you alone. Let us adjourn to a more private chamber.'

Before Caredig could comply with the King's wish, a courtier stepped in. With his hand, the courtier shielded his mouth but it did little to conceal the conversation.

'Is that wise Your Majesty?'

'Wise? What makes you think my request foolish?'

The courtier glanced at Caredig before directing his lips closer to the King's ear.

'Under the circumstances of recent happenings Your Majesty, this boy has been gone some months, and we do not know what influences he has been under during his absence. Would it not be safer to resume council with him here amongst the faithful watch of your subjects?'

'Ronald…' began the King.

'Donald, Your Majesty. Ronald stands to the right of you.'

'Is that not Reginald?'

'No, Your Majesty, Reginald was hanged for treason.'

'Well, thank goodness for that. At least I got the right man.' King Henry gave Ronald a polite smile which Ronald reciprocated as only a man who might have been accidentally hanged could.

'We believe so, Your Majesty.'

'Well, that's comforting. Scottish are you?' The King attempted a smile which caused the compact features of his face to tense awkwardly.

Donald appeared momentarily taken aback by the question, but kept his poise long enough to deliver the answer without too much hesitation. 'Aye, by my mother's birthright I am, Your Majesty.'

'Does that not bring into question the fealty of your loyalty then?' The King hoisted an eyebrow which in turn wound down the smile.

Caredig watched the King's face with interest as every gesture tautened prompted another to then slacken. It was like watching the facial features of an abstract puppet.

'I am loyal only to you, Your Majesty,' said Donald.

The courtier swayed and bobbed as he answered. It was as if this little dance might enable him to duck the oncoming volley of the King's examination. At this point, Caredig considered changing knees but the uneasy exchange provided little opportunity to do so without being noticed.

'But are the Scots not enemies of the Crown?' said King Henry slapping his hand down on the armrest of the throne.

This startled the courtier but he steadied himself before answering.

'Some of us are, Your Majesty, but I am not the sum of us.'

King Henry's eyes squinted at the courtier as if seeing him for the first time, 'have I not had private counsel with you before?'

'On occasion, Your Majesty.'

Caredig could visibly see the courtier's face constrict into an awkward knot.

'Then what makes your private counsel and this boy's private counsel any more precarious than the other?'

'I dare say it doesn't, Your Majesty.' Donald flashed Caredig a spiteful glance, the principle of being usurped by a messenger clearly touching a nerve.

'Then I shall have private counsel with this boy. Let there be no more about it.' King Henry folded his arms and thus wrapped up the matter.

'So you shall, Your Majesty.'

'And if it is not safe, as you seem to suggest, then I shall have your head for the treason of not having convinced me enough otherwise.'

The courtier seemed to shrink ever so slightly into his otherwise sizeable frame. 'If it pleases you for it to be that way, Your Majesty.'

'It does not, but I hope it demonstrates that I am considerate of your advice .' King Henry got to his feet and instructed Donald to fulfil his duties while he was absent.

'No pressure,' said the King patting the courtier on the shoulder.

Accompanied by two other courtiers, King Henry disappeared through a door at the side of the throne room leaving Caredig still kneeling at the base of the steps. Not knowing quite what to make of the situation, Caredig stayed put until a courtier rushed back and, pulling sternly at Caredig's arm, managed to drag the messenger like a parent tugging away an impertinent child whose finger found its way into someone else's cherry tart.

Donald turned to the crowd and saw that next in line was a portly gentleman wearing a scold's bridle, his face as red as a beetroot and tears streaming down his cheeks. The gentleman appeared to be mumbling as loud as he could muster and flourishing his arms about in a most exaggerate fashion.

'Whose that then?' said Donald to Ronald who had moved in closer once the King had gone.

'That's the town crier,' said Ronald, 'censored for airing some of the King's private particulars.'

'Oh, I didn't hear about it,' said Donald.

'And *that* would be the reason why,' replied Ronald signalling the maffling town crier to come forward.

CHAPTER SIX

Caredig, accompanied by an entourage, moved swiftly through a series of short corridors that twisted and turned as if built by masons suffering from topographical agnosia.

'Much further?' croaked Caredig fearing that the King was planning something a little less like a quick chat and more like something of a drawn out interrogation.

'Nearly there,' said the courtier nudging Caredig with a poke of his bony knuckle.

Eventually, they arrived at a plain wooden door and no where else to turn. Caredig was ushered in behind the King while the remaining courtiers stood outside. The door was closed, and King Henry took a seat in the corner of the room on a modest chair. Caredig observed that the quarters were barely furnished and there was no opportunity for exit apart from whence they had entered.

'Take a seat,' said the King.

Caredig looked around and could see that the one and only chair was occupied by King Henry.

'There doesn't seem to be one.' Caredig for a moment questioned whether the King was offering his lap.

'Oh really? How inconsiderate of me, please take this one. A stretch of the legs will do them good.' King Henry got up and nudged the chair towards Caredig with his foot. 'I entrusted you with a task did I not?'

'You did, Your Majesty, and I intended to carry out that task to the letter had I not been thrown from the saddle.'

'They say a poor rider always blames his horse.'

'Well, I didn't throw myself off it Your Majesty.'

'It's a shame we have not the horse as witness.'

'Can a horse be a witness?' Caredig failed to conceal the look of disbelief.

'They have in the past made very good witnesses given the right question,' The King said matter of factly, 'but on this occasion we must rely on your testament and ...' King Henry presented, from under his robe, Caredig's pouch. '...This.'

'Oh, that,' said Caredig trying to hide the fact he visibly squirmed for a second or two.

'This may very well be treason, and you, at this moment, are looking very much like a traitor.'

Despite the King's threats, Caredig felt the yearning to possess the pouch once more. 'Your Majesty, I have much to say, I have seen many strange things ...'

'No doubt such aptitudes would sadly be missed if you were to lose them. I must therefore carefully consider the future of your eyes and mouth, so I will give you some time to reflect upon their *sine qua non*.'

'Your Majesty, I would never knowingly betray the crown.'

'That may be so. However, even an unknowing betrayal must be accounted for.'

'But, Your Majesty, I'm sorry for what I've done. Whatever it is that I've done. Er, what have I done?'

'Sorry is a word for bad-mannered children and clumsy servants, not traitors. You will wait here until I am ready to … well, delve deeper into this matter.' King Henry's thin lips pressed together so tightly they merged into a single red strip across his face.

'But if you please, Your—'

King Henry's face turned a plum red as he snarled through gritted teeth. 'No ifs, no buts and certainly no pleases.' The King opened the door, left and slammed it shut.

The grinding of a key sealed the messenger's fate. Now that the royal presence had vacated the cell, Caredig took a moment to take in his predicament. Having so intently focussed on the King since entering the room Caredig had neglected to see, that above was a round hole set with gridded iron bars. Caredig peered into the dimness beyond. A face as insalubrious as a dilapidated folly popped into view from behind the bars.

'Guest at His Majesty's request aye?' The folly crumbled as it spoke.

'Pardon?'

'Holiday or business trip?'

'I'm sorry I don't quite-' Caredig, with neck straining to see the visage above, noted that the furrowed brow of this neighbouring inmate was frayed like worn leather, eyes washed out like soapy water, a nose speckled like a quail's egg, and a mouth laden with teeth resembling gritstone tor.

'Never mind, I am waiting to check-out. Any day now I imagine.'

'What brought you here?' Caredig said straining his neck toward the dull eyes peeking through the bars.

'What didn't bring me here? Larceny, perfidy, a general disregard for personal hygiene.' The face made a grimace. 'Although you wouldn't think it ten years ago. Ten years ago I had me own stool in the minstrel's gallery and a fancy stool it was too. Carved from a single maple trunk.'

'So you're a musician?'

'Was, was a musician. The King's father used to treat me like royalty you know. No instruments to play in here though. Occasionally I'll whistle and thump me head against the wall for concussion.'

'Percussion?'

'No, concussion, makes me feel better.' The minstrel sucked back through his uneven teeth to emulate a form of whistling which sounded more like water being thrown over hot coals.

'So what detains you at His Majesty's displeasure?' The minstrel ceased the sucking sound with a clack of his tongue.

'I've come from the Welsh Marches,' said Caredig.

'Hilly this time of year I hear.'

'I got lost in the mountains trying to follow the rebel Owain Glyndwr. I was to bring him news of a treaty.' Caredig kicked at the stone floor in annoyance at the failure of fulfilling the deed.

'Nah, he wouldn't have liked that. What I heard he didn't have much of a sweet tooth.'

'I missed the opportunity to deliver it. My horse threw me and bolted at the sight of a brightly burning light drifting towards us. I must have passed out with the fall because when I opened my eyes, I was in a house the likes I've never seen before.'

'A house?' said the minstrel in unwarranted astonishment.

Opposite me was a creature asleep upon a rocking chair, its face heavily bearded with an upturned nose and large glistening nostrils. Small tusks poked out from its furry cheeks. It'd ears twice the size of a man's ears, and it wore an acorn hat upon its head. I was rigid with fear and could not move.'

'An acorn hat you say?' the minstrel said before letting out an affected whistle.

Caredig took a deep breath trying to remember the events through the cloudiness of confusion felt at the time. 'The room was filled with strange artefacts. A skull containing a burning candle. Its glow similar to the one I had seen floating outside. There was a rack of glass tubes filled with living organisms of which I knew not, a basket of crystals of every hue, machinery of baffling invention, and a pot stewing a mystic liquid that shone like all the stars in the cosmos.'

'A pot?'

'Yes, a pot,' said Caredig showing a little irritation.

'Hmmm, interesting,' said the minstrel, 'tell us more.'

Caredig continued. 'On top of a stack of papers, I saw a shiny black stone. Something about it beguiled me. I gently touched it, and it brightened. Some sort of eye stared back at me. It spoke, yet it had no mouth. What it said I understood not until it called my name. It began to speak of things I knew not. I pleaded in a whisper for it to stop its devilment and it became black again. I don't know why I did it. I can't say what prompted my action but I took the stone and concealed it in my pouch.'

The minstrel began to speak. 'Yes, a pouch,' said Caredig cutting him short. This seemed to satisfy the minstrel who once again fell silent.

'Then out of nowhere appeared a blackened beast, a dragon, as black as death. I didn't waste any time. I made for the door. The creature in the chair opened its eyes, and I heard it say, "Don't go". I could hear footsteps coming from another room. I ran and I ran and kept on running until I could see no more of that place.' Caredig had been walking around in circles as if caught up in the maelstrom of memory. 'Well, that's about it. I do not mean to startle you with my recount.'

Caredig looked up to glean what reaction the minstrel had made of the story. The minstrel's open mouth was pressed against the bars, a droop of spittle suspended from which, before quite reaching the floor, was then sucked back up with a nasally snore reminiscent of the sound a shawm makes. Disheartened by the lack of interest from the one and only audience, Caredig slumped onto the chair and with some effort managed to nod off.

Back in the great hall, the King looked decidedly bored from the nugatory proceedings of the day. He had finally gotten to his last subject, and the tone in his voice signified impatience to have him dealt with swiftly.

'How dare you demand even a penny more for that paltry lot. You get what I pay for. I'd have more meat off a flock of finches. Get out of my sight.'

The cart driver who was last to have counsel with the King stormed out of the great hall. The doors were shut, and all but two courtiers remained by the King's side.

'Now what to do about this? Is it dangerous?' King Henry once more produced the pouch holding it up for inspection.

Ronald eyed it off with suspicion. 'A cursed stone perhaps, Your Majesty? I have heard on the island of Môn in Gwynedd that such stones are cast into sacred waters and take on magic properties all of their own.'

'Barbaric stuff and nonsense,' scoffed the King, 'we must have it tested by someone with soundness of judgement. You must take it to the Abbot and request that it be examined under the protective watch of our

Lord.'

Ronald took the pouch holding it at arms length.

'And what do we do about the boy?' asked Donald.

'I will decide that once I have heard his confession. Send in Isembard the Ignominious.'

Donald hailed a guard and serviced the order as Ronald hurried off to locate the Abbot. Soon enough, the minstrel came rattling in, a guard at either side. His chains dragging across the stone floor.

'Kneel before the King,' snapped Donald.

'I am kneeling.'

Isembard was once quite a tall man, at least as tall as King Henry. But now, at only fifty-three inches, he was at least two feet shorter. This was due to missing the parts of his legs that would typically be found below the knee.

'What happened to your — ?' Donald waved his hand at the lower half of Isembard's body.

'Removed as a precaution,' said the minstrel, 'the Abbot, in his foresight, proposed to the King's father that lopping them off would greatly inhibit me chances of escape. Inhibit yes, prevent, no. From 1405 to 1412 I have managed to escape no less than twenty-two times.' Isembard did a little jig on his knee-caps.

King Henry was about to speak when Isembard interrupted.

'Once, I even managed to make it as far as the outer moat. They did consider removing my arms at that point, but, we came to an understanding after I told them I needed my arms to hear with.'

King Henry was about to speak again but Isembard just carried on regardless of the glaring monarch.

'You see, I'd overheard two brigands in the cell above me discussing the resurrection plot of the exiled King Richard.'

With a growling sigh, King Henry slumped further into his throne resting his chin upon his fist.

'Strange, I read the trial transcript, and it only mentioned the punishment of amputation as a footnote,' said Donald.

'Exactly, it was, strictly speaking, a note to the feet,' said Isembard wistfully rubbing his knees.

'Enough,' barked the King, 'were it not for the information you are about to impart, I'd have that flapping clap-dish for a gob clean off.'

The hall fell silent. The King tapped his foot. The steady tapping soon caught the attention of Donald and also Isembard who was about to speak but then thought better of it.

'I am sorry, Your Majesty.' Donald bowed his head in reverence. 'Let us proceed without further delay.'

'Are you not my loyal subject?' said the King ceasing his foot.

Isembard went to reply but instead turned and looked at Donald for consent.

'That's a question,' said Donald, 'you may answer it.'

'I am indeed, Your Majesty, loyal to the Court and on Sundays, the Church,' replied the minstrel.

'And were you not chief minstrel to my father but having displayed certain unfavourable characteristics now disgraced?'

'Very much so disgraced, Your Majesty,' the minstrel grovelled, 'irreproachably so.'

'And did this boy confess to you without duress and in plain speak?'

'That he did and I plain listened to every word.'

'Do you feel the boy was truthful?'

'Well, he did go on a bit in somewhat of a blethering rant. Am I to judge such gubbins as a fevered rant? Some of me own rants are cack. When I was a royal court musician, let's see? That was about ten years ago now, I had me own stool in the minstrel's gallery and a fancy stool it was too ...'

Suspecting it was going to be a long conference King Henry sighed and commanded Donald to fetch him some roasted sweet chestnuts to nibble.

CHAPTER SEVEN

The Abbot's quarters were to be found amongst the priory buildings along the South wall. In countenance, the Abbot was a mealy man, considering the sun to be one of the sinful indulgences better left to the flowers and the hay harvesters. He was also unnaturally skinny, gluttony being another of his favourite sins to avoid. He fed mostly on groats mixed with warm milk. His sober temperament and fondness for austerity placed him highly in the King's esteem as a reliable intermediary between man and God. Ronald found the Abbot lying on his bed with his eyes wide open, his shirt parted. Every few minutes, he would flail his chest with a wreath of nettle.

'Have I interrupted something Abbot Jupp?'

'I'm warding off the temptation of sleep. To my shame lately, I have been exhausted. Tiredness that can only be the ploy of the devil trying to slow me down in God's work.'

'I have something from His Majesty that may arouse your interest enough to shake off this devilment.'

The Abbot yawned and then shouted to himself shaking his fist as he did so. 'Curse thee, and thy yawns thou fiendish figment of the fires below!'

Ronald observed that the Abbot had deep dark half-circles under his eyes. He wondered how long he had gone without sleep. The Abbot upped and turned onto the edge of the bed and strung up his shirt.

'I must repel the lure of warmth and all its sinful proclivity by charging the soles of my feet with the precise temperature of rectitude.' The Abbot let his bare feet bask on the cold slabbed floor much in the same way someone might luxuriate their toes in the sand.

He reached for an empty eggshell which sat on a small stool beside the bed. It reeked of a mugwort and garlic mixture that had been left sat to go rancid. The Abbot, with one deft mouthful, shot down the contents and gave a rigorous shiver throughout his whole body. He suddenly went stiff and each of his toes stood for some time all in different directions.

Ronald, for a moment, thought the Abbot had taken poison and was dead. He flurried his hand in front of the unblinking eyes until the sound of prolonged wind squealed from beneath the Abbot's buttocks and he once more resumed a natural sitting position.

'Ah, that's much better, the fiend is expelled,' he said with a renewed spirit, 'now, what can I do for you Reginald?'

'It's Ronald actually,' said Ronald covering his nose to prevent the fiend from entering via his nostrils.

'Oh, I thought the King hanged you for treason, no less.'

'No, that was Reginald,' Ronald said starting to wonder if his existence rested with some sort of clerical error.

Ronald handed over the pouch. The Abbot opened it gently, shaking it over his hand until the smooth black stone popped out.

'It is nothing but a rock,' said Abbot Jupp, 'tell the King, I recommend a boiled tincture of wormwood, feverfew, and the bark from an ash tree. He is to sup on this every morning for three days without having breakfast.'

'You only have to touch it,' said Ronald, 'to see that the King is still in his right mind.'

The Abbot pressed one of his stringy fingers against the surface. The eye appeared and blinked quizzically at Abbot Jupp. The Abbot nearly dropped the stone as his hand tried to hold it steady. He stared at it for a moment before a voice spoke his name. On hearing his name spoken from a stone, the Abbot, with one quick gesture, dropped it back into the pouch and pulled the leather drawstrings tight.

Meanwhile, Ronald, without appearing to move, found himself at the door of the Abbot's bedchamber.

'I'll leave it with you then?' Ronald closed the door behind him leaving the Abbot gazing at the pouch.

'Yes,' huffed the Abbot, 'leave it with me.'

The corridors beneath the priory were narrow and dank. They were carved out as a series of secret passages when the grounds had been a Roman fort. Cistercian monks discovered them by accident and kept the knowledge concealed within private texts. Not even the King knew of their existence. The matrix of tunnels consisted of crudely dug out rooms at various points along the way. These rooms, although small, were used as manuscript archives, cellars, storage vaults and meditation cells.

The Abbot and three of his friars scurried through the crooked passages. They held their torches at a safe distance between each other as they contorted through the narrow chinks and kinks of the uneven walls before reaching the largest of the networked rooms, a room equipped with all the necessary instruments for empirical divination. Fitted to the room was a heavy iron-clad door. Abbot Jupp inserted an oversized key into the lock and, with both hands, cranked it open with a heavy clank. Wide steps led down to a space filled with an assortment of various apparatus used primarily for experimental purposes. Down descended the Abbot and the three of his most able and trustworthy friars.

'I recommend we use the methods of Doctor Mirabilis as opposed to Aquinas for the duty of making this examination,' said the Abbot to the friars, 'for what we have here may undoubtedly be a device of the devil.' Abbot Jupp placed the pouch in the centre of a long stone table resurrected out of the very ground itself.

'This,' sneered the abbot with a kind of reverse reverence, 'is potentially lethal, not just to us but to Christianity itself.'

The friars set about the business of preparing the stone for examination. A furnace roared to life, drapes were hung, measuring implements arranged to weight and size, wooden frames with glass curvatures stacked in units of magnification, books opened and pages noted, parchments laid, inkwells stocked, tinctures stirred and minerals spooned. The friars, heads bowed, ascetically taking each task at a time with the upmost attentiveness. After an hour or so, the Abbot, who had been overseeing all the silent activity, finally spoke.

'I must leave you to the business at hand,' he said, 'my absence for any short time might jeopardise the secrecy of these tunnels and our work.' Abbot Jupp left, quietly closing the door behind him.

The friars all donned stained glass visors to repel the evil eye. They put on leather gloves to avoid infection when touching the stone. Round their necks hung heavy silver crosses to ward off evil spirits.

'Are we supposed to say the *Qui habitat*?' said one of the friars.

'Psalm ninety? Yes, I think under ecumenical health and safety it's now a legislative requirement.'

'Wasn't back in my day, in my day all we'd do is make the sign of the cross and get on with it,' said the eldest friar.

The stone was dropped into a copper-alloy balance pan and a small lead weight placed on the other. The eye lit up. The friar noted the scale weight and scribbled on the parchment, pennyweight sixty. A voice called into the air, 'One hundred grams.' Each friar backed away from the stone. They looked at each other questioningly. Then from behind one of the visors came a muffled voice.

'What did you say, Brother?'

'I did not speak, Brother.'

'Is there another in the room?' said the eldest of the three.

Each friar scanned the room before concluding that the voice had come from the stone. In unison, they turned their attention to it.

'Abbot Jupp Bennett born 1350 died 1417. Height five foot nine. Suffered from occasional constipation and mild eczema. Had a son Jack Bennett, lived with mother, Adelid Webb, the child kept secret …'

Before the voice could continue, all three friars had stashed their protective clothing and exited the room as fast as their garbs would allow. A few hours later only two returned wearing cushions, made of hessian fastened by twine, over their ears. They put the visors over their faces and donned the gloves once again. One friar tapped the other on the shoulder, the other lifted the cushion over his ear.

'What do you think will happen to Brother Godwin? His threat to go to the Bishop about the bastard son didn't go down too well.'

'By the look on Abbot Jupp's face, I should think it not worth thinking about lest we lose the very thing upon which to think it. Shall we get this over and done with?'

'Aye, I think so. I shan't be heading anywhere, I have nowhere else to go but up.'

The friars resumed their work by smothering the stone heated minerals. The impact created a fantastic snap followed by a blast of billowing smoke. One friar noted the result. Once again, the voice reacted. 'Nitric acid with a sixty-eight per cent water content fuming to the point of an explosion.' The friars dipped the stone in a tincture. The voice carried on throughout the room, 'juice of rue, cumin and powdered pepper …'. Next, they examined it through magnifying panes … 'Four inches times one hundred magnification equals four hundred inches …'. The friars silently made their notes, and the voice kept on speaking … 'this room was used to keep olive oil and wine during the period 307 of the common era.' The friars busily worked on the stone well into the night.

CHAPTER EIGHT

Caredig, having slept uneasily, paced the cell. Every few steps, the messenger idly fiddled with the stonework for any crevice that, despite its impregnability, entertained the idea of an escape. The fortification of the stonework felt stoic. It was hardy, it was weathered stone stuck in time, forever bearing the comings and goings of anguish, fear and guilt. Eventually, a loose thin stone jiggled free, susceptible to hope, it allowed Caredig to displace it. By means of a squint, Caredig could just see beyond the outer wall. A gasp of cold air swallowed in through its gap. The messenger momentarily enjoyed its breath of freedom before being alerted to a guard on the outer wall sounding an alarm. Caredig eyed as best possible through the slit trying to see below, but what the incarcerated messenger failed to spy were two cloaked figures darting across the grounds.

'Hurry, hurry, hurry,' whispered Grimoire his cape flapping about him like the wings of a disturbed duck.

Gyffe was trying to balance unsteadily on an elevated wooden plank hovering above the ground. 'I can't quite get the hang of this … perhaps it would be easier if …'

'There's not enough time for perhaps.' Grimoire dashed towards the priory attempting to stick to the shadows.

'Wait for me,' cried Gyffe balancing on one foot and propelling himself with the other.

'If I'm not mistaken … ' Grimoire stood before a tomb in the graveyard. He pushed the tombstone and it fell back as if the dead were expecting them. 'Squits first,' he said with a smile.

Gyffe who was still wobbling on the plank managed to hop off. It dropped to the ground in some display of relief. Gyffe bent double and eased his way into the hole. Grimoire gave Gyffe a push further into the darkness and then followed holding a crystal which illuminated itself.

'Keep moving,' urged Grimoire.

Gyffe who had no means to illuminate his path felt slightly cheated at being the one to lead them into the blackness. 'How's my back looking from back there? I can't see anything from up here,' said Gyffe fumbling for any surface that provided leeway into the unknown.

'Oh, I'm terribly sorry. Here, take this.' Grimoire passed Gyffe the crystal which shone brightly enough to see several yards into the distance.

'Where exactly are we going?' asked Gyffe.

'Forward,' replied Grimoire giving Gyffe a good nudge.

The two of them snaked their way through the constricted shaft until they came to a wedge where the exit was a mere gap.

'Squeeze through,' said Grimoire more as an instruction to his portly self.

Gyffe scraped his way through and Grimoire kneaded his body, one appendage at a time, until he finally uncorked himself. They both emerged at a junction leading left and right. Gyffe shone the crystal in each direction.

'Which way now?'

'Whichever way seems right,' said Grimoire.

Gyffe veered off to the right but was suddenly yanked to the left. Grimoire had his coat grappled in a fist. 'Always go the right way. The right way in this instance is left.'

Grimoire snatched the crystal and pulled Gyffe along with him. Eventually, they came to the large iron-clad door. 'It needs a key I suspect.'

'We don't have time for a lock release spell. Instead, I shall use my boot.' Grimoire raised his leg and with one mighty kick had the door swinging open. The pair leapt inside almost tumbling down the steps. They steadied themselves.

'We've found it,' said Grimoire. He dashed down the steps and peered at the stone. It was locked in a metal cage. He muttered …

'ᚹᚣᚻᚣ'

The bars slackened and quivered like the strings of a broken bow. Grimoire grabbed the stone. The eye lit up. 'Grimoire aged …'

'Oh shut up,' said Grimoire stuffing it into his pocket. He darted back up to Gyffe who was still standing at the top of the steps.

'We have one other thing to do before we leave.'

'What's that?' Gyffe had already had enough of things to do.

'Rescue the messenger.'

* * *

Caredig was lying on the ground looking up the grate above. It was awfully quiet up there, and the messenger wondered if the minstrel was still alive. Gazing at the grill, the bars seemed to shift and merge into each other as if dancing in patterns. The harder Caredig stared, the more the bars began to blur and swim about each other. Before long the bars had faded entirely and Caredig blinked hard to get them back. It was a feeling between sleep and wakefulness until a length of knotted rags eased their way down, just to the tip of the messenger's nose. Caredig sat up.

'Climb boy,' called a voice.

'Minstrel, is that you?' said Caredig.

Without further enquiry, Caredig promptly placed each hand along each coloured rag of the braid. About halfway up, the messenger was hoisted by unseen hands into the adjacent cell. Caredig scrambled into the darkness and stepped back to avoid any close contact with the rescuers or, feasibly, would be captors.

'Come with us.'

'Who are you and where are we going?' asked Caredig.

'No time for introductions, we need to get away from this wet and odorous cell to begin with. Follow us and keep close.'

The door to the minstrel's cell was already open, and the three of them snuck out through the castle corridors until, descending some steps, they found their way to the inner moat. Once in the moonlight, Caredig tried to get a better look at his two liberators, still feasibly but looking less likely captors, but their hoods obscured their faces. Anyway, it was too late now to turn back. If caught, he would be convicted for having attempted to escape.

They approached the main gates of the outer bailey. Two guards, with frozen faces, stood stiffly at either side. They gave not a peep nor a twitch at the sight of the three escapees.

'How to do you propose we get through?' said Gyffe.

But Grimoire had already begun winding the wheel mechanism that lifted the gates. 'Give us a hand, Gyffe.'

Finally, one of the guards, with some effort, managed to move his mouth. 'Stop,' he murmured, 'stop or I'll—'

'What,' said Grimoire, 'stop doing this?' said Grimoire winching the gate up some more, 'Or you'll what? Breath on me?'

As the sentries were unable to move, Gyffe boldly stepped in, and with a little effort, the two of them had managed to wedge the gate open a few feet off the ground.

'Now, stick the plank under the gate,' said Grimoire.

'I wouldn't do that if I was you,' said the other guard through the corner of his mouth.

'What? Do this?' Gyffe said stepping back from the wheel and leaving Grimoire to hold it steady. He slid the plank under the gate and wedged it open just enough for all three to slip through. Once the plank was wrenched away, the gate came down with a heavy thud.

A cry came from one of the castle turrets. 'I seen 'em,' shouted a guard.

The drawbridge creaked into ascent and steadily began to rise faster than the three could manage to cross it.

'Across the moat,' Grimoire said ushering Gyffe and Caredig to the water's edge.

Gyffe placed the wooden plank he had been carrying onto the ground. 'Squeeze on.'

'This will never float,' said Caredig.

'It doesn't need to,' said Gyffe tugging at Caredig's arm.

With all three of them onboard, it gently rose into the air. Grimoire gave a little push from his foot, and the plank glided over the moat with ease. Once on the other side, they disembarked.

'What is it?' Caredig said shuddering from the thrill.

'Enchanted wood,' replied Gyffe tossing it into the water.

The messenger now feared greater danger here than being in that miserable cell. If caught, Caredig might as well have been parading around in a pointy hat and screaming prophecies in the village square.

'We'll never outrun them,' said Caredig.

'We don't have to.' Grimoire pointed to a horse and cart waiting beside the track. All three leapt into the back, and the driver kicked off. The wagon had not been cleaned since, and there was much sliding and slipping on hen muck before each one could steady themselves for the ride.

'I don't believe it,' said Caredig, 'I am back the same cart.'

'Are you all in?' called out the driver.

'And we are also in your debt,' shouted Grimoire above the din of trampling hooves and rickety cartwheels.

'Don't think it,' replied the driver, 'if the King can't thoil settling up with his subjects what they be worth, then he'll get nowt from me.'

The horses picked up speed and the jolting cart threw its passengers from side to side as it fled Portchester castle.

'Grimoire, what did you do to the guards at the gate?' asked Gyffe once he had managed to upright himself.

'Nothing more than a paralysis spell. It will wear off in a few hours but for now they'll be supping their lunch through a reed.'

It was at that moment Grimoire, and Gyffe both raised their hoods. The look on Caredig's face could not have been more in shock if it wasn't for the passing sight of a legless man bounding along the wet ground on his knees with his arms propelling him forward at a ferocious speed.

'Ha-ha, I'm free, free, free again!'

CHAPTER NINE

A night and day's travelling in the cart did not produce the most restful of journeys. The driver had dropped them off by a river, said his goodbyes and with a cheery wave headed off into the distance.

'Is it possible we have outrun them?' Caredig asked as soon as they had found an out of the way spot by the river.

'Outrun? No need,' said Grimoire, 'it was your minstrel friend they were after. They won't discover your empty cell until some time this evening which puts us almost a day ahead of them.'

'So, where are we now,' said Caredig, 'and what is that thing I had taken by accident, a Llech Lafar I think they call it?'

'By accident?' Grimoire dipped his beard in the waters and wrung it out as best he could. 'Llech Lafar? I suppose you could call it that. We are now in a most suitable place as any, alongside the Wye. The river that forms part of a natural border between Wales and England.'

Gyffe was leaning against a tree.

'Talking stone you say? That thing which you stole you mean.' Gyffe looked at Grimoire, waiting for the chastisement toward Caredig.

'Come now Gyffe, what's done is done, and the stimuliris has been safely recovered.' Grimoire patted one of his inner cloak pockets assuringly.

'But what is the stimu—?'

'—Liris? … Well, what is it indeed.' Grimoire sat down next to Caredig his beard still dripping. Caredig inched away, but Gyffe noted this may not have been out of unease for his safety, but more to do with Grimoire's toilette. 'It's an apparatus functioning from a type of magic unheard of by people in these times but someday, my boy, it will be magic for all people at all times.'

'What does it do?'

'Why so many questions?' snapped Gyffe, annoyed that he couldn't think of any to ask and then he realised he just did and fell silent.

'It tells you things, and it shows you things.' Grimoire gave Gyffe one of his disapproving looks.

'Like a crystal ball?' asked Caredig unflinching at the exchange had between Gyffe and Grimoire.

'Not exactly, it doesn't foresee the future like a crystal ball. Instead, it provides insight.'

'Insight?'

'Yes, it provides insight into the present and the past. Perhaps, even the future, but not just on one thing, it can tell you much about many things or many things about one thing.'

'We better get moving,' said Gyffe eager to change the topic and the topography.

'Can you show me?'

Gyffe threw his hands up in despair. Grimoire succumbed to Gyffe's noises and stood up. 'Another time perhaps, for now, over that bridge we must go. Chepstow Castle stands before us and we must tread carefully, lest, we end up knowing nothing about anything worthwhile.'

Caredig remained seated. 'That plank of wood, you called it enchanted wood.'

Much to Gyffe's annoyance, Grimoire sat back down again. 'Ah, well, that is, well, it's actually just a plank of wood, with a few extra attributes.'

'What can it do?'

'It rises above the ground,' Grimoire boomed, demonstrating the act of levitation by trembling his hand up and down in front of Caredig.

'Can it do anything else?'

'Um ... No,' Grimoire said scratching his head, 'well, you could hit a ball with it, or burn it, or shelve some books on it I suppose.'

'And the floating powers it possesses? Is that a kind of magic that someday we all shall have?'

'Er, no, not without wheels of some sort, it's just a bog standard enchantment cast upon a piece of driftwood I'm afraid. You see, most people view magic as something spectacular, even sinister. In fact, magic is just the opposite, it's mundane, ordinary but at the same time, special.' Grimoire patted the messenger on the shoulder in a fatherly way.

'Righto,' interrupted Gyffe, who felt the tree he was leaning against was beginning to lean on him, 'shall we get a move on? We'll be forced to camp otherwise.'

'As good a suggestion as any,' Grimoire replied, creaking his knees several times before locking himself into an upright position, 'the moving on, not the camping.'

'To the castle,' announced Caredig.

'He's coming with us?' Gyffe gave Grimoire a look in which he expected a negative reaction as a response.

'Well, you are both either absolute loonies or prophetically sane but what choice do I have?' Caredig uncomfortably laughed to break the tension.

'There's your answer, he has no choice, and if he has no choice than to come with us, then we have no choice but to let him,' said Grimoire with a seriousness in which its tone could have buried the dead.

'To the castle then,' repeated Caredig.

'No, we don't want to go to the castle,' said Grimoire, 'there are no friends of ours there. We must find an inn and enquire upon adequate transport for the rest of our journey.'

Dusk was upon them and they made their way through the town, inspecting every inn along the way. The town folk were settling in for the evening, hurriedly returning to their homes, taking tipples in the candlelight, shutting shop and sweeping the horse muck from the street. The three moseyed through the streets but the looks they received hastened them onwards. Luckless, they trudged along the river for a good hour or two before they came across a remote ferry crossing. Next to it was a small building, its windows brimming with the warm light from within, the gentle chatter and clink sounded the suggestion that it was a tavern of some sort.

'We are not far from Tintern Abbey,' said Grimoire, 'this must be a drover's respite. We'll blend in like any other travelling stray.'

Inside the tavern, chatter fell to a murmur. It wasn't crowded but the few who were inside, grazing over their drinks, looked up at the three travellers with a temporary glare of suspicion.

'Just act natural and whatever you do, don't mention the Welsh revolt. It's caused enough trouble at the Abbey as it is,' Grimoire muttered through a gritted smile.

The interior of the tavern had all the simple asceticism associated with the Cistercians, an inglenook fire provided a hug of snugness, modest furnishings and plain walls. Grimoire suspected that the tavern had connections with the Abbey as the monks there were keen brewers of cider and the sweet waft of apples could be detected in the fug. He walked directly up to the landlord who was idly chatting to a man who had the appearance of a bearded angler with a tad fishiness to his mistrusting face.

'Three beds for the night,' said Grimoire.

The landlord stopped his chatter and looked at Grimoire from the top of his pointy hat to the bottom of his raggedy boots.

'And three large ciders,' Grimoire added.

'I've never seen the likes of you around here before. You a prophet?' said the landlord.

'From time to time I have been known for my accurate predictions.' Grimoire was aware that announcing oneself as magic folk could result in unpleasant nuisances such as being hanged by the neck.

'Let me show you something. Give me three cups.'

The landlord appeared intrigued at what sorcery might be revealed to him on this quiet night. He fetched three wooden cups and placed them before the mage. Grimoire took a roasted chestnut from a bowl on the bar and placed it under one of the cups. With swift movements, Grimoire switched the cups several times. He flapped his arms over the cups trumpeting, 'Abracadabra!'

'Now tell me under which cup lies the chestnut?'

The landlord pointed to the middle one. Grimoire lifted it up and quickly put it back down again.

'Guess again.'

'It was there I saw it.'

'No, it wasn't,' said Grimoire.

'Yes, it was. I saw it. Didn't you see it?' The landlord nudged the angler.

The angler nodded without taking his eyes off the cup.

'I did see it, it was the middle one,' said the landlord pointing in exasperation.

'Choose a different cup.' Grimoire said without much confidence.

The landlord raised an unimpressed eyebrow. The angler snarled and hovered back over his drink.

'I'm sticking to the middle one,' said the landlord.

'Really,' said Grimoire, 'don't fancy any of the others?'

Eventually, the landlord was so frustrated at Grimoire's hesitation he lifted the cup himself to expose the chestnut.

'See, I told you so.'

'I'll do it again.'

'Don't bother.' The landlord poured three tankards of cider and shoved them under Grimoire's nose. 'Cheapest lodgings to fit three people we have here are the stables. If you're happy with that, I'll take a penny.'

Grimoire handed over a penny and carried the drinks to his companions who by that time had found a table by the hearth. He placed the tankards down and dragged a seat to the table for himself.

'What was all that blottorum-blottibus back at the bar then?' Gyffe asked.

'Blottorum what?'

'Just a phrase I use for occasions such as these.'

'Yes, but what does it mean, Gyffe?'

'Whenever there's mischief afoot.'

'That mischief is a tried and tested method of throwing would be witch hunters from the scent,' said Grimoire.

Caredig sipped slowly at the cider casting an eye around the tavern. It was clear that the glint from several rough looking men, who although preoccupied with their orders, made no bones about showing which table sat the elephant in the room.

'Now all we need to do is find someone who can take us Westward,' said Caredig.

'Us?' Gyffe turned to Caredig with a puzzled squint.

'If permitted? I have nowhere else I can go, and now there's a price on my head.'

Grimoire took out his pipe and fired up the sweet wafting mugwort mixture he liked. 'You must have relatives who would protect you surely?'

'I have neither friends nor relatives close by. My parents were not young when I was born, and they died not long ago. I believe I have a cousin in these parts. I am unsure of his exact whereabouts.'

Grimoire released a puff of smoke. It danced above the table before dispersing itself throughout the room. 'Hmmm, you are asking much of us to harbour a known fugitive let alone invite that fugitive into the province of magic.'

'And how do we know you aren't a spy? You did after all take the stimuliris straight to the King,' Gyffe added.

'Why did you rescue me then? You could have left me where I was, knowing full well that in due time your secret would be silenced forever.'

'That's not entirely true, ghosts can be such insatiable gossips, too much time on their hands. It's an ethereality that makes them susceptible to overhearing what they shouldn't. To make matter worse, they also have a propensity to blurt out whatever they've heard at the most inopportune moments.' Grimoire stopped to puff on his pipe.

'You should be grateful for the bruiting of phantasms,' said Gyffe.

Grimoire let out a quick succession of smoke rings. 'That, however, is not the reason for your rescue. Aside from taking what was not yours, you did not deserve to die for the knowledge you kept. It was the just thing to do. So I guess in keeping with that principle, be it that you are still marked for death, we shall provide you with the refuge you need.'

Gyffe prevented himself from responding to Grimoire's acquiescence by filling his mouth with a long drawn out swig. As Gyffe went to swallow, a hefty slap on his back shot out a spray from his lips. Before Grimoire could decry the displeasure of being showered in cider, an equally solid slap on his own back discharged a billow of smoke. This was followed by a succession of coughing and spluttering from sides of the table.

'Greetings strangers,' said a man, whose hands now gripped their shoulders. He towered behind them and presented his leathery face with its broad forehead and pebbled eyes glazed with the dew of too many tankards. When he opened his mouth a warm odour of ale accompanied his deep throaty voice. 'Couldn't help over-hearing earlier you fellows are looking for a ride.'

'We are at that,' said Caredig who had managed to avoid the outburst of fumes and liquid.

The villager grabbed himself a seat pulling it up close to the table. 'I go by the name of Hunch.' He didn't so much as offer his hand as force it into the hands of all three opposite, shaking each one vigorously.

Eventually, Grimoire had composed himself. 'You have a horse?'

'I have two acceptable steeds and a cart.'

'And what goods would you be transporting? Hay? Aggregate? Livestock?'

'Deadstock.'

'Deadstock?'

'Yes, that's right, I'm handing the deceased to their rightful kin for a proper send off.'

'And what would be the fother of your load?'

'Two corpses, husband and wife, after he went she followed, so got to take 'em both.'

Grimoire, Gyffe and Caredig all looked at each other before Grimoire took charge of agreeing to the terms. 'What would this cost us?'

'I can take you as far as Aberystwyth for just over a penny.'

'We'll take it then.'

'With pleasure. That will be a penny now, the rest you can pay when we get there.'

'How do we know you aren't going to swindle us out of our fare?'

'Well, for starters,' said the man, 'me cart is parked by the stables and me horses are in 'em. That's where you'd sleeping tonight isn't it?'

'The very spot,' said Grimoire, 'although, we paid a penny for the privilege.'

'Then I won't be going nowhere without me load, so you lot can keep an eye on it for me.'

'Very well,' Grimoire grumbled handing over the penny, 'you look like an honest man.'

'Do I?' The man grinned broadly.

'Not entirely,' said Grimoire, 'but the remark is intended for you to consider it a goal to pursue.'

'That settles it then. See ya in the morning,' called Hunch taking leave of the three.

Caredig and Gyffe said nothing as they stared into almost drained tankards.

Grimoire took one last contented swig. He then licked his lips with a pronounced afterthought. 'The Benedictines sure know how to make a fine brew.'

CHAPTER TEN

In the stable, aside from the rats, mites and horse manure, the hay provided some moderate comfort. All three found their nesting spots among bails stacked against a wall. In the stalls beside them, the odd snort from a couple of horses could be heard. Caredig dug deep within the hay but kept one ear poking out to make sure Gyffe and Grimoire were doing the same. The sounds of the night crept in with the nightingale being the first to announce the switch between evening and the witching hour.

'Goodnight, Caredig,' whispered Gyffe but no response came. Gyffe shifted himself to see if Caredig was still there and on seeing a single ear poking out, satisfied himself that their companion was still present.

'Goodnight, Grimoire,' Gyffe whispered again.

'Nos dah, Gyffe,' said Grimoire who had found a trough to recline in.

Gyffe struggled to get comfortable. He pointed his limbs in every conceivable direction. Flipped himself on every side of his person. Eventually, through the exhaustion of tossing and turning, he too was muttering softly in repose of much-needed rest. It was only Grimoire who stayed alert. He stretched his legs out in the trough, the brim of his hat pulled over his eyes, giving thought to the great journey which lay ahead of him. Grimoire was all too aware of the tremendous physical and mental feat involved in getting there.

'Must remind myself to pack a few jars of medlar compote for the journey,' Grimoire said under his breath.

Usual magical modes of travel would have to be abandoned as the profusion of magi, all embarking on their individual journeys, would amass a significant concentration of power. If this power were to be summoned in such numbers, it could cause a rift in the fabric of the world. What worldly chaos could follow might savage the very foundations of humankind (it would be an interminable inconvenience at the very least).

'Oh, and must not forget to pack a few bottles of nettle wine,' he said to himself, 'one never knows when one will get thirsty on such a long hike.'

He pulled out his pipe, tampered it with mugwort and with a deft flick from his finger produced a flame which he held to the flakes until they rasped with a soft crackle and trails of smoke wound their way into the air. He let his thoughts unravel in the same manner. The Tree of Oracles, a towering primordial yew, formed within the cavity of a mountain in Snowdonia. The tree had stood hollow for thousands of years. What of the magi who would be present at this sacred meeting ground? Would Ma Gwrach be there?

'My dear friend, Ma Gwrach,' Grimoire said quietly with a smile.

Grimoire had fond memories of her potent brewed sarsaparilla which they would drink together in vast quantities and then attempt to cast spells (often getting the incantations completely wrong causing frequently amusing results).

'He-he,' Grimoire chuckled, 'oh I will never forget the look on her face when, miscasting a time dilation hex, she turned herself into a clock.'

Ma Gwrach was the only magi he had ever encountered who had, as a familiar, a plant. It was potted into a goblet with a cloche on top. Its name was Prunewick, and as far as Grimoire could tell it didn't really do much except needing the odd sprinkle of fertiliser. However, Ma Gwrach told him that it had a psychic connection with all botanical organisms which gave her a vast scope of knowledge. She would regularly visit the Knucker's Knest and then one day she just stopped coming. He never knew why.

'Popped her clogs, perhaps?' puffing out smoke with each word.

Grimoire gave the lip of his pipe a saddened chew. A bat suddenly appeared in the stable, did a circular dance and then shot out again. Who would the four elemental magi be? He had pondered this often, having known a few fire sorcerers and aquatic shamans in his time.

'Maybe, "weirdly-bearded" Bardolph?'

Whoever it might be, all Grimoire could think about was that he was glad it would not be him. He sighed as he gazed at what starry twinkles could be seen through the uneven boards of the stable wall. His reverie was disturbed by a clanking. It was still very much dark outside.

Grimoire covered his pipe to mask the smoke, got out of the trough, went over to the sprawled Gyffe and gave him a gentle nudge with his boot.

'Shhh.'

Gyffe sat up dazed. He turned to speak but Grimoire put a finger to his lips.

'Shhh.'

Taking Grimoire's abrupt shushing as a cautionary warning, Gyffe slowly made his way to the stable doors. Through a gap, he caught sight of Hunch bridling up the horses. For a long stretch, there was relative silence interrupted only by the steady pitter patter of rain. Then came the chatter of men. Hunch's drunken voice seemed to dominate the discussion with incomprehensible slurs.

'We've been betrayed,' whispered Gyffe.

'It seems so,' replied Grimoire, 'wake the boy.'

Gyffe clambered over the hay bails but could not see Caredig anywhere. He hissed his name into the darkness, but there was no response. In a frantic search, he began plucking out the hay in great chunks.

'The little Judas has legged it,' said Gyffe covered in the golden grass, 'we've been double-crossed.'

A voice came from outside. 'No time to explain, we've got company in the way of the King's men no less.'

Grimoire and Gyffe startled as Caredig's head poked between the stable doors. Grimoire must have been so lost in thought that he hadn't even noticed the messenger slip away during the night.

'I've hitched their horses to the railings, it will take them some time to undo the knots.'

'And what about that fellow, Hunch?' said Grimoire.

'He'll be sailing with three sheets to the wind.' Caredig mimed draining the contents of a bottle. 'I snuck a cask of cider into his room, I doubt he would have returned it full.'

'Good work lad, we'll take his horses and head for the hills via the drovers' road.'

They all crammed onto the driver's high seat, and with a flick of the reins, Grimoire had them cantering down a rutted track. Behind them, a staggering Hunch shouted "Shlop!" and fell face down in the mud. The lanes narrowed as they traced their way alongside the River Anghidi, this caused the horses to drop speed to a steady trot.

'What's with these horses? We're being pursued, so they slow down.'

Gyffe checked over his shoulder at the shadowy trail behind them.

'Thought they had some sort of common sense?'

'It's their sense of equanimity.' Grimoire slackened his hold.

'Maybe they've lost us.' Gyffe's nerves subsided.

The sound of thumping hooves broke through the stillness and Gyffe's nerves were bundled back onto their tenterhooks.

'This track leads straight to us,' said Caredig, 'we'll never outrun them.'

'Let's take a little detour shall we?' Grimoire steered the cart off the lane and onto a track running through a field. 'We'll follow the river for a bit, then head North Westward and try to lose them in the mountains before daybreak.'

'Lose them,' said Gyffe, 'how can we lose something that's trying to find us?'

The cart bounced along ill-suited tracks as Grimoire thrust his face towards the path ahead. Caredig and Gyffe jounced beside him, straining their ears for the encroaching threat.

'Maybe we've lost them.'

Gyffe gave a little inward hurrah at Caredig's remark, as it certainly seemed that the clomping of the horses had begun to peter out.

'A river, must be the Usk,' said Grimoire, 'the mountains are close.'

Gyffe strained his ears over the din of the cart to hear the gushing of water. Onwards they rode, the wheels of the cart struggling with the uneven ground. As the cart brushed through a patch of ferns, a falling star caught Gyffe's attention. 'Look, luck is on our si—'

The falling star lit up the sky, and as it did so, a silhouette of men on horseback flashed before their eyes.

'Get them,' shouted a guard.

A glint of steel was thrust into the air. The guards charged.

'Can this thing go backwards?'

'Unlikely,' roared Grimoire at Gyffe. He whipped the reins, charging directly at the oncoming guards. A bitter wind cut across them as they sped, the cold numbing every joint and limb, icy shards of rain stung their faces. Grimoire then did something very odd indeed.

'Take these and keep them steady.' Grimoire passed the reins over to Caredig.

Standing up on the high seat, and not without some difficulty, Grimoire disrobed and stood naked with arms outstretched. At once ,Gyffe felt a flush of fear and embarrassment, as it appeared that Grimoire had lost not only his clothes, his sense of decency, it appeared he had also dropped his marbles.

'Dare you to strike down a man who is bollock-naked!' Grimoire beat at his chest and roared.

Who were more in shock, the guards or the horses, Gyffe couldn't decide, as he was too much in shock. The baffled pack dispersed, letting the cart soar through at flying speed. Grimoire, with some effort, returned his clothes to their proper place and resumed control of the reins.

'A combat tactic taught to me by an elder of the Gaesatae people.' Grimoire's earnest clarification was lost on Gyffe who was now trying to blank out the additional assault of a pair of bewhiskered butt cheeks.

The cart's wheels crunched over grass and stone. They slid and sloshed through mud and puddles. The dim terrain a swish of darting shadows, but it wasn't long before Gyffe noticed that the guards had reassembled and were continuing their pursuit.

'They're gaining on us. Shall I hold your clothes?'

'Trouble is, it only really works once. They get desensitised to it, you see,' said Grimoire.

Up galloped a guard, a gust of mud thrown up from the skidding hooves, his sword cutting through the air.

'In the name of the King, surrender or die,' shouted the guard.

'Any chance of some magic?' Gyffe burbled through a slurry of brown gunk now spread over his face.

Grimoire ignored Gyffe's plea even as the sword landed hard against the side of the high seat.

'Not worth the risk,' said Grimoire, 'magic is a red flag we can't afford to wave at every present danger.'

'Risk?' Caredig held steady as the cart ripped through a patch of gorse.

'There's no risk of surrender, they've decided to skip that bit straight to the dying part.'

Another guard galloped to the front of the cart, the eye of his sword poking close to Gyffe's face. Gyffe attempted to outstare the tip but, as the blade loomed ever closer, so too, did the river and Gyffe knew this was their only chance.

'We'll never cross it with this load. Got to lose it somehow.' Caredig sucked in a chilled breath and clambered towards the harness that held the cart shafts to the horses. The cart bounced over a stone and nearly threw him to the ground. 'I can't unfasten it, it's too tight.'

A sword sliced inches from the messenger's head. Caredig ducked back onto the seat. The guard raised his sword for another strike.

'Grimoire, if you don't cast a spell I'll be forced to try one of my own,' said Gyffe.

The guard's sword still hovering at his face. Gyffe blew at it as if repelling a fly. Were it a fly, it would have had marked results, but the unbothered blade was implacable.

'Follow me,' shouted Grimoire.

'Where? There's nowhere to go forbye the length of sharpened blade,' said Caredig.

Grimoire heaved himself onto one of the horses, Caredig managed just to mount the other.

'I've never been on a horse,' cried Gyffe 'and I'm decidedly unexcited by the prospect.'

Caredig took no heed of the musing as the messenger yanked Gyffe up.

Another guard galloped into view. 'In the name of King Henry …' He raised his sword and swiftly struck.

At that moment, surrounded by three guards, the only saving grace was the uncertainty of the cart's trajectory. Each time a sword was brought down, the cart would shimmy and bop over the coarse ground, leaving it to slice aimlessly through the air.

'We're going to end up joining those two in the back.' Gyffe held tightly onto Caredig, so much so that Caredig could only gasp in protest. A sword lunged towards Grimoire.

'Grimoire, watch your back.'

But before Grimoire could catch Gyffe's words, the sword's tip plunged into the mage's side. For a moment time stood still, the steely thrust poised in its target. Grimoire's face was a mix of surprise and indignation, Caredig held out a hand to try and pull Grimoire back, and Gyffe cried aloud the one spell he thought would appease the assault.

'Die wizard,' roared the guard, plucking the blade from its fleshly sheath.

Grimoire collapsed onto the mane. Lightning struck the shaft of the cart. A boom of thunder rolled across the heavens. The guard's horse reared back, with hooves dancing against the flashing firmament.

'Grimoire?' With an outstretched hand, Gyffe tried to stir him, but the horse pulled away, carrying Grimoire slumped on its back.

A second lightning strike shot from the air. It splintered the second harness, releasing the cart altogether. With a tremendous crash the cart was dumped before the guards, its contents broke open, and two gruesome figures jolted upright from their caskets.

'The wizard has summoned the dead,' cried one of the guards.

Two dead bodies, hollowed eyes and flaking skin, faced the stumbling horsemen who had now come to a breaking halt. The eerie assemblage of decaying corpses swayed before them. The jaw of one of the bodies became unhinged. It dropped neatly into the corpse's lap. A trembling yowl echoed out of the gaping chinless cavity.

'Away! Away!'

The guards quickly about turned and launched their steeds in the other direction. But it was not the dead who had yowled, it was Gyffe trembling at the ghostly figure of Grimoire returning that gave rise to his fright.

'Will you be quiet,' said Grimoire tugging at twisting the reins. 'Across the river we must go.'

Grimoire turned his horse, Gyffe cupped a hand over his mouth, Caredig took in a lung full of air, and the horses descended the cobbled embankment. The waters were shallow enough but the current too strong to make the crossing with complete ease.

'We're going to sink.'

'Oh please do be quiet, Gyffe.'

'We're going to be swept away by the current …'

'For goodness sake Gyffe …'

But before Gyffe could elucidate on the particulars such a plight might lead to, they had reached the other side. For a moment all three fell silent, listening for any sign that the guards might have recovered and resumed the pursuit.

'We make our way towards Castell Crucywel. There we can find rest for the time being before embarking Northwards.'

Caredig wriggled out of Gyffe's clutches. 'Can the squit ride with you?'

'Well, at least my spell worked,' said Gyffe, reinvigorating his sense of curiosity, 'it actually did work.'

'Your spell,' said Grimoire, 'what spell would that be?'

'I summoned a divine intervention, I wasn't sure if it would work but —' Gyffe's words were drowned out by a mournful chorus of mooing coming from the other side of the river.

'Hmmm, I believe what you summoned was a bovine intervention. It was, instead, the rainmaker. I still had it in my pocket. The impact of the blade must have set it off, like steel to flint.'

'But I saw the blade thrust deep,' said Gyffe reenacting the horrified expression he had at the time.

'I wouldn't say that.' Grimoire displayed the abrasion and bruise.

'You should have that treated,' said Caredig.

'They'd only smother it in pounded leaks and honey, nothing a bit of comfrey won't comfort until it heals over.' Grimoire patted his side with a slight groan. 'Come now, at least we have horses. My wounds may not be so forgettable had we to make this journey on foot.'

CHAPTER ELEVEN

The horses kept a steady pace over the countryside and by the early afternoon they had reached the abandoned ruins of Castell Crucywel. The castle had been ravaged by Glyndwr some thirteen years earlier and was never reclaimed. The crumbling frame, an overture to its once glorious past. In those days, royalty rested in its walls, now it was home to hedgehogs and migrating house martins. Its ramparts covered in ivy and its stones like the decayed molars of a decrepit golem. The horses were led inside a cracked turret. There they had plenty of grass and thistles growing up from the earthy floor. This provided much sought after feed for the evening. The three then allocated each other supper gathering duties, Caredig went off to collect some hazelnuts and haws seen along the way and Gyffe busied himself with collecting bittercress, dandelion leaves and burdock root to accompany their meal. Grimoire wandered off into the capsized bailey mumbling something about mushrooms. By the time Caredig got back, it was getting dark, Gyffe had constructed a pile of dry leaves and twigs with the intention of casting a fire spell.

'I haven't done this in a while,' said Gyffe.

Caredig emptied pockets bulging with the collected berries and nuts. 'Done what?'

'Conjure up the flames.'

'Should I prepare myself for a flock of sheep?'

'It's quite difficult casting a spell while saddled on a horse fleeing from Kingsmen wanting to kill you, you know. Mostly, we fribblings, are delegated the duty of serving those with magic. Although, there has been quite a few magically endowed squits whose prominence among the higher order of magi is something to be revered.'

'Squits? I've heard that word before. I think a friar used it at Portchester.'

'Unfortunately, as with the tylwyth teg and other such fay, our best intentions to remain concealed do not always go unnoticed,' said Gyffe.

Gyffe placed his hands above the mound of twigs and muttered a few words of which Caredig didn't quite catch. Nothing happened. Gyffe outstretched his arms once again, waving his hands over the twigs, repeating the incantation. Again, nothing happened. After the fourth time Caredig began to get impatient and got up to wander around the remnants whilst Gyffe continued his attempts. By the time Caredig had returned, a small fire was crackling underway with a very pleased looking Gyffe, charred about the face, with his waggle slightly singed.

'You did it.'

'Told you I could do it.'

Caredig sat down to the burgeoning warmth. 'Where's Grimoire gone?'

'No idea, probably got lost in his own thoughts somewhere.'

'Does he do that often?' Caredig took a handful of hazelnuts and placed them beside the burdock root Gyffe had put on the coals for roasting.

'Frequently, he always finds his way back though.' Gyffe popped a handful of haws into his mouth and chewed uncomfortably as the thin husk fell away, picking out and flicking away the pits as he came to them.

'After this, where are we heading then?'

'Straight for a hot bath and a comfy bed I should think,' said Gyffe.

'Back to that wizard's lair?' Caredig did not sound entirely sure that this was where he wanted to end up.

'It's not a lair, it's our home,' said Gyffe, 'and he isn't a wizard, he's a mage.'

'What's the difference then?' Caredig said.

'Wizard is spelt …'

'I know there is a difference in spelling but what's the actual difference between the type?'

Gyffe flicked the remaining pit over the wall of the alcove. 'Type? Wizards work alone and dress pompously.'

'And a mage?'

'A mage is the other way around.'

Caredig with bent knees, maximised the warmth by huddling as close to the flames as possible. The night was setting in and Grimoire still wasn't back. 'Do you think we should go looking for him?'

'It had crossed my mind, but he'll only be upset if we do.' Gyffe rolled some bittercress inside a dandelion leaf and chewed it without much satisfaction, but it was food.

'What if he's been captured or worse, slain by the Kingsmen?' Caredig also tried some bittercress and dandelion but spat it out and reached for a hazelnut.

'He wouldn't let it happen without letting us know first,' said Gyffe.

'He'd have little chance of that if he were dead or has he some magic to speak beyond the grave?'

'Not that I know of, he'd probably just scream loud enough for us to hear.'

At that point, Gyffe wondered why he felt no urge to prompt Caredig with questions of his own. This was very unusual behaviour for a squit and something that sat uneasily in his mind. Was he losing his essential squitness? Or was there something about Caredig he just couldn't trust? Squits were not only highly inquisitive but also notoriously suspicious. It was the diametrical extreme to their curiosity. In most cases, squits were unstoppably curious about what other squits were up to, and then unremittingly suspicious about it. This meant that fribbling squits were very bad at buying gifts for each other.

'Have you served Grimoire long?' asked Caredig digging out some more of the roasted nuts to let them cool off.

'Long enough. I wouldn't say I serve him exactly. I sort of help him out.'

'In what way?'

Gyffe leaned back against a hummock as if consulting the stars for consultation on what "help" exactly meant in the circumstance of serving Grimoire.

'The ancient craft requires much preparation, the gathering of ingredients, the mixing of potions, the blending of powders,' Gyffe said forking a few baked burdock roots from the fire, 'the rituals require much arrangement, artefacts unknown to common man. Mysterious and unpredictable relics must be properly handled by someone who is familiar with the secrets.'

'And that's you is it?' Caredig said as he gave one of the burdock roots a try.

'Mostly, I also do all the cleaning, washing-up and sweeping when required.'

'Sounds privileged.'

'Hmm, that's what people say until they themselves encounter the trial of scrubbing a pot of burnt porridge.'

'Sorry, I didn't mean about the cleaning. All that other stuff, the magic, the mysticism …' Caredig tossed the burdock root away and removed the rest with a hefty spit.

'Oh, I knew that, just thought I'd mention it though. The magical ways are not as all glamorous as folk like to make out.'

A loose stone dropped from one of the walls causing Gyffe to jump.

'Maybe you are right.'

'Right about what?'

'Going to find Grimoire,' Gyffe said jumping to his feet armed only with a burdock root, 'if someone strangled him he might not have had a chance to scream.'

At that moment the shadow of Grimoire appeared at one of the shattered doorways. 'Scream? I don't scream. Who ever heard of a mage screaming?'

He wasn't alone. Behind him stood a broad outline of another man.

'Watch out there's someone behind you!' Gyffe madly swished the burdock root like a dagger.

Grimoire raised his hand. 'For goodness sake Gyffe, take hold of yourself. I'm well aware there is someone behind me as I brought him here. It's Owain. He's been hiding out here ever since Crinkum mislaid the treaty on the unfortunate spot of a burning campfire.'

Grimoire entered the alcove letting Owain pass.

'Shwmae,' Owain said.

Gyffe, and to some extent, Caredig were too surprised at Owain's unexpected appearance to return the greeting. Instead they turned to Grimoire who just shrugged. 'The youth these days don't uphold the same values concerning manners. I apologise if their faces appear as surprised as a fish on a hook.'

'It is I who should apologise for my abrupt presence. I have a request and it may not be in your favour but I must ask it as my time is wearing thin.'

CHAPTER TWELVE

On the second day of Grimoire and Gyffe's absence, Patch was, as arranged, taking the odd collection of valued items down to the sunken fortification below. The task was not entirely suitable for a hognome as the turret steps, accessed via a trapdoor at the back of Grimoire's house, were steeply set and the passage below narrow. Patch stumbled to and fro as he hauled Grimoire's items down the steps until he reached an almost lightless passageway save for the lantern he had fastened on his head with a strap beneath his chin. It was on returning from the fifth lumbering haul that he sensed a sound coming from outside the house. Hognomes have extremely hairy ear-holes, and it took him a bit of effort to comb them open with his long fingernails to get a better listen.

'Foxes?' Patch debated on whether or not to close the trapdoor, should he and Crinkum need to take refuge below sooner than Grimoire had stated.

Once inside he put the thought of foxes behind him and, besides, Grimoire's house was looking considerably less cluttered. This achievement pleased him immensely. With the use of a small trolley, he had almost cleared all of Grimoire's most valued possessions. Including, the possessed chess set, carved from the bones of the actual people the pieces represented, except for the rooks which were carved from the stone of the ancient castles they inhabited.

'Good old heave-ho,' said Patch, patting his invention as if it were a living thing.

The trolley was basket shaped, woven with wicker, and painted initially in a fun splash of yellow which over the years had turned into a rather mundane mustard colour. It was hooked onto the back of a little pot-bellied steam cart. As Patch pedalled, two bellows fanned the burner, it burped and wheezed its way through the house blowing steam from funnels sticking out of the rear. The only drawback to its design was that once it had gained speed, putting on the brakes would risk it upending. To arrive safely at a halt, Patch needed to steer it continuously in a circuit until he reached a safe velocity upon which to apply the braking system. This braking system was, more often than not, his legs and an unfortunate piece of furniture.

Once again, a sound coming from somewhere interrupted his duties. Patch was just about to pack some wool into the clappers of Grimoire's leg bells to prevent them from jingling during transport when, once again, his duties where interrupted from a persistent sound coming from outside.

'Not foxes, no.' Patch crept to the entrance. 'Dragoyle?' He strained his ear. A snort opposite indicated that Crinkum was near, blending in with the hearth by having a dust bath in the ashes.

'Dragoyle is here. Yes, safe here,' said Patch returning to his duties.

Just as he had filled the trolley with Grimoire's sacks of ceremonial incense powder, the mudroom gate rattled causing Patch to drop a sack. It split on the floor and the room filled with clouds of thickly scented meadowsweet. The thought of foxes returned.

'Somebody there?' called out Patch in as foreboding a tone as he could muster.

The answer came in several deliberate knocks. Clunk … clunk … clunk.

'Go away. No one to know here,' said Patch warbling the words for effect.

The knocks repeated. Clunk … clunk … clunk.

'Only I,' continued Patch, 'wild … err … giant and …' Patch looked around at Crinkum. 'Black … err … death dragon …'

A wicked laugh resounded from behind the door. 'Enough hognome, open the door before I turn it to dust.'

On this being said, Patch conceded he was dealing with a magical being and since he served a mage it would be unwise to dismiss it. After several attempts at opening the door, Patch was soon face-to-knee with the unmistakable appearance of a sorcerer. The sorcerer's knee was forbidding enough, but as Patch took in the full form, he felt unnerved. The face looking down on him was as pale as the moon, the eyes as dark as the night sky, a mouth like the hollow of a tree and a wormy tongue imprisoned behind crooked stained enamel bars that served as teeth.

'I smell,' said the sorcerer flaring his nostrils, 'I smell, meadowsweet.'

'Have it, take it,' said Patch hoping this was all the sorcerer wanted.

'Don't be worried,' said the sorcerer, 'I'm not here to cause any fuss.'

Patch stumbled backwards. 'Mind not yours to read.'

'I hazarded a guess, by the fret of your frown.' The sorcerer prowled around the living quarters examining the near empty room.

'Where's Grime Wear then?'

Patch looked at the sorcerer quizzically.

'Grit Wart Fusty Pants?' The sorcerer eye-balled Patch.

Patch repeated his quizzical look without blinking.

'I'm talking about your master, the mage, Grimoire.' He prolonged the name with a foul waft of breath that had the faint scent of spearmint indicating either some awareness of oral hygiene, but ultimately a failure to upkeep it, or a penchant for spearmint tea.

'Gone out.' Patch didn't flinch.

'It's just that I was wondering, as I saw him not long ago at the Knucker's Knest. He was chatting to a person of interest. A person I myself intercepted, albeit briefly. I'm a little intrigued at the particulars of that conversation had between Grimoire and the fellow in question.' The sorcerer slurped back the words as if to prevent them from trickling down his chin.

'Person of inter—' Patch begun but forgot the third syllable.

'Yes, yes, I have a list you see. A list concerning the once and future

…' The sorcerer hesitated. 'Persons of interest.'

'You … from below?' Patch seized the moment to lure the sorcerer into revealing his purpose by distracting him with chatter. Patch was a hognome of few words and he found this to be an absolute boon when engaging in small talk. He, therefore, acted as casually as he could. He took a remaining bottle of whortleberry wine from the shelf and poured two drinks.

'Much obliged,' said the sorcerer taking a drink and eying the choice of drinking vessel bemusedly, 'from below you say?'

'No mugs,' said Patch downing a mouthful.

For a moment they both sat in silence cradling clogs full of wine.

'Below,' said Patch, 'in that place. That place of dwarfs.'

'You mean have I been fraternising with foul-faced Ffinnant, that squat dwarf in his sodden warren? Unlikely, life's too short for dwarfs.'

Despite sharing the prejudice of height, Patch couldn't help but smirk into his clog as he took another sip.

'So what's he up to then? Has he taken his leave to the oracular yew?'

'Can't say. Haven't heard,' said Patch.

'Hmm, a lot more spacious than it was last time I was here.' The sorcerer looked about the room, 'Seems a lot less cluttered with hocus-pocus. I must admit, it even appears, dare I say, tidy.'

'Last here?' Patch knitted his eyebrows into something resembling a bristly shawl. 'Never heard a word of you.'

'That doesn't surprise me, Grimoire likes to compartmentalise people. ' The sorcerer took swig from his clog.

Patch thought about the word. He knew what Grimoire liked and didn't like. Such things as enjoying growing seers sage because it would stupefy the tylwyth teg on balmy days. He didn't enjoy sheep because he had once been bleated at by an undead black-faced flock in his youth. He enjoyed a gentle back scratch from Crinkum. He disliked settling onto the privy with a good book only to realise all the mullein was gone. However, Patch couldn't think of a dislike or like which needed such a long word.

'Likes oats.' Was all Patch could think of to say.

'Oats, indeed,' said the sorcerer once again looking about the room. 'He didn't mention anything about a crystal did he? You haven't perchance noticed on your travels, while decluttering and sorting, a chipped and scuffed jewel embedded in the jacket of a tatty leather bound book?'

'Not heard, not seen.' Patch had no idea what the sorcerer was on about and felt the best plan of action was not to seek clarity with the sorcerer's meaning lest the hognome admit to something he shouldn't.

'Where's it all gone then? All his ... stuff?'

Patch contemplated the question as he understood this one. Then he considered the situation which he was still coming to grips with. A sinister sorcerer turns up looking for Grimoire. If Grimoire had been here, the sorcerer would have queried Grimoire in person. Did the sorcerer know that the mage would be absent? Patch mulled over the thought until he concluded that the best option would be to put himself in Grimoire's shoes and answer as such, however undesirable that might be.

'Well,' said the sorcerer, 'pawned then?'

'Down below.' Patch cupped his mouth realising that answering in Grimoire's shoes was a terrible mistake.

'I see,' said the sorcerer, 'in the dwelling of Ffinnant.'

'Yes,' mumbled Patch cupping his mouth again but this time with his other hand.

'I see,' said the sorcerer grinning and drawing out the vowels along with it, 'that's all I wanted to know,' he snapped.

He jumped to his feet and headed for the exit but took a moment before leaving. 'Oh, and if you're worried about what lurks below ... I would be.'

The sorcerer slipped through the door. Patch sat in silence. A minute passed and the door creaked open again. The sorcerer stormed back in pointing a wispy finger at the hognome.

'One last thing, when Grimoire does return, if he returns, tell him Mygodorth Pfft was here.' The sorcerer slipped away again.

Patch was about to get up when the door creaked open for the third time, and the head of the sorcerer popped into the room. 'Oh, and if you do come across that crystal, put it aside for me, I shall return one day. Ta-ta,' he said giving the door a good slam behind him.

That night Patch rocked back and forth in his chair with all the calmness of sea vessel in a tempest. The sorcerer's words echoed in his mind; *lurk*, *return*, and oddly enough - *Pfft*. Patch then wondered if he'd latched the trapdoor.

'Think.' Patched pressed fingers against his temples focussing on the moment of closing the trapdoor, nothing came of it. He let go and stared at the silhouette of a mouse who had triumphantly discovered the piece of bread and cheese Patch was saving for a midnight snack.

Patch forgave the rodent as the near and present danger was much more deserving of his attention. 'Hear noise. Climb steps. Close trapdoor. Close?'

Did he leave it wide open? In a flurry of guilt and fear he propelled himself from the chair and tiptoed to the kitchen. 'Spoon.'

Patch grabbed a wooden spoon, parried it a few times, reconsidered, and then grabbed a ladle as it felt deadlier, indeed, he recalled the impact it made on some of Gyffe's stodgier soups. The hognome made his way out the back to the trapdoor.

'Closed, aha, not latched.'

He descended the stairs and entered the long corridor. He heard several muted thumping noises that indicated that his ears were not playing tricks on him and it may be coming from beyond the fortress itself.

'Badgers? No, not badgers.'

Patch raised the ladle and held his breath for several minutes.

'Maybe Ffinnant?' Patch whispered at the same time as letting the air out of his lungs.

The noise again echoed in the distance. Patch had never been beyond the point where he stood and was not sure he wanted to actually discover what was making the noise.

'Foul dwarf.' Somehow, telling himself this bolstered his nerve to carry on.

Patch could barely see as he trundled cautiously down the corridor. He couldn't see its end but it felt long. With his hands he could feel that it was fronted with oak panelling, and he came across several ruptured windows peeking out to clumps of earth and broken stone with tangled visiting roots pushing through. Patch hurried down it in the fashion of a hognome, which was in all respects an unhurried event. Eventually, he came to a platform with wide steps leading down into pitch blackness. An impressive window, albeit fogged with moss, cut with elegant but cracked glass, looked out into the cavern. It was a struggle to shift himself up onto the small sill below, but he just managed it by scrambling up the wall. Peering into a widened crack, Patch scoured the gloomy cavern beyond.

'Where is dwarf?' Patch whispered.

Patch's eyesight was poorly but mostly in the longsighted sense. When it came to distances, he had to squint and focus for a while until the intended object was satisfactorily visible if not a little blurry. He spied what appeared to be a boat bobbing in the waters below. Along a small jetty, moved a cloaked figure. By means of a dim lantern, it guided its way across the smooth pebbles of the embankment until it reached the grand stone steps leading up to the house.

'Not badger, not dwarf. Man, too tall for dwarf … too-too … sorcerer.' Patch rolled the thought around in his mind, 'Pfft?' He let the word deflate from his mouth. 'It returns.'

Patch eyeballed the figure until it was out of sight. He stood where he was for a moment before he heard the thud of a door closing. This made him topple and slide to the ground with a panicky jiggle of his legs.

Must get back.

He brushed past the straggly roots eventually finding the turret steps and with every effort heaved himself up to the top, slammed the trapdoor and bolting it for good measure added the additional weight on top of a failing potted aspidistra Grimoire was trying to cheer up.

'Good and shut.'

He made haste to the living room and pouring himself a large clog of wine noticed small white flakes were tumbling onto his head and shoulders. Looking up he saw Crinkum on his perch munching seashells from a cloth-bag and dropping the crumbs as he did so.

'Manners,' said Patch.

Crinkum gave the hognome a sideways glance and then resumed his feast. Patch was feeling unnerved, unlike Gyffe, the hognome would rather the curiosity went away. But something had told him he ought to have a peep if only for Gyffe's sake who wouldn't have been able to help himself despite the obvious danger. This being the quandary for any fribbling squit, as it is for cats, who upon confidently clawing their way up a tree find themselves in abject terror once they discover they can't get down.

Patch took a long sip from his glass and, drawing his knees in close to his chest, awaited the intruder.

CHAPTER THIRTEEN

Owain was indeed strong, he held Grimoire on his shoulders as if he were nothing more than a bale of straw. Grimoire, who was not so physically able, held a sturdy stick lengthways across his shoulder. Caredig balanced on the stick stretching up towards the cowering Gyffe.

'Let yourself down slowly, I've got you,' said Caredig.

'I'd rather be floated down like a feather,' said Gyffe with only one footing for support and a weak branch to hang on to.

'I'm not wasting magic just because you've gone and got yourself stuck up a tree,' barked Grimoire.

Gyffe wobbled his way to Caredig's clutches, then he was passed down to Grimoire who ignored the offer, and the squit fell into Owain's arms, who delivered him to the grass with a clumsy wallop. Once everyone had reassembled on terra firma, Grimoire turned to Gyffe pointing the stick directly at him.

'And what impelled you to do such a troublesome thing as that?'

'Eggs.'

'Eggs? What eggs?' Grimoire tossed the stick away.

'These eggs, we can boil them.' Gyffe produced from under his short cloak a handful of speckled green eggs.

'A ploughboy's meal,' said Owain with a laugh.

'I've heard they are a delicacy amongst the aristocratic Dutch.' Gyffe produced another handful and placed them on the ground.

'This is a bad omen,' said Grimoire.

'Food is never a bad omen.' Owain knelt down and picked one up as if to measure his belly to egg ratio.

Grimoire cast his attention back up at the tree. 'The eggs in themselves may simply signify supper, but this flock of rooks recently left the tree. It could mean for whoever lingers, death awaits.'

'Then you will agree to take me to my daughter?'

'I said I would sleep on the matter, as it would greatly delay our journey, but since we have been warned by our friends in flight that whoever stays here or near here may be marked. I then agree that the appropriate course of action is to escort you to your daughter's residence where you may find sanctuary, and we shall carry on from there.'

'What is her name, this daughter of yours?' Caredig scooped the eggs into a cloth and fastened it with a hemp rope.

'One of my daughters, for I have several, but she is the only one not born of the same mother as the others. Her name is Gwenllian.'

'And where would we find her?'

'Cwm Hir. It is not far from Llandrindod. Half a days ride away.'

'There was an abbey there that your men burnt to the ground.'
Caredig looked ill at ease as Owain responded to the question with a snarl.

'Never mind,' cut in Grimoire, 'there will be plenty more dissolution to worry about with future Kings.'

'Over the mountains, you say? More than half a day's ride I should imagine.' Gyffe looked at Grimoire for agreement.

'The day is already half gone so I imagine we shall be forced to camp somewhere. So possibly I'd think it will take day us a day and a half,' said Caredig joining in the welcome change of topic.

'Have you seen the condition of our horses?' added Gyffe.

'Two days then,' Owain conceded, 'but we shall ride as if we had only half a day to do it, all right?'

The horses let out a neigh as if to veto Owain's determination. They were Shire horses and had more than enough room to allow all four passengers position enough to sit two-by-two on each horse, Gyffe sat behind Grimoire and Caredig behind Owain.

'We shall head towards Ystradfellte where Llywelyn Bren gave up arms. Then head Northwards towards Tirabad,' said Owain.

On Owain's command, the horses lurched forward leaving the battered Castell Crucywel languishing behind. As they rode, the land about them began to dip and fall like green waves in a sea, hills staggered against hills, horizons staggered against horizons, and the unlikely caravan staggered against each other on the narrow tracks. Further along, the very stone actually began to change in appearance, it was if like crossing borders from country to country, and witnessing the alteration of cultural raiments. The reddening stone signified their approach to the substantial range needed to be crossed to reach Ystradfelte.

'So wizard …' said Owain now satisfied they had gathered a steady trot.

'Mage.'

'Sorry, mage, what lies ahead for you now the English have taken hold once again of my country?'

'We must not talk too loudly about such things as these hills carry voices to unwanted ears,' said Grimoire, 'technically referred to as an echo chamber.'

'I beg your pardon,' said Owain dismissing Grimoire's comment, 'I am, however, curious to learn why such gifts were bestowed upon me. Such as the stone that could call the very rains from the heavens, a cloak which blinded men from my presence and the mask which could turn my features to any soul living or dead.'

Gyffe perked up, he had been waiting all the while for his chance to speak about his contribution to the whole affair. Squits, in general, liked to hold the floor when speaking of their deeds. This made attempts in sharing stories around the campfire an event which often ended up in messy tussles. And being that their physical prowess was not fit for such sports, the outcome often resulted in a few accidental self-injuries. This usually was followed by a chorus of sulking sobs and at the very worst a bitten ear. In this case, however, Gyffe was not among his own kind, and besides, he felt that while on horseback his listeners were less inclined to be able to mob him.

'If you must know, it was I who planted those extraordinary objects within your reach,' said Gyffe nearly sliding off the saddle as he half twisted to discern Owain's reaction.

'What he said,' grunted Grimoire from in front and slightly irked to have Gyffe clinging to his back.

'You?' Owain laughed.

'Yes, it was I. Not sent by Grimoire but by Myrddin himself.'

'Ahem,' coughed exclaimed Grimoire objecting to how this explanation might confuse Owain. It was duly noted by Gyffe.

'It was Grimoire who sent me to Myrddin, of course. This was because he was too busy with …'

'All right, get on with the story,' said Grimoire, 'no need to dot and dash everything. Otherwise, we'll be at Ystradfellte before it's told.'

'Let the young man speak,' said Owain.

'I'm eager to hear of these happenings too,' said Caredig.

'Well, then,' resumed Gyffe quite pleased that some of his audience, not including the horses, were prepared to hang on his every word, 'I was granted access by Nymue to meet with Myrddin beneath the enchanted stone which had become his imprisonment.'

'Why would she let you see him?' Caredig asked. 'Her jealousies and possessiveness are well reputed.'

'Ah, it is a little known fact that Nymue is part fribbling squit, on her mother's side. She served Myrddin with all the dedication and diligence which we squits are prized for.'

Grimoire rolled his eyes and groaned.

'Her keenness to be an apprentice eventually led her to become a sorceress well in her own right. I knew of her well before she apprenticed under Myrddin. Indeed we never called her lady of the lake back then, we always knew her as the squit of the pond.'

'Was it not she who presented Excalibur to Arthur?' said Owain. 'I'm confused.'

'Actually, it was her half-sister but I believe Nymue gave it a polish before it was held aloft. However, I digress ...'

'Prattle is the word I think you are looking for,' said Grimoire.

'I was granted access to Myrddin's cave,' said Gyffe ignoring Grimoire's aside, 'surrounded by the most beautiful crystals one could ever imagine and then as if drawn by an invisible hand, I was urged into yet another cave. This one was furnished modestly and sat upon a chair carved out of the stump of an oak tree ... was Myrddin.'

Gyffe paused, he waited while listening out for any ooh or aah that might be forthcoming from his dramatic effect. The horses lumbering clop, twigs crunching, the canopies of trees swishing in the wind, trickles of water from far off cascades, all these sounds abounded, yet, an ooh or an ahh, there was none.

'He wasn't at all surprised to see me,' Gyffe continued, 'actually, he knew I was coming and had prepared a warming brew to welcome me.'

'I imagine the poor fellow is rather lonely,' said Owain.

'You might think that, but it is not the case as I asked him the very same question.'

'You asked the great wizard Merlin if he was lonely?' said Caredig.

'Well, I didn't use those exact words. I phrased it in the sense of being satisfied without needing people around him.'

'I assume you took your own company out of the equation?' said Grimoire.

'Interestingly enough,' resumed Gyffe' Myrddin is spoilt for companionship having all the past and future spirits, human or beast, at his council whenever he so needs or desires. He has this crystal ball see …'

'Carry on with the story and don't get caught up with details,' Grimoire interrupted.

'But the crystal …'

'Enough with the crystal, no one here needs to know of it. If you don't tell the story the way I think it should be told, I'll tell it myself the way I think you should say it.'

Gyffe hesitated for a moment to hopelessly try and grasp Grimoire's meaning before proceeding.

'Anyway, it was Myrddin who told me …' Before Gyffe could

continue, a surge of coal-coloured clouds swept in from the West, they were marbled with dashes of white light glistening within the puffy folds. A thunderous roar drowned out the heavens, and dark rain spectres sailed across the sky.

'They're on the move.' The horses jolted, and Grimoire steadied his rein.

'Who?' Chorused the other three.

'The magi are moving.'

'How can you tell?' Gyffe was loathe to change the subject but felt that this was a moment of momentous importance.

'Those cannot be ordinary rain clouds. That's magic, and it means at least from these parts the pilgrimage has begun in earnest,' said Grimoire.

'What must we do?' Owain shouted over the din of thunderous bellows.

'A little more riding, a little less talking,' said Grimoire.

In silence they pushed onwards, the idle mood for conversation halted by the spectacular scene above. All except Gyffe who in his mind was rephrasing some of the things he was going to say before the vast cloud of magic interrupted a perfectly opportune speech.

Myrddin then looked at me, and he said, 'your visitation is timely as I have a critical task to bestow upon you.'

'Me? But I am just a fribbling squit.'

'Squit, squit!' Myrddin bellowed. 'Fribbling or not, a squit is not just a squit. No, it is you Gyffe I sent for. I would not entrust this to any old body.'

'What must I do?'

'You may have heard of the Tree of Oracles, perhaps Grimoire mentioned it?'

'Of course, I have. I am Grimoire's most relied upon confidante. In great detail, we discussed the nature of the tree, but you may wish to elaborate on any particulars I may have missed.'

'In that case, there is not much I can impart of which I suspect you already know. The yew germinated not from a natural seed but from a source of magic so powerful that it induced conditions ripe for all life and indeed, and also death. The Empyrean Tear we called it. It was sowed by one of our ancients, a druid by the name of … Dab Woollyfoot.'

'Is it true that through some primordial sorcery he was able to manifest the nucleus of an idea into a solid living organism?' I asked.

'Ah, no, nothing as involved as that. Whisperers and poets have bent the origins, I believe. He actually obtained the handful of yew seeds from the apothecary Crow Harebell. It was she, through some hydrodynamic stratification, impregnated the kernels with a sentient genetic esse. A rudimentary quasiprobability, or so I'm told.'

I pondered on his last sentence before deeming that the most erudite response would be, 'Oh, right.'

'Yes, to bring to life something from the very substance that could destroy it. The fire of knowledge, some called it. Just as the age of information began with a spark, the occult was fired with the imagination.'

Myrddin then got up and went to a woodworm eaten chest, lifting the lid he withdrew a smaller box which he placed in front of me. He seemed to be searching for something, tossing out unusual items onto the floor and making important rummaging sounds. Finally, he presented three things for me to see. They were, a stone, a cloak and a mask. Of course, I knew what these were, but before I could tell him I knew, he told me anyway. I guess, he wanted to explain their characteristics in his own words.

The horses clambered up a narrow track following the ridge of a steep incline cut from the earth by wind and rain. The air began thinning, shortening the breath of the riders, and stinging their eyes gelidity. The whistling wind cut through the landscape in bleakly cold tones, reflected in the balding grass and pockmarked rocks. Grimoire eyed the path ahead sternly with Gyffe huddling behind him, still reflecting on his encounter with the great wizard.

'With these three mystical artefacts, the order of the magi can be sanctified within Cambria as the rest of the world goes about its ruthless persecution of our kind. It will, of course, all come down to you.'

'Why me?' I said.

'Because you are destined to be one of the most celebrated frits within the fold of the magi …'

'I didn't quite catch that. Can you repeat it?'

'Because you were there,' shouted Grimoire against the toll of the wind.

'What?' Gyffe straightened up looking around for the speaker.

'You were there, I said. Myrddin consigned the task of delivering the artefacts to Owain because you were the only one there. You've been muttering to yourself the whole way, and it is really rather irritating.'

The day was beginning to tire, a fine mist settled just above the ground, and the sky was dimming. Onwards they travelled until the precipitousness of the track dipped into dense woodland. The bulky horses struggled to pass through the foliage with varicose roots clawing at the slopes and soaring trunks spearing out from all angles seeking a prime position at the canopy. Owain and Grimoire both breaking off wayward branches, some sought their revenge by whipping back with a satisfying snap across their impartial assailants. Soon they could hear the tireless croon of water flowing close by.

'It must be the fall of crooked Einion. We are close. Let's give the horses drink and rest before we continue to Ystradfellte,' said Grimoire swatting back the lash of a willow's catkin.

Owain took to the front and guided his horse down the narrow wooded ravine. The horses stumbled and tripped on the uneven ground, gaining speed by the simple gravity of their weight. The riders held on tight even though if the steeds were to topple they risked being crushed beneath. Fortunately, the horses seemed all too aware of the potential messy predicament and began a strange backwards, sideways dance all the way to the end of the slope. At the bottom, both horses skidded in unison before reaching the waterfall beating its wet threads against the rocks. Soon enough, the riders dismounted and led the horses to the pool of water where they drank heavily.

'Invigorating,' said Caredig.

Grimoire and Gyffe appeared perplexed, but Owain simply smiled.

'Ah, my boy, you have the making of a knight if such peril stirs your blood,' Owain heartily slapped the messenger on the shoulder.

In return Caredig modestly bowed and then looking at Grimoire turned his attention to the eggs Gyffe had retrieved. 'I'll get a fire going, and we can partake of these eggs.'

Owain busied himself collecting dry twigs and leaves for a fire. When he returned, Gyffe was preparing himself to cast a flame spell.

'You shouldn't be doing that,' said Caredig, 'did you not pay heed to what Grimoire said about using magic at this time?'

'Just a little one, I thought,' said Gyffe eagerly rubbing his hands together.

Owain unravelled a cloth he had fastened to his belt containing a fire-steel and flint which he struck together to get a flame going. 'Not this time,' said Owain, 'better stick to what the old man has said.'

Caredig took out the eggs and punctured them at the tops to be placed in the hot ash once the fire had burned for a while.

'Why not just boil them? We've plenty of water,' said Gyffe.

'I'm going to bake them,' said Caredig, 'I was advised by Grimoire not to use the water, something about disturbing the unnatural flow of things.'

'Oh,' said Gyffe, 'it's all Grimoire, Grimoire, Grimoire today.'

Grimoire had wandered up to the waterfall and stood entranced gazing into its whitish gush.

'He worries me sometimes,' said Gyffe.

'Worry?' Caredig said.

'Well, sometimes he doesn't seem all there,' said Gyffe.

'All where?'

'In his mind,' replied Gyffe.

'He's obviously got a lot to think about, the whole upheaval of his way of life and the evolution of science. All very distracting I would imagine.'

'Perhaps,' said Gyffe picking up a smooth flat stone and skimming it across the pool. It bounced once and then vanished. Gyffe, puzzled, picked up another one and threw it across the water. Once again, the first contact it had with the water caused it to vanish.

'Something not quite right here,' he said.

'It just takes practice.' Caredig picked up a stone and flung it towards the pool. It too vanished. Both Caredig and Gyffe picked up a stone each and pelted them across the water.

'Stop!' It was Grimoire's unmistakable voice shouting over the din of the falling water. Caredig dropped his stone and Gyffe slyly tossed another.

'I said stop,' Grimoire bounded towards them, 'you are hurting it.'

'It?' Caredig gave Gyffe a puzzled shrug.

'Yes, it …'

But before Grimoire had time to explain Owain called out, 'the horses.'

All three looked around to see that with each slurp the horses were fading away. Their present form wavering and gradually becoming aqueous. At last, they stood as two watery beasts at the pool's edge, the rippling translucent muscles of their hindquarters flexed as they reared with a gargled whinny spraying a shower from their manes.

'Ysblennydd …' said Owain his mouth pouring out in almost wordless wonder at the splendid beasts.

'Ignore them,' said Grimoire, 'they are enchanted by a powerful magic.'

'Enchanted, you say? If I have one of these I would surely take back Wales from that false Welsh King.' Owain could barely control his infatuation.

One of the horses splashed its way towards him bowing its head down. Owain stroked its face, his fingers trailing through its watery features. 'Such beauty …'

'I advise you to stay well away, Owain.' Grimoire stepped in. The horse glared at the mage with disapproval.

'Step back wizard.' Owain drew his sword pointing it with a glint of death reflecting in his eyes.

'Mage,' said Grimoire holding his ground.

'We must stop him mounting that horse,' Gyffe said turning to Caredig for support but Caredig had left his side and was bobbing up and down on the other horse's back.

Grimoire eased himself away from the quivering tip of Owain's sword. 'Go on then. Take back what you think is yours.'

'Now I shall ride on land and sea. English King nor Frenchman will prevent me from reclaiming this land.' Owain leapt onto the horse and slopped into it bareback.

'You can't let him do it,' said Gyffe running to Grimoire's side.

'No, unfortunately, you're right, I can't,' said Grimoire, 'I can't prevent him neither.'

The horses brayed once again before diving into the pool carrying both Owain and Caredig with them.

CHAPTER FOURTEEN

Patch filled up the waterskin with hot water. He liked to place it between his feet when he went to bed. Crinkum sat on a cushion in front of the hearth, watching the flames intently.

'No more rounds. When wood burnt, fire out.'

Crinkum cast a wistful look at Patch.

'Waste to burn all night. Get square eyes, looking at fireplace too long.'

Crinkum hung its head and shifted uneasily where it sat. The concealed stash of split wood was not the most comfortable thing to sit on despite Crinkum's stony backside.

'Nos dah, Crinkum,' said Patch heading off to the kitchen where, in the pantry, on the second shelf, was an empty potato sack and an onion net stuffed with the down from wood pigeons. This was Patch's bed. He put on his nightshirt and slipped into the thick hessian bag. The waterskin warmed his toes sufficiently enough to elicit one of those comfortable yawns that signal the drift into sleep. He spent a thought for Grimoire and Gyffe and hoped they would return soon.

A hognome on its own is not much use to anybody but himself.

Patch put the thought out of his mind, thankfully his feet were not cold, and nothing could be done about anything else and so, between his feet and the beckoning troubles of the immediate universe, Patch found that glorious little space which provided the contentment of sweet nothing. He blew out the candle which was held in a truckle of cheese and closed his eyes.

Suppose they are all right. Grimoire can look after himself mostly, except when it comes to meals and Gyffe ... well, Gyffe can get himself out of a fribble like most squits can.

Patch reached out into the darkness, plunged his fingers into a jar and popped a pickled onion into his mouth. He chewed it squeakily for a while before pulling the sack up to his chin.

But what about that thing I saw in the darkness below? No, must not think of things below. How I wish I were warming Grimoire's slippers and preparing his evening mulled wine ... at this very moment, I might instead be trimming Gyffe's waggle as I do when it gets too straggly and irritates his Adam's apple.

The pickled onion's acetic juices tarted around his mouth, and he reached for another, but before he could pluck one from the jar, he heard a snapping crack coming from outside. Then came a thud, followed by yet more noises, then the splintering of wood, a succession of bumps, a smack of clunks, a clangour of din and finally, thudding footsteps clonking clumsily inside the house.

'Crinkum?' Patch knew very well that it wasn't but, by asking the question, somehow he allowed the very narrowest of likelihoods to be entertained as a vague possibility of reassurance. He slid further into the sack, but in burying his head, his feet popped out through a gash in the other end with attentive toes on the qui vive.

What could it want?

The footsteps crept through the kitchen momentarily stopping just outside the pantry where Patch lay in resigned retreat. He hoped whatever lay beyond the door had no appetite to appease from entering the larder. He heard a succession of deeply drawn-out sniffles and then the footsteps faltered away.

How did that banishment spell go? Bugger something. Out? Forth? Oh, what are the exact words Grimoire used to say to compel Gyffe to make himself scarce?

Patch waited and then heard what sounded awfully like snails being crushed. After a while, the noise ceased and the footsteps resumed until he could hear to them no more.

It's going after Crinkum.

Ever so slowly, which was by all accounts quick for a hognome, Patch eased himself off the shelf. He fumbled in the dark. 'Must protect hognome home, must be brave.'

As he was responsible for stock-taking all the goods around him, his poor vision did not hinder finding an object which might prove useful in defence. Should there be, of course, any need to engage in …

Combat.

'Combat.' The word didn't feel so exhilarating when thought with the expectation of actually having to partake in it. The hognome laid his hands on a hock of mutton, the weighty meat could prove a lethal weapon if handled correctly. Patch practised a little swing in the dark and whacked over a pouch of millet.

'Oh, oh,' exclaimed Patch suddenly motionless, mutton held midair. The coursing grain clinked on the floor like the sands of an hourglass counting down the possibility of being uncovered.

Ever so quietly, Patch crunched his way over the mess and pried open the door. He snuck into the kitchen and saw by the moonlight, a bowl of broad beans he had stewed for tomorrow's breakfast decimated. Beyond the cleaned out bowl were a trail of chewed husks leading out of the kitchen.

Thought those beans had gone over ... ha-ha, first strike ... bellyache.

Patch followed the trail of legumes to the living room where he found Crinkum curled up on the embers of the hearth. Patch pulled a candle from its holder and by placing the wick on a bright ember managed to produce a flame. He saw that the carefully aligned cushions on Grimoire's favourite chair had been dishevelled.

I'll teach this sorcerer some manners ...

With renewed determination, Patch looked around for armaments. He took the scuttle next to the hearth and secured it on his head, he grabbed a poker and slid it into his belt, hock in hand he clambered to the attic where he suspected the sorcerer was seeking out Grimoire's chamber.

I hear the wicked foulness with its black-hearted snort ...

The snorting was indeed coming from Grimoire's bedchamber. Gently, Patch pushed open the door and spied on the bed a lump so horrifically lump-like, it caused him to inch away with fright. He raised the hock in anticipation of an attack.

'Sheep? I smell sheep. Come here little sheep.'

The wicked foulness speaks. It wants to turn me into a sheep and then ... eat me.

The hock held above his head, Patch closed his eyes and prepared to bring it down on the lump. He then felt the mutton relieved from his grip, followed by a nibbling so greedily ravenous he had to bite his lip to prevent a gasp. His knees, however, began to tremble and the clacking they made could not be silenced.

'Rather good, better than those tough old beans. Got me a little windy they did.'

Patch stared into the darkness until the lump began to take shape. The outline of a gnawing witch feasting on a shank of bone became apparent under the strain of the hognome's poor eyesight. Patch pulled himself together. He groped for the box of sulphur sticks beside Grimoire's bed and struck a light. He put it against the wick of a candle, as the light brightened it became clear it was not the sorcerer. It was Ma

Gwrach, her wrestle of tousled hair wrangling over her pointy shoulders. She smiled a toothless smile and ignored the illuminative intrusion and carried on eating.

'Dear Patch, you are always considerate and always kind. Not like you to be sheepish, have a nibble if you please.' Ma Gwrach offered the whittled piece of meat.

Patch recoiled trying to find the words for finding an estranged witch chewing on mutton in his master's bedchamber.

'Where's Grimoire then? Out collecting graveyard dust?' Ma Gwrach said through a mouthful of meat.

Patch then noticed Prunewick, Ma Gwrach's familiar, encased in its glass shell staring at him with its hollow unblinking eyes. He immediately stiffened, his place within the magi reconfirmed and his usual stiff decorum fell into place.

'Gone, gone to take back stone.'

'Stone?'

'Stim ...u... —' the word passed uneasily and unsuccessfully through his lips.

'Oh that thing, fall into the wrong hands did it?'

Patch considered the general rightness and wrongness of hands before replying, 'stolen.'

'Careless,' said Ma Gwrach returning to the mutton and savouring a tough, stringy bit, making sure it met its mark.

'Not Grimoire's fault, boy was here, boy took it.'

'Taken? Not like Grimoire to invite a thief across the threshold. Usually, they invite themselves. That's the preferred modus operandi of most thieves, swindlers on the other hand ...'

'Not invited, found.' It were times like these that Patch wished he had the verbal faculty of being able to unabashedly blurt details out.

'He found a thief, did he? Well, if you find a thief, bring it home, expect to be robbed.'

'Not at first thief, was messenger at first, then thief.'

'What kind of messenger? One who dispatches the unfortunate tidings of the missing things he took.'

'Boy had treaty.'

'Stolen?' Ma Gwrach carelessly dropped the stripped bone.

'No, had King's mark on it. Sent by messenger.'

'Ah, now we are getting somewhere,' said Ma Gwrach with a fatigued sigh, 'it is the prophecy, six Kings in total. The mole has made a pact with the wolf aye?'

'Almost.'

'I see. Almost being delivered but mostly not at all received?'

'I think,' said Patch, wondering if he actually thought it or just blathered the word for reassurance.

'Well, that was quite a voyage but I'm glad we finally got to the bottom it. When can we expect Grimoire's return?'

'We?' Patch said.

'You and I, and also that winged thing Grimoire calls a familiar.'

'Us?' Whether he wanted to actually acknowledge the fact, Patch had, by uttering the word, now fulfilled Ma Gwrach's wishes.

'Yes, yes … I have some news for him dear, which he might not want to hear, but he ought to listen just the same.'

Patch had always oddly respected Ma Gwrach. She was one of Grimoire's oldest friends and her comings and goings, although not always embraced with the eagerness one should perhaps show, were in the bygone days so routinely lodged in daily life that any attempt at discontent might as well have been put in the too hard basket.

'How long?' The words stifling in his neck.

'How long what?' Ma Gwrach grabbed the hock off the floor and finished what remnants remained on the bone.

'How long … stay … you?'

Ma Gwrach put the bone down again, she shifted sideways on the bed and stared at Patch. He felt his awkward question would produce an equally awkward response, at least awkward in the sense of having to accept it.

'It's a good question and one that must wait until after I have left.'

CHAPTER FIFTEEN

The waters lay still with no sign of Owain or Caredig, not even a burble or bubble from whence they went in. Gyffe stood at the edge peering at nothing more than his own concern.

'Where have they gone?'

'They have been led to Poseidon's paradise, a maritime netherworld.' Grimoire stroked his beard thoughtfully.

Gyffe tugged at his waggle, but the action failed to mimic the desired contemplative effect. 'Lost forever I imagine.'

'Possibly but I hope not. There is little I can do, such spirits use the streams and rivers to pass through to other planes, other worlds even.'

'Is there no strong magic which can bring them back?'

'It is not a matter of strength Gyffe, the *ceffyl y dwr* is born from the same seed of fire that spawned the Tree of Oracles. A procurement spell would serve no purpose here, nor would a restoration spell be any good, even the long overdue spell which I've used countless of times on fellow magi in order to get my books back would be a mere drop in the ocean. No, we must call upon the elemental spirits themselves to reverse what we have just witnessed. Now, where's my wand …?'

Grimoire rarely ever used his wand and was tempted to cast a procurement spell to find it until Gyffe, who had been all the while watching the patting down of pockets, thought to pluck it from his boot from where he regularly tucked it. He held the twisted knot of ivy within Grimoire's reach.

'Here it is.'

'Ah, I knew I had it somewhere.' Grimoire gave it a quick polish with his cloak, he then picked up a piece of quartz spotted on the river's edge and began walking in a circle.

'Let me see, north, south, east, west … where's west then?'

The wand quivered ever so slightly as Grimoire waved it around the crystal. Grimoire began a chant of whistles and clicks which Gyffe recognised as the song of the sea, the ancient language used primarily by dolphins but also understood by all aquatic spirits and demons.

Phsssssst,

Tchick, tut,

Tck, tck,

Phssssst,

Tsk, tck.

The crystal began to perspire a dazzling dew as it took flight from Grimoire's hand and plunged into the waters. Grimoire raised his hands to the river and chanted …

I call to crooked Einion,

The yearning and forlorn,

Lost spirit of the falls,

Grant me my thirst,

To drink upon your form.

Gyffe watched intently as a figure parted the cascade, it waded across the surface of the pool. Its sloshing mass made up of tumbling flab and dripping ligaments. A hairless head glinting like a puddle, one eye plugged full of aquatic debris, a hole at the side of the head dribbled where an ear would normally protrude. One arm was but a stump covered in fragmented stoney caddisfly carapaces and the opposing leg shaped from bandy wood, burnished by the caress of flowing water.

'Who summons me from my dankness?'

'My name is Grimoire,' said Grimoire.

Einion belched a bubble of foam. 'Why Grimoire have you stirred me from the deep?'

'I can assure you that your reveries are but temporarily interrupted as we have lost our companions to the *ceffyl y dwr* and fear we may never get them back.'

The water spirit bobbed on the spot before wadding slightly closer. 'What need have I to be sprung from the gurgles and gargles to be told of such happenings?'

Grimoire pursed his lips. It was always baffling to him why spirits insisted on asking, in different ways, the same question repeatedly.

'Have our companions drowned?' Gyffe asked with the hope of changing tack.

'And who are you to haul me from the lathering froth and—?'

'I am Gyffe, the fribbling squit,' Gyffe interrupted.

'A fribbling squit,' corrected Grimoire.

'Drowning won't save them. The pool is enchanted, I should know, the river beguiled me once I discovered it had taken my true love.' The water spirit stooped in its sodden sadness. 'I lost her in the numerous cascades. Sometimes I catch a glimpse of her reflection, sometimes only my own, but we are both here, for all time.'

'I'm sorry to hear that,' Grimoire mumbled behind the cloak of his beard, 'we may be able to help, but that all depends on whether you can you help us.'

Einion turned to Grimoire, his working eye opened wide and gushed several watery blobs as it winked into focus.

'It is possible, but in return, I ask one thing of you.'

Grimoire felt he was getting into the rhythm of this repetitive spirit talk.

'Summon Gwladus's father and plead for his blessing, as once given the waters will merge.'

'We shall indeed give it our best shot but only if I can request a small detail from you.'

'Be my guest,' said Einion.

'Tell me where he is buried and we will do our utmost to make sure that although still eternally wet, you will at least be forever wed,' said Grimoire.

'The graveyard of St Mary's church at Ystradfellte, you will know his tomb by the crest of a hare. If you are successful in gaining his blessing, can I ask one thing of you before I go?'

'Most certainly,' said Grimoire.

'Where would you like me to drop off your friends?'

'Hmmm, the banks of Clywedog Brook, the nearest bend past Cwm Hir Abbey?'

'I know it. It shall be done.'

Einion then stepped into the pool and was gone.

'It shall be done? As if all he's got to do is pop downstream and fish the poor sods out. Meanwhile, we've got to persuade an angry dead parent to forgive his estranged daughter into tying a watery knot with a fluvial swain, whose appearance makes sitting in the bathtub for too long positively rejuvenating,' said Gyffe.

Grimoire shrugged. 'Well, if he's been dead long enough, he may have had time to think things through. Let us depart immediately, Ystradfellte is not far away.'

'Can't we use a transportation spell to quicken our journey?'

'I suppose the urgency of the situation allows for it, although, the accuracy of a geographical peregrinate spell is not always dependable, something to do with atmospheric conditions.'

Grimoire raised both arms to the sky, and Gyffe huddled in close. Grimoire chanted the spell towards the heavens.

'✓Իᛮ'

A wild wind swam about them beating down in thunderous cracks above their heads, it tore into the sky as if the earth itself was to be pulled into a vacuum.

'Hang on to your hat,' bellowed Grimoire.

A ray of blueness shot through the sky and enveloped their bodies, swirling and swirling like a spinning top, gathering force until within seconds they were sucked up through an opening in the atmosphere which closed with a sudden whoosh.

CHAPTER SIXTEEN

A tidy gathering congregated in the Ystradfellte village square. So neat in number that the congregation happened to be only two puzzled villagers and an equally bemused tomcat. From above in a willow tree, they were staring at two figures caught spectacularly in a tangle of cape and legs.

'No one said anything about a hanging did they?'

'Nay, not officially, then again Llywelyn never got the official go-ahead when he got his honorary necktie.'

'That was almost two hundred years ago.'

'True. Although methinks, this isn't an official condemning.'

'What makes you say that?'

'Nobody is trying to sell us spoiled meat.'

'More tavern wreckage perhaps?'

'Looks that way.'

'Told Lobkyn to stop selling that stuff to tourists. What did he call it?'

'He didn't see the point in giving it a name since after the first tankard you'd be unlikely to remember it. Besides, he can't read nor write, makes putting labels on things a waste of time.'

'Well, it ought to have some kind of warning as it not only makes 'em as blind as bats but hangs 'em over that way too.'

The two villagers moseyed away, with each idle step seeming to tut-

tut along the path.

Once the coast was clear Grimoire and Gyffe did a tremendous amount of wriggling which found them both falling feet last to the ground with a clappering dong. Gyffe checked his head for any sign of a detached cerebral lobe.

Shuffling himself upright, Grimoire corrected his hat. 'Well, that didn't go so badly.'

'Could have been worse,' said Gyffe still holding his head.

'Has been,' Grimoire got up as the second dong resounded.

Gyffe lifted himself to his feet, and they both stood in front of St Mary's Church surrounded by the forever resting, of which one, would soon be stirred.

'Well, let's go wake him up,' Grimoire marched forward followed by Gyffe, both of them keenly eying the gravestones for the crest of Gwladus's father. Gyffe was the first to find it by tripping over the thick stone edging and finding himself face-to-face with the meanest depiction of a rabbit he had ever seen. On the headstone was an inscription suggesting the general mood of its inhabitant.

I cannot see

I cannot smell

So, your wretched flowers

Do not serve me well.

Grimoire hurried over and placed within Gyffe's open palm a small pouch and silver spoon.

'What do I do with this?'

'Take a sample of the dust, and then we must leave quickly before we are spotted loitering amongst the dead,' said Grimoire.

Gyffe scooped up a spoonful of the earth and slipped it into the pouch. They both hurried out of the graveyard with its slanting stone slabs and parting epitaphs but on spying two men walking towards them, Grimoire pulled Gyffe by the collar, and both leapt into a thicket which unfortunately turned out to be a bramble patch.

As the men passed, they stopped briefly to eye the two, in a tangle of cape and legs, untangling thorny twines. Shaking their heads, one of the men said to the other, 'Remind me to have another word with that Lobkyn.' The two men then walked off, leaving Grimoire and Gyffe to their ouching and cussing. Finally free of the spiky snare, they waited until the tut-tut of the disapproving villagers was at a distance.

'What do we do now?'

'I have an idea concerning that chap Lobkyn,' said Grimoire, 'we must get to the tavern before those two do.'

They only had to turn down a small lane before seeing the wooden banner with the words The Old Inn. Grimoire and Gyffe stepped into the tavern with outbound chests and the distinct air about them of having arrived. The innkeeper failed to notice the mage and his assistant enter. He was busying himself behind the counter weighing portions of pork scratchings into several earthen jars. A fire, the only sign of life in the threadbare public room, did its best to liven up the quarters.

'Could this be the very same Lobkyn we've heard so much about on foreign soil?' Grimoire bellowed, outreaching his arms as if to offer a hug to the establishment.

'Do what?' Lobkyn looked up from a scoop of crackling he was about to pour. His rotund face was pearled with perspiration that drizzled down rosy cheeks, the thin circle of hair about his head was ruffled, and a distinct aroma of strong drink wafted from his breath despite him standing a good several yards away.

'Word of you has even reached the ears of King Henry himself.'

'What word?' Lobkyn scratched his head in confusion. 'What is all this?'

'Have you not heard?'

'If it be me own words then surely I've heard 'em as it would have been me that said 'em but any others I can't account for,' said Lobkyn.

'Did you hear that, Gyffe? He's not yet heard even of his own words, but by all accounts of who said them, it would be he that spoke them.'

Lobkyn eyeballed Grimoire for at least a few minutes and the perspiration dripping from his brow doubled as if Grimoire's words had caused his brain to melt. 'Look, what do you want? And what's with the All Fool's dress?'

'Ah, these garbs be not jests,' bellowed Grimoire, 'they are the very latest attire worn at the royal court, anyone who is anyone has followed suit in wearing apparel such as these.' Gyffe tugged at each loose section of his clothing to highlight the earnestness of Grimoire's claim.

'Anybody?' Lobkyn swabbed his brow with the end of his sleeve.

'Everyone,' Grimoire smiled warmly, 'except those who wish that their dissenting garments be bequeathed as goods and chattels through the deceased estate.'

'What has all this got to do with me? Whatever it is you are selling I can't afford it.' Lobkyn tossed a hairy piece of rind into his mouth and ground it with his jaw as a routine of stress relief.

'We are not here to sell, we are here to buy.'

Lobkyn slowed his chewing, he wiped a streak of sweat from his neck and craned it towards Grimoire as if the protrusion might assist with magnifying further details of the words, "Here to buy".

'Let me elaborate,' said Grimoire who was starting to feel a bit more comfortable in the role of a royal merchant, 'it is this nameless brew, this *labeless* liquor, this anonymous ale, that has become the King's fancy of late, and presently he is on his way here to commission a special batch for the royal court.'

By now, the half-chewed lump of pork was almost through Lobkyn's throat as he prepared to verify his potential fortune.

'Here? King Henry in this here tavern? Prove it.'

Gyffe was at a complete loss as to what Grimoire was planning. He stood at Grimoire's side nervously, awaiting what proof he had in mind.

'Indeed, the King shall probably be standing in this very spot and to prove it, I shall show you His royal dispatch.' Grimoire produced from his pocket a scroll which he handed over. Lobkyn took the scroll, unravelled it and pretended to read.

'Handwriting is a bit messy.'

'Do you think the King has idle time for matters of the quill?' snapped Grimoire whose excuse for his own slovenly handwriting had always been that by the time his hand responded, his mind was already twenty words ahead.

'Here, what are these numbers at the bottom?'

'That's how much the King is prepared to pay.' The memory of trying to solve the move-the-bench problem in a narrow castle stairwell gave him a pang as he remembered those formative calculations before he managed to solve it.

Lobkyn's eyes widened as he glared at the length of numbers inscribed.

'And what does this word mean?' Lobkyn held up the scroll and pointed to a series of repeated scribbles.

'Er, his signature written for good measure, many, many times.'

Grimoire had always been dissatisfied with his mark and it was his habit to doodle many variations repeatedly while ticking over his thoughts.

Lobkyn knitted his brow and when he did a bead of sweat found the funnel of his nose and trickled down it. 'They don't look the same.'

Gyffe stepped in with a haughty laugh betrayed by tones of a spooked crow. 'The King goes by many names, the King mainly, the King, then there's King Henry and Henrique when he visits the Kingdom of Portugal. He also likes to be known as Good King Henry, Henri when in France and it is said he sometimes signs his secret love letters as Hen —,'

'In a matter of hours,' interrupted Grimoire by placing his foot on Gyffe's toes, 'you shall have his full council to yourself, but in the meantime, my companion and I are tired and could do with a short nap. Have you a room we could make use of until the King, as he is mostly known, is due to arrive?'

'Don't normally house guests but there's a small drying-out room up top, not linen, locals.' Lobkyn finally caught the dangling sweat bead from his nose with a quick lick of his tongue.

'That will do nicely,' said Grimoire.

'I should probably give the place a bit of a dust if its to receive royalty. Maybe, I could drape a tapestry or two.' Lobkyn surveyed his business as if having just procured it.

'Good idea,' said Grimoire, 'but the most important thing is that you are dressed fit for a King. Have you something similar that you can adorn yourself with? Otherwise, I'm afraid the King may have to choose a suitable shroud instead.'

Grimoire could see that this last remark had caused a jittery reaction in Lobkyn who didn't so much as scratch his head, being that Kings had a peculiar cure for such an itch, but held it in place lest King Henry was in a curative mood.

'I'll see what I can come up with.' Lobkyn for a moment seemed to be willing his brain into a state of clarity. 'Years ago, we used to hold an open stage for minstrels and the like, some of them left their belongings in the cellar … err … dressing room. They wore outfits not unlike the ones you've got on.'

'What luck, now if you could kindly show us to our room, we'll retire for an hour.'

Lobkyn, huffing and puffing up the narrow stairs, led them to a room which was furnished with a single quilted mattress on the floor, a washbasin and a bucket. Once Lobkyn's heavy breathing was no more than an indistinct pant, Grimoire hastily shut the door.

'Suppose this is a trap,' Gyffe said, noticing the room only had one window too small for either of them to fit through should the need to escape arise.

'Hmm, a trick within a trick,' Grimoire replied, rubbing his hands together. 'Then, in that case, we must get to work, time is of the essence, and the dead tend to be a bit groggy when stirred.'

'Should I prepare the spell circle?'

'No time, I am going to have to cast what is known in the trade as a pell-mell spell. Pass me that bucket.'

Gyffe picked up the bucket and held his nose. 'It's got vegetable soup in it, mostly carrots.'

'Toss it out the window, we've no need for carrots.'

Gyffe opened the window and bailed the contents outside. From below, came bellows of disgust, followed by a duet of retching. Gyffe poked his head out the window to see the two men from the village square.

'Curse you and those drunkards Lobkyn,' one of them shouted, raising his fist.

'We were just about to have stern words with you Lobkyn,' the other chimed.

'We will be back within the hour. For now, we shall have to bath and change, but we promise you our mood shall not.'

They both dripped away like snails leaving a sticky alkaline glaze across the cobbles. Gyffe shut the window and pulled the curtains tight. Grimoire took the bucket and placed it before him on the ground. He knelt beside it and cast his hands over it.

'Haven't done this one for quite some time, not since summoning Grandpa Clapfart to ask him where he last put the house keys before he died.'

The bucket began to rollick as if possessed, dark flames shot out from its mouth, twisting and twirling like the tongues of black devils.

'Pour in the dust,' said Grimoire.

Gyffe opened the pouch and standing back, poured in the contents. The flames ate them up, and as Grimoire danced his hands in the air, swirling red smoke followed his fingers as if Grimoire was composing a requiem. He then cast the spell.

'ᚺᚱ◇'

The outline of a figure appeared. The aura gradually taking the shape of an elderly man, eyes adjusting to his predicament, jowls sprinkled with ghostly fibres, a sour expression drooping above his prickly chin. The foul face did not seem surprised nor curious, in fact, its dour expression was so morbid Grimoire considered extinguishing it and resorting to plan "b" which for all intents and purposes had not been devised yet.

'Wha–, where am I? Is this the after ... afterlife? Who dares to undead the dead? Damn it, why am I in a bucket?' The spectre growled before laying its eyes on Grimoire.

Grimoire shifted uneasily on the spot while Gyffe backed away into the shadows. Grimoire turned his palms at the spectre. 'Oh, the augury of man's one true fate, herald of our present future past, the watchman of the damned, living soul of a bygone life ...'

The spectre's face screwed into a grimace. 'Enough! Dead and buried will do. Now, why do you disturb my everlasting grievance?'

Grimoire took off his hat and held it to his chest. 'I call upon you for a request?'

'Put your hat back on, stand up like a man and speak properly. And even then, I am not able to grant you a request as I have no life left in me to give. Go pester another who lives.'

'It is only you who can fulfil this deed,' said Grimoire with a huff as he put his hat back.

'Only me? There are thousands who die each year. What did you do? Put a name in a hat?'

Grimoire was tempted to kick this man's bucket but then realised the man already had.

'Concerns your daughter.' Grimoire was eager to get to the point.

'I had three daughters, two of sense and one without.'

'I speak of only Gwladus.'

'Oh, that one, she is no longer my daughter. I've disowned her. That power was invested in me when I gave life to the insolent brat.' The spectre screwed up its face with the bitter memory. 'She gave up her father for a river. I have two others, admittedly both their spouses are wet behind the ears but not as much as Gwladus's intended. And intended he shall remain.'

'I am told she wanted to give her heart to the young man called Einion.'

'The pauper who asked for my blessing? He too gave himself to the river. Seems to be a very popular river for impudent children.' The spirit grimaced again, but this time the grimace was from one of whom was wizened in the way of grimacing.

'That boy has asked me to summon you.'

Gyffe eyed the spectre curiously as Grimoire's words took effect. For a moment, the apparition appeared curious, concerned almost.

'Do they live?' he finally said.

'Yes, but in such a way that without the blessing, they shall be eternally unhappy.'

A different sort of grimace returned on the spectre's face. It occurred to Grimoire that this man must have spent a lot of time practicing such grimaces in his eternal confinement.

'Why should I bestow such a thing now? Are they not forever locked in each other's saturated pockets? Seems like a typical marriage to me.'

Despite wanting to give this man a piece of his mind, the piece he reserves for dullards and dolts, Grimoire continued with the diplomatic approach. 'They are of the same river, but of different streams, they shall forever flow together but for always be apart.'

The apparition's wispy arms weaved together in defiance. The expression deadened as much as a dead man could. 'Why should I provide them with the satisfaction that was denied me?'

'Because you're the adult.' Gyffe's remark was quickly put to rest with a firm poke of Grimoire's elbow.

'Because it has been asked for again in the hope that you may on reflection have changed your mind,' said Grimoire.

'Reflection? You think death is one prolonged glare in the looking-glass of damnation? The matter has not changed, and I heard that remark from your friend. One more squeak out of you and you'll both be in this bucket.'

Grimoire took a long breath, longer than expected, as he prepared himself for a bit of a speech. 'The matter has changed a great deal. Your other daughters are long gone, their husbands also laid to rest, you are bereft of earthly riches and now must count your worth only in memory and those who remember after you. If you amend your decision, you will always have a river that flows in honour of your goodwill.'

The apparition also drew a long breath, and it seemed that to follow might be an equally lengthy rebuttal. 'A river? Hmm, doesn't sound so eminent an afterthought. A sea perhaps, or even an ocean, but a river? Why have you been sent to persuade me to give my name to a river? If my daughter, and this Einion whom she fancies, be spirited, could they not have approached me personally?'

Grimoire was tempted to light his pipe and expound on the

difference between the underworld and the otherworld but decided against it. 'Technically they are not dead, and Einion, at the moment, is busily at task rescuing some friends of ours who were taken by the falls. Owain Glyndwr and a messenger called Caredig.'

'Owain Glyndwr?' The apparition lifted a smouldering eyebrow.

'Do you know him? Is the name familiar?'

'No, I do not know him … but, the name is familiar, yes. Just because we deceased no longer trifle in the affairs of the living does not mean we don't hear whispers from that world. Yes, I have spoken to some of his allies long-since slain.'

'Forgive me, but I posed my question bluntly. I am to understand this of the dead but what I meant was if the name was in your favour?'

'It is, and if Einion is indeed undertaking this noble act, I will relent and give my blessing for the only reason of backing the revolt, not I should disclaim, for that irritating squirt, Einion. But only on one condition.'

'And that is?' Grimoire hoped there would not be yet another wish to fulfil.

'You let me bloody well be.'

'I can assure you we will,' said Grimoire trying to think of even the most unlikely situation where he should wish to share this man's company again.

'Does that mean we can bring him the good news?' blurted out

Gyffe.

'You can,' sighed the spirit who then proceeded to grimace as well he could under the circumstances of just having relented, 'I, therefore, albeit reluctantly, give my blessing between my so-called daughter Gwladus and that tadpole Einion. But …'

Grimoire and Gyffe gave each other a withering look.

' … Only if Einion succeeds in bringing back your companions … or at least one of them … the important one. And I shall be watching from beyond. Can I go now?'

Grimoire nodded, and the spectre faded away into the black flames, which in turn shrunk until they were no more.

'Can we trust him?' Gyffe stepped towards the bucket and moving it away with his foot.

'Hmm, I'd think faith rather than trust is required, it being a feuding family and all. We'd better hurry to Clywedog Brook to see if the other end of the bargain has been upheld.'

Gyffe seemed to acknowledge what Grimoire was saying, but it wasn't until a kindly hand was placed on his shoulder that Gyffe appeared ready for the next move.

'Let's go rescue our accidental friends,' Grimoire said, almost with a smile.

Grimoire and Gyffe bounded out of the room, stomping down the stairs to the public bar of the tavern. There, they found Lobkyn sitting on a chair looking somewhat glassy-eyed. He had fixed upon his person an outfit, not unlike Grimoires, a large pointed hat but brightly bound with colours of orange and purple, he also wore a cape, bright with myriad cuts of colourful cloth. He had even gone so far as to wear upon his feet coloured rags tied in a knot. In his hand, he was holding a tankard of ale and beside him a jug …

'Nerves,' Grimoire said as he hurried past him. Just as Grimoire pulled open the door, the two men Gyffe had managed to drench in the bucket slop marched into the tavern. They ignored Grimoire and Gyffe and strode right up to Lobkyn who staggered off his chair and bowed down ungraciously before them. Lobkyn raised his head and cocked a blood-shot eye.

'Yer foiled slyness … I Lob … y … kin …' and before he could muster another word, he promptly fell flat on his face.

This gave Grimoire and Gyffe a much-needed diversion upon which to slip away. Slamming the door shut behind them, came a barrage of angry shouting by the two men inside. The last words being heard, 'Lobkyn, you are a fool.'

'Poor Lobkyn,' said Gyffe thinking back to the times he found himself in similar predicaments without the allowance of strong drink to help pardon his actions.

'He'll live to serve another ale, but our friends won't live to savour one if we don't use some magic to get to Clywedog Brook fast.'

'I'm quite glad you said that.' Gyffe smiled hunkering down under Grimoire's cloak. Grimoire once again raised his arms to the sky. The world around them blurred, the twisted rays wrapped around them and whisked them through the parting. This time their arrival was less incongruous, and they found themselves more or less upright on the shady bank of a brook. They wandered along the bank for a while before Gyffe spotted something up ahead bobbing on the water.

'Might it be them?'

Grimoire urged Gyffe forward with a gentle shove. As they approached, they saw two figures slumped in a coracle fastened to a stone by a thick rope on the bank. On closer inspection, it was clear that in the boat was Owain and Caredig, but no movement was to be seen. Gyffe ran up and tried shaking them, for a moment there seemed a stir, but whatever enchantment had bewitched them was still at work.

'What can we do? Is there magic to reverse the effects?' said Gyffe wandering if Grimoire might resort to water or a slap over the face.

Grimoire surveyed the two slumped bodies and stroked his beard. 'Hmmm, perhaps I could try this.' Grimoire produced a brown clay bottle from underneath his cloak.

'A potion?' said Gyffe.

'Of sorts.' He leant over the two bodies and forced a good portion down each of their throats before standing back. Gyffe too stepped aside for whatever potion Grimoire had used to take effect it would surely be strong stuff. Before too long, there was spluttering and whooping. Both Owain and Caredig shot up like hares in the long grass. They spent a few seconds bobbing their heads around in shock before trumpeting a song of belches and finally slumping back down in the coracle.

'Where are we?' Owain grunted at last.

'What has happened?' Caredig croaked rubbing his head.

'As promised,' Grimoire said proudly, 'we have brought you somewhat safely to Cwm Hir. Where you may find refuge with Gwenllian. As for what has happened? We had to take a slight detour to get here.'

'One involving a grumpy old ghost and a bucket,' added Gyffe.

Soon the sun was setting and it wasn't long before all of them had ample rest at the hospitality of Owain's daughter. The next morning it was time to say goodbye and Owain came to greet them. At first, they did not recognise him, he was dressed in simple stockings, tunic and a sheepskin coat. His hair had been roughly chopped, and his short beard was gone. He looked younger and not unlike any shepherd, one might pass on the slopes.

'Of course, I will take some time in thinning out,' he said, extending a muscly arm, 'but swapping a sword for a crook will no doubt slacken the thew.'

'Will you be adequately shielded here?' said Grimoire.

'Shielded? Am I not now the wolf in sheep's clothing? Will I not have every scope upon on the hills? I will tend to the bleating lambs and the bards will tend to my story.' Owain extended his hand. 'It will be sad to no longer have your company, my dear wizard.'

'Mage,' said Grimoire, 'I'm sure our paths will cross again.' Grimoire shook Owain's hand firmly.

'A pleasure to ride with you sir,' said Caredig also offering a firm handshake.

'Likewise young messenger, perhaps one day we shall ride side by side for Cambria, on steeds made of flesh and bone, the way it should be.'

Gyffe stepped forward to shake Owain's hand.

'Hywl fawr Gruff,' said Owain with a wave.

Gyffe lowered his hand and pretended to scratch his knee.

Into view rattled a horse and cart driven by a young farmhand.

'Don't fear, he only understands Cymraeg.' Owain gave the farmhand a friendly wave, 'Your cart awaits. If the weather holds up, you should arrive home by morning.'

Grimoire turned to Caredig. 'Is something on your mind?'

The messenger hesitated. 'Is it that obvious?' Caredig said unsure to whether it was an answer befitting the statement of which was never made.

'I knew it. The boy wants to stay,' shouted Owain. 'Good, I did offer, but perhaps he felt obliged to go ...'

Grimoire permitted his face one of his rare genuine smiles.

'Of course, he does,' said Grimoire. 'He was up half the night chatting with Gwenllian.'

'I'm not sure I'm quite suited to a life of magic,' said Caredig humbly.

'It's the hanesion, Grimoire, it calls to us all,' Owain added.

'Very well, it is for the best. If ever you do need further refuge do not hesitate to come to us.' Grimoire was about to turn and leave but felt his elbow grasped.

'How will I know where to find you? I have little memory of that day I awoke in your house,' said Caredig.

'Take this.' Grimoire took from his pocket, a small silver pendant with a necklace attached and passed it over. 'When the time comes that you may need us, open the pendant and consult the inscription within. You shall know how to find us.'

Gyffe helped Grimoire step onto the back of the cart, and the two of them did not look back. The cart lurched in the direction of home, they sat in silence for a while, the jolting of the cart, prevented any easy opportunity for words. The countryside crept along with its continuous wend and slade always obscured in part by copses and escarpments, at every turn unfolding in a feast of teal, russet and taupe. After some time Gyffe turned to Grimoire. 'What was that potion you gave them to lift the enchantment, it must be powerful magic?'

'That was no magic Gyffe, that was a bottle of Lobkyn's ale I absconded from the bar before we left.'

'Oh, right, of course, and what about the silver charm you gave Caredig.'

'Also not magical,' said Grimoire.

'What was it?'

'The inscription inside is our address.'

CHAPTER SEVENTEEN

Ma Gwrach's cackles could be heard coming from the kitchen. She was in the midst of casting a conundrum spell. Patch hadn't the foggiest idea what a "conundrum spell" was, so after fetching ingredients for her, he decided to attempt a clean up of the living quarters which since Ma Gwrach's arrival had become an obstacle course of strewn about bits and bobs, molehills of candle wax and incinerated incense, mugs of half-drunk tea, bunched feathers, pots of steeping decoctions, salt rings, and protective crystals on every surface.

'Start where?' Patch stood in a swamp of mystical debris.

He had just about unpicked all of Ma Gwrach's hair strands from the banshee-claw comb when he heard the outside gate rattle. His attempt to get at the door was hindered by catching his foot in one of Ma Gwrach's wicker baskets left carelessly on the floor. Hobbling, he tried to kick the basket away, he banged his head on one of her dangling spirit bells and at the same time stepped in a tray of pond scum she had been fermenting.

'Eek,' said Patch wiggling the slime from his shoe.

The outside gate clanged as it was swung open by force. Patch finally made it to the door and placed his footstool down to grasp the handle. Just as his hand reached it, the door opened, sending him flying with it and pinning him against the wall. He held on tight to the handle as Grimoire and Gyffe spilt into the room.

'What on earth has happened here?' Grimoire roared picking up off the floor a box containing a pile of his old broken wands. 'Must get around to fixing these,' he muttered trampling his way across the mess.

Gyffe closed the door with Patch still dangling from it.

'Where's Patch then?' Gyffe said nimbly hopping around the clutter.

'Here.'

Both turned around to find Patch trying to wriggle his feet back onto the footstool.

Grimoire sharply about turned and made his best impression of a march up to the hognome.

'At least no windows are broken,' said Gyffe as Crinkum smashed through a pane and swooped up onto its perch. 'At least only one,' he said, correcting himself as he went to find a brush and scoop.

'Now tell me, Patch.' Grimoire sternly held his gaze upon the hognome balancing on the stool. 'Why if I leave you with the great responsibility of orderliness do I return to see that it appears you have been responsible for the very opposite?'

Grimoire leaned in close to examine the hognome as if evidence of culpability. 'I didn't take you for the sort Patch. However, it seems to me that hidden beneath that reclusive aged hognomeous self is an animal of the worst partying kind. Would this be true?'

'Not a hognome, was a Gwrach.' Patch tried to hide watery eyes beneath his bushy eyebrows.

'A witch did this?' Grimoire widened one eye until Patch could see his entire cowering face in it, 'a witch did this? Is that what you are trying to say?'

'Not any witch, a Ma Gwrach witch.'

'Really? How intrusively fascinating, Ma Gwrach? Here? Hmm, this wreckage is the hallmark of one of her typical visits. I must admit, in retrospect, what I know of revelry for you Patch mostly consists of one perry pear wine too many and a stack of pice bach. However, I have not heard from Ma Gwrach for many years.'

At that moment, a shrill cry of surprise came from the kitchen. Grimoire hopped his way across the room and entered the kitchen to find Gyffe, pointing at three equally dismembered parts of Ma Gwrach. Her head was upside down on the table, torso balancing on a stool and her legs warming themselves by the kitchen hearth.

'Ah, my dear friend Grimoire has returned. I'd warmly welcome you with a cwtch, but as you can see, I've come undone,' said the severed head with a wobble.

'This is a conundrum,' said Grimoire.

'Wasn't supposed to be,' replied Ma Gwrach, 'but instead of a tidy entrapment cast upon the house, I've gone and done it on meself.'

'The house? Why on earth would you want to cast a conundrum spell on the house?'

All three of Ma Gwrach's body parts became animated. 'To

confound intruders of course. You've already had one, or so I'm told, can't afford another. Besides, you can't leave this lot behind without some kind of assurance that we have made provision for their wellbeing. For goodness sake Grimoire, lesser magic folk don't mean less important.'

'I had considered the latch on the door might have sufficed,' said Grimoire arms now firmly behind his back.

Ma Gwrach's legs crossed, her arms folded, and her head not knowing quite what to do, rolled around a bit. 'Patch told me about your recent burglary, and as we are to be away for some time ...'

'We?' Grimoire turned to Gyffe but showed no reason for doing so, 'you're accompanying me to the yew?'

'That I am.' Ma Gwrach smiled, but from the position of her head, it appeared as a scowl.

Grimoire took a few long seconds to think about this. 'But I haven't seen you for ... I thought you were ... I considered you might have passed on ... to ... wherever it is you, witches go ... when you do.' Grimoire cleared his throat. 'To be honest, I had planned on attending the meeting alone.'

'Never mind. There will be plenty of time for catch up. For now, I was wondering if something might be done about my disparate bodily parts. I'm beginning to feel an itch on my nose that my hand, unhelpfully, is currently scratching at the other elbow.'

Gyffe twisted his head to the side as he examined Ma Gwrach's upturned head. 'Can she be put back together?'

Grimoire gave a wilful sniff at the air. 'Is that betony I can smell?'

'Don't think so, no betony in the potion. Woundwort though, the main ingredient it is,' Ma Gwrach said with another wobble.

'Who collected your ingredients?'

'Patch, it was your gnome-servant Patch who was kind enough to offer his services.'

'Ah, I see. Woundwort would be found farther afield, betony, however, grows closer in abundance. You do know Patch has poor sight?'

'I did ask him if he ...'

'And what did he say?'

'He said yes, and off he went.'

'You do know his hearing is none the better?'

'Well, he might have told me.' Ma Gwrach's head almost toppled off the table.

Gyffe stepped in before another tangent took hold. 'Yes, but can we put her back together?'

'Hmm, tricky but yes we can. We can put the parts back together, and they will be whole again.'

'Just like that?' asked Gyffe.

'Not entirely, we must make sure that her parts are facing the right way in under six turns ...'

'I can do that,' Gyffe stepped in about to turn Ma Gwrach's head upright when Grimoire grabbed his collar and yanked him backwards.

'But we must only turn two parts simultaneously.'

'If I turn the head upright and then turn the legs upside down, then we'll be back where we started.'

'Exactly, that is why dear Gyffe it is called a conundrum spell.'

'Aha! If we turn her torso and legs upside down, we can put all the parts together and then when she is whole turn her upright.'

'If we do that she will fall over on her head. A conundrum spell fathomed wrongly may never be righted. Better leave me to it Gyffe, I need time to think.' Grimoire stroked his beard which by all accounts meant he was either thinking or he'd found a flea.

Gyffe hesitated, not because he really thought he might be able to help Grimoire unravel the effects of the spell, but more so he was curious how it was to be done.

'Off you go, Gyffe,' said Ma Gwrach cheerily. 'Go and make yourself a strong mug of sundew tea, we've been stuck in more baffling pickles than this haven't we, Grim?'

It was her pet name for Grimoire, and he hated it. Grimoire choked upon hearing it. 'Err, yes, we've been in some fine messes.'

'Go on,' said Ma Gwrach to Gyffe, 'make yourself a pot of tea, a strong pot of tea.'

Gyffe reluctantly left them to it, closing the kitchen door he made his way back to the living room. 'Tea, tea, tea, is all she thinks about that witch.' Gyffe poured a heaped teaspoon in the kettle and hooked it above the fire. He sat down and stared at it. It had been a long week.

'Won't boil.' Patch had resumed his comfortable spot rocking back and forth in his chair.

Gyffe, in his weary state, had failed to notice him there. 'What?'

'Kettle, won't boil watched.'

Gyffe had forgotten that the kettle was cursed. Grimoire had picked it up cheap from a travelling swynwyr in the Knucker's Nest, and if looked at it would never boil. Gyffe averted his eyes and turned his attentions to Patch.

'Have you ventured underground … yet?'

'Aye,' Patch replied, adjusting the throw over his legs.

'Do you think it's safe?'

'Safe? Don't know. Not home for hognomes nor squits. Too long to be there. Feel danger.'

'It's only for a few centuries.' Gyffe knew that it was unlikely to be so short a time, but there was no point in worrying Patch about such things. 'You could take up embroidery again? Or whittling?'

'Hmm, humming,' Patch cleared his throat in the manner of a melody. 'What about dragoyle? Only gargoyles on Ffinnant's place.'

Crinkum snarled from its perch. Dragoyles disliked gargoyles. Dragoyles were shaped by the elements, born from wind and stone.

Gargoyles were made by humans, and enchanted gargoyles were forged by masons working under the guidance of enchanters or sorcerers. Dragoyles considered them to be glorified waterspouts with dubious motives and repellent algal halitosis. Gargoyles were either bad-tempered, stupid or sometimes inconveniently both.

'A lot of windows in that house,' Gyffe sighed.

'Cut hole in door,' suggested Patch.

'What do you mean?'

'Put flap on it.'

'Oh, good idea, a dragoyle flap?' said Gyffe.

Crinkum shook its head. It had been trying to hint for years at the need for such a flap and it was only now they had finally cottoned on. Gyffe noticed Prunewick placed on the mantle above the hearth. It seemed to wave at him without moving its tiny branches.

'Prunewick will need light.' Gyffe examined the twiggy shrub considering whether or not he should be looking out for canker or leaf curl.

'Not like light,' said Patch.

Gyffe stared once again at the motionless shrub. He remembered Ma Gwrach telling him how she had picked it up from an onmyōji who had rooted the elm over an enchanted rock and clamped it with the silk from the antheraea yamamai. Ma Gwrach dubbed her familiar according to the mystical Japanese tradition of Kotodama, but the chosen name of

Runewitch, as she choked from a horehound sweet, ended up as the unintended name of Prunewick, and as with the predicament of the lozenge, the appellation stuck.

'But surely all plants ...'

'Got sensitive bark,' said Patch.

Just at that moment, Ma Gwrach, reassembled in one piece, swanned into the room lifting her skirt as she did a little jig. 'All together now ...' she squawked. 'Well, at least Prunewick can get into the spirit of it.' She pointed, falling backwards into a chair.

They all looked at Prunewick who stood motionless in his chalice, the same wooden expression on its face.

Grimoire shuffled into the room and although appearing together in the bodily sense had a look upon his face which seemed to express that he was at a loose end.

'How did you do it?' Gyffe asked.

'With great difficulty, exacerbated further by itchy feet and a gabby head.' Grimoire slumped down in his usual chair. He reached for a clay jar which held his favourite pipe mugwort mixture blended with coltsfoot to soften the grassiness. Taking out his pipe, he popped a thimble full into the chamber and ignited it with his finger.

Gyffe poured himself a clog of sundew tea. 'Well, at least we now have the Stimuliris back.'

After a couple of puffs, Grimoire cleared his throat. 'The Stimuliris has been stolen.'

Gyffe recalled his concern to Caredig about Grimoire losing his mind. 'Was stolen,' corrected Gyffe taking a sip of his tea.

'It has been retaken. I had all but forgotten about it, but its thief had not. I should have concealed it better, but I thought to place it within my cloak, any pickpocket would need days to rummage through the hundreds of pockets, and indeed the circumstances were ripe for the picking.'

'Careless,' Ma Gwrach grunted pouring out a clog of whortleberry wine. 'Can I tempt anyone else with a drop?'

Without looking at her, Grimoire held his hand out, and Ma Gwrach found a cracked vase, half filled it and placed it there.

'We went through all that to get the Stimuliris back only to lose it again.' Gyffe cradled his mug.

'And I know who it was, and they know where we are,' Grimoire growled into his cup and taking a long sip of the wine. 'However, its whereabouts do not concern us now. There will be no time to go after it again. Although, the theft does mean that those who resist the Order of the Magi are shaping the future faster than I thought. It seems their spies have no qualms in getting right up under our very noses.' Grimoire stared hard at Gyffe.

For a moment, Gyffe was busy attempting to dislocate the thought of what it might be like under Grimoire's sinuous conk with its crusty floccus and perpetual leakage when preoccupied with a head cold. It was only after the thought was banished, did Gyffe pick up on Grimoire's stare. Astounded and a little offended at the implication, Gyffe turned away to look at Patch, which was always unhelpful as the hognome was now fast asleep.

'It does, therefore, mean that you can't stay up here much longer and sooner rather than later, you must go underground and await further instructions.'

'How soon? A hundred years?'

'Nine hundred and ninety-nine years, two hundred and thirty-three days sooner, I should think.' Grimoire blew a ribbon of smoke across the room.

'That's tomorrow,' said Gyffe.

'It may very well be as soon as that,' Grimoire said matter of factly, 'I have a feeling that somehow the stimuliris will be returned but with it will come tremendous peril. We cannot take any chances.'

Ma Gwrach, who couldn't keep still at any one time, had removed the cloche encasing Prunewick and was proceeding to trim its foliage with a small pair of spring scissors.

'Even as we speak,' she said with a snip, 'there are opportunists who are planning on using the time when magic sleeps to strengthen the presence of all-round wickedness.'

She placed the cloche back over Prunewick and gave it a polish with her sleeve.

'Ma Gwrach is right. I know of several dark shamans from the East who have refused to meet at the yew, there are undesirable wizards in the South who will no doubt follow their lead, and most of the sorcerers I've crossed paths with will boycott the gathering out of principle.'

'Where does that leave the rest of us then?' Gyffe sloshed the remainder of his tea around.

'Vulnerable but not without some protection, that is why the lesser magic folk have been excused from the gathering. The dabblers, the ellyll, the tylwyth teg, hognomes, the bwca, coblyns, the aes sídhe, fribbling squits, and yes, even the homunculus piskie, for they have been delegated the duty of guarding the dolmens of the equinox once the vote has been cast.'

Gyffe shuffled uneasily on his chair. He had witnessed firsthand some of the devastating effects turned-wizards had produced, not always through malice but sometimes just because they were feeling a little out of sorts. He also suspected that the higher beings of magic, although in all other respects endowed with a collective wisdom one could only aspire for, had not really thought this one out.

'The plan sounds premature to me,' said Gyffe who on preparing to bite his tongue, missed and the words tumbled out.

Grimoire's face became a scowl. Ma Gwrach intervened by pouring more tea into his clog.

'No one planned it this way,' she said topping up her own clog with wine, 'no one planned anything, it was written in the stars. The lore of magic has, for now, run its course. Those who continue to practice will face horrific persecution, harrowing trials and unthinkable torture.'

Grimoire feeling the warming effects of the whortleberry wine closed his eyes and spoke in hushed tones. 'From Annwyn a seer named Drab Greyling travelled to Ynys Dywyll to give council to the druids there. He told them that their way of life would be challenged and that a Roman General would arrive at the isle and destroy them if they didn't go into hiding along with the many who already were. They ignored his warning, some say they felt their magic had the strength to defeat a legion, some say that one of the high druids had cracked a druid's egg and was bitten by a serpent within which had put a curse on the isle, others say that Drab struggled to be convincing in his prophecies due to having the unfortunate mannerism of smiling when he tried to be grave. The army did arrive, and the druids were all but wiped out. It was to be the first epoch, for almost four hundred years magic lay in wait, waiting to return. Each equinox will be different, each more dangerous than the last, we cannot predict what we will find when we are awakened, but we will depend on those who have survived the backlash to bring us up to date.'

'We will be of little use hiding underground,' said Gyffe.

'You will be free to come and go as you please, but you must avoid being seen or heard. You must make the shadows your friend and the moonlight your guide. Above all, you must be patient and stay out of trouble.'

Gyffe considered the commands with slight disdain as he felt, as a squit, being impatient and staying well within reach of trouble was, although potentially far more dangerous, much more satisfying. However, he now began to feel sleepy. He looked over at Patch who continued to snooze contentedly in his rocking chair, Crinkum was crouched on his perch in stony silence, and turning to Prunewick he thought he spied a yawn, but then Prunewick's mouth was perpetually gaping. Gyffe felt the room begin to spin, a dull blurriness glazed over his eyes as he caught Grimoire getting off his chair. He saw Ma Gwrach lean towards him, her bendy nose pointing at him. She cackled. Before darkness descended, he thought he heard Grimoire say,' Leave them be, your tea has done the trick.'

CHAPTER EIGHTEEN

The next morning Gyffe awoke to find Patch in the living room holding a chamber pot at arm's-length.

'Last one,' Patch said, going outside and tossing the contents with a splash. He came back in, giving the door a shove shut with his foot.

Gyffe spied on Grimoire's chair, a wooden box with the words "Fribbles for Squits" scribbled on it. Gyffe lifted the lid and examined the contents.

'A wand,' Gyffe held up the crudely shaped rod, 'it's made of bronze. And what's this?' He picked up a silver sleeve which had stamped upon it "Crafted by Wonderful" there was a note attached to it in Grimoire's handwriting.

'Wand dongle,' Gyffe read aloud, 'adaptor that fits on the grip of the wand. Instructions not included.' He plugged the adaptor onto the wand and a thin display lit up along its length. He noticed there was a round button above it which he pressed. The word "Menu" appeared in muted green text. He pushed the button again. "Saved spells" appeared, he pressed the button again, "Spell intensity". He pressed the button once more, "Spell range".

'Well, I never,' said Gyffe ogling the wand before returning to the box and its contents.

Inside there was a pair of simple shoes. The note attached read, "The

Feat of Flying, does what it says. Instructions also not included. Purchased secondhand at a horse and cart boot sale, hope they fit".

There were more things in the box. Gyffe pulled out a quill made from a feather the likes of which he had never seen before. The plume, a bright chevron of sapphire and silver. The note attached read, "Quill made from the feather of the Tattle-tale tit, write it, and I shall read it." There was a black corked pot for its use with the label, "Think; thought-provoking ink".

Gyffe couldn't help writing the word "test" on the back of the note.

The last item in the box was a small velvet-lined container full of colourful potions. Gyffe read the labels, "Centuary Vulnerary; for wounds and abrasions", "Eye of the Owl; cat's gall and hen's fat", "Mind Febrifuge; rue seeds, vinegar, old ale", "Evil Repellant; rue, cumin, powdered pepper, honey", "Antidote for a Shaman's Curse; rosin, white wine, bay laurel gum", "Evade Foes; scent of vervain", "Ear of the Bat; ram's urine, oil of eels, houseleek, wild clematis, boiled egg". Gyffe held up the last potion, it read, "To Make one Merry; brandy".

Gyffe saw that Patch also had a box. 'Are you going to open it?'

Patch lifted the lid and eyed the contents.

'And what did you get?'

'Socks.' Patch held up a pair of socks rolled in a ball.

'Maybe they are enchanted socks.'

Patch sniffed at them. 'Not enchant … ing to me.'

He rummaged some more and held up a neatly folded cloth. 'It's ... handkerchief.' He attempted to unfold it, but it was glued together. 'Also used.'

'You're not reading the notes,' Gyffe said, grabbing the note tied to the socks and reading it aloud, "Socks; cold feet curative". He then took the note attached to the handkerchief, "Remedy rag for a runny nose". Gyffe saw that also in the box was a chew stick, several bars of basil scented soap and a phial containing nail clippings labelled "Domarth's Claw". Gyffe held up the phial. 'Ah these might be useful,' he said shaking the slivers of trimmed nail.

Patch handed him the accompanying note. It read, "Domarth's Claw; not sure why I collected them, might be useful for something, believe they taste a bit like fennel".

'Hmm, maybe not, well you can have these flying shoes, they look a bit small for me.' Gyffe handed Patch the pair before opening Crinkum's box. 'Let's have a look at what Crinkum got.' Gyffe lifted the lid. Inside the note simply read, "Volcanic Bites" with a little slogan underneath, "If you lava your dragoyle, treat it with volcanic bites".

Crinkum dropped from his perch. Grabbing a clawful of the rocks, it popped them into its mouth and munched pleasurably before spitting something out which hit Patch on the snout. It was a nut. A hazelnut to be precise. Crinkum scooped another clawful and carried on munching while Gyffe and Patch continued to watch the spectacle in a somewhat mesmerised state of disdain. Gyffe turned to Prunewick to see what it was making from all this. He did not expect Prunewick to be particularly animated, but he noticed that it had a peculiar way of expressing itself without actually having to do anything. He noticed that several of Prunewick's branches were sagging.

'Have a look at Prunewick, do you think it's poorly?'

Patch went up close to the glass and inspected the little tree.

'Do you think it needs water?'

Patch shook his head. 'Doesn't like water, likes tea.'

'Tea? What sort of tea?'

'Bogbean tea.' Patch patted his pockets as if to check to whether any was at hand.

Gyffe for some inexplicable reason waited until Patch had finished patting. 'Do we have bogbean tea?'

'No, nor a bog, no bog, no bogbeans. Glad.'

'Why so glad about that?'

'No Boggards neither. Horrible things.' Patch cringed at the thought.

Gyffe couldn't take his eyes off Prunewick. 'One of the branches moved, I'm sure of it. Did you see it twitch?'

'Not a twitch, saw nothing,' said Patch.

'It's pointing to the window,' said Gyffe.

'Was already. Never moved.' Patch went to sit down but stopped in his tracks when he felt a distinctly unfamiliar presence in the room.

Gyffe's line of sight followed Prunewick's lateral, which had always been pointing that way, to the window. Crinkum had all but finished the volcanic bites. It held the last one in the air and was about to drop it into its mouth when it caught sight of Gyffe and Patch staring unnervingly towards it. Crinkum hesitated, slackened its arm and went to put the bite back into the box before tossing it into the air and catching it between grinning teeth.

'Look,' said Patch.

Crinkum flinched its neck to catch a glimpse of what they were so fixated on. Along the window crept what could only be described as a root of a tree, its knobbly limb sliding across the glass followed by smaller roots snaking in through a small crack in the window.

'It's an enchantment,' cried Gyffe racing to the door. He flung it open to find an ivy had enveloped itself around the bars of the outer gate. On the foot-worn mat with the faded words "croeso" was a note, Gyffe snapped it up and closed the door quickly behind him.

'Say?' Patch found himself poking Gyffe on the arm.

Gyffe opened the note and read it aloud. 'Down is the only route to leave.' Gyffe scrunched up the note.

'Uncondrum spell?' said Patch.

'Successful this time. They've forced our hand.' Gyffe grabbed Grimoire's somewhat worn armchair cushion and pushed it into a basket. He took Prunewick and laid it carefully onto the padding. Patch readied his trolley to put in some last-minute supplies but Crinkum seeing the opportunity for a free ride jumped inside.

'Well, that's it then, down we go,' said Gyffe feeling the walls begin to quiver.

Gyffe led the way as creeping roots sprung from the cracks in the stone tiled floor. Patch fired up the steam cart, smoke sputtered from the funnels, it rumbled and shook. Patch began pedalling forwards just as a taloned branch smashed through one of the windows. The walls began to squeeze inwards, creaking and crunching from the embrace of the encroaching foliage.

'Quickly,' said Gyffe.

They made it to the garden steps where in an alcove used for storing mops and brooms lay the trapdoor. Opening it, Gyffe stumbled down the narrow steps, Patch steered the steam cart down the hole losing complete control as it bumped its way down with Crinkum jolting to each clomp of the trolley behind. Finally, they reached the dark corridor in a less than graceful pile. Gyffe and Patch helped each other from the wreckage while Crinkum leapt out of the trolley with an eagerness it could not hide.

'Look Crinkum, candles.'

Crinkum bounded along igniting each and every one along the way. Soon the corridor was aglow unveiling its oak cladding and patterned frieze. Between each set of candles, hung paintings of druidic dwarves

toiling over alchemy in caves equipped with fiery furnaces, enormous
bellows on great stands, bendy tubes of glass, iron racks flanked with jars
full of flaked and liquid minerals.

'Crach Ffinnant's kind,' said Gyffe peering at each one as they
walked down the corridor.

'Not his real name,' muttered Patch ignoring the row of passing
scenes. 'Not interes … ted,' confidently mouthing the last syllable.

The relationship between hognomes and dwarves had always been
somewhat strained, although both had a passion for mechanical driven
industries. The leading factor of this tension was caused by dwarves
being slightly taller. Dwarves and hognomes were expert miners, in fact,
like dwarves, most hognomes lived in complex warrens dotted along the
verges of mountains and cliffs. They too liked to work with metals
producing many fine implements, but unlike dwarves, they abhorred the
smelting of ores for the manufacture of weapons.

Patch couldn't help but stop at one portrait displaying a dwarf
smelting a quadruple-headed axe. 'Pah!'

Hognomes had no inclination for physical combat of any sort, even
playful wrestling amongst youngsters was frowned upon. In earlier less
civilised times, one tribe of hognomes wishing to invade another tribe
would go about it in a distinctly non-violent way. The unaggressive
would-be attacker sauntered up to the warren they wanted to take-over,
carrying with them all of their possessions, then as soon as the

opportunity presented itself, they would just move in. With an air of ambivalence, they would place their own furnishings next to the ones already in place and proceed to go on with life as if nothing was amiss. The defending hognomes would continue to ignore the invaders until they had firmly settled into their space. Following this would begin routine petty, annoying behaviour.

Patch stopped at another painting and glared at it. 'Not art.'

'Come on,' said Gyffe, 'I thought you weren't interested.'

'Not,' said Patch shuffling along.

In these scenarios one hognome would affix a kettle above the hearth while the other hognome would come along and replace it with his own. The invading hognome might find his mug of perry pear wine suddenly in the hands of the invaded hognome being casually sipped as if he had poured it himself. This habitual irk would go on for as long as each tribe could bear until all of a sudden, the invaded or invading tribe, would find the other upped and gone. Some of these invasions would last many years and to an outsider watching, the lack of ferocity and confrontation would be enough to send that person completely mad.

'This!' cried Patch pointing at a painting that showed a dwarf leading a group of hognomes into a mine.

It was the first time Gyffe had heard Patch declare abhorrence with such clarity.

'Ignore it,' said Gyffe, 'we've got to locate the room.'

Patch shuffled onwards throwing his arms up in despair. 'Fakes, all fakes.'

The dwarves referred to hognomes as "emongoh" which being hognome spelt backwards was how the dwarves viewed them in the way of enlightenment. The hognomes referred to the dwarfs as "frauds" which they felt was a much more amusing backward spelling of the race's title despite the semantic adjustment to achieve the desired result. This longish history of distaste for one another was also partly the reason Patch felt so ashamed at having to reside in the keep of one.

'And this—' Before Patch could continue, Gyffe had him by the shoulders and was urging him steadily forward.

Eventually, they came to the door Patch recognised. Entering, Crinkum once again did the rounds of igniting candles. One by one, they infiltrated the room with light. The piled assortment of crates and sacks took up but a small portion of the large living area. The room was resplendent with an enormous hearth, its cast-iron surround featured black dwarfish imps peeking out from behind moulded rubble, a great chain also wound itself around the entire frame representing the druidic dwarf "chain of events" with each loop signifying each progressive era in dwarfish history.

'Well, here we are,' said Gyffe, 'our new home.'

'For now,' said Patch seeing the room in enough light for the first time.

The rest of the room was fitted with impeccably crafted, if not slightly damp, dark varnished furniture. From corner to corner, the floor was covered with woven rugs creating a sea of blended colours and patterns. The walls were adorned with tapestries that wove the history of dwarfish civilisation throughout its mythology. Above the fireplace was a large portrait of a dwarf, who had by means of a comb made some attempt to represent an air of sophistication, but there was no doubt that the artist struggled to ornament the grisly features painted on the canvas.

'That's him,' said Gyffe placing Prunewick on the mantle, 'our absent landlord.'

'Absent. Good. Not wanted here,' said Patch checking that all the crates, boxes, chests and miscellany were accounted for and undisturbed.

'Crach Ffinnant kept his true heritage hidden,' said Gyffe getting the fire going with a candle, 'he went about mankind as a poet and confident of the sorcerer Hopcyn ap Thomas. He endured ridicule for his small stature, but despite this, he made friends with powerful men, even Owain had crossed paths with him several times and heeded his prophecies.'

As soon as the fire sputtered to life, Crinkum, who until then had been cradling a candle, seized the opportunity to curl up by its side.

'It's fair to say that this place has had its ups and downs, quite literally you know. Designed by a renowned dwarfish architect, or so I am to believe. When the King found out about it, he organised a skirmish and attempted to smash it to the heavens. Unbeknownst to the King, and to Crach at the time, the architect had it constructed from material mined from beneath its very foundation. The explosions weakened the earth below and the entire building sunk in a billow of smoke as if it never stood there in the first place. The soldiers feared magic had caused the disappearance and retreated to the King with the news that Crach Ffinnant and his castle had vanished into thin air.'

'What became of dwarf?' said Patch placing himself on a footstool.

'The fate of Crach was never known, some say he returned to his race who had long retreated from mankind, preferring the deep caverns which gave them access to Annwyn.' Gyffe strolled alongside the tapestries examining the imaginative scenes of great battles and journeys. 'Others say Hopcyn ap Thomas turned him into a familiar, an owl no less, as a way to conceal him from his persecutors.' Gyffe noted one tapestry showing an exceptional display of complex mining machinery. 'A few think that Crach was actually a shapeshifter who was damned as a terrifying beast ...'

'Really?' said Patch with a yawn.

One particular tapestry showed dwarves and hognomes working together as they built a bridge over a deep ravine, the bridge to the Tree of Oracles. It was one of the few times both races worked side by side in harmony, or so they say. 'While a handful mentioned that he had a penchant for balmy weather and was sunning himself somewhere in the tropics. Whatever the case may be, he never came back to this place.'

Gyffe hesitated as he had noticed that one of the tapestries was blank. It was if it was waiting for yet another chapter in dwarf history to be sewn upon its fabric.

'That's odd,' Gyffe turned to Patch but the hognome having begun listening to the fate of a dwarf had found it riveting enough to nod off.

CHAPTER NINETEEN

Grimoire looked back at the caved-in castle, he could see a dim light coming from inside and knew it was time to leave.

'Ready now,' he said to Ma Gwrach, she took his cue and pulled the rope loose from the pier.

The boat wafted onto the steady river carrying them further away through the belly of the cavern. It continued to drift as a narrow pass loomed ahead. Grimoire pinched a shag of mugwort, stuffing it into his pipe and lighting it with a snap from his fingers. The trail of smoke floated behind them, giving the rowboat the impression it was being powered by steam.

'It's been a long time since I voyaged through the snarls of Annwyn, I'm assuming the dangers that lurked in my day are still very much the mainstay peril across these waters?' said Grimoire.

Ma Gwrach pulled the yoke and shifted the rudder as to correct the boat's alignment, they were heading straight into the mouth of the snarls.

'Doubled I'd say, dear Grim, ever since the call to congregate at the Tree of Oracles. Many foul wizards and dubious wyzen have ventured to the snarls where they may dip in and out of the otherworld without notice. That means all sorts of unsavoury sorcery is being smuggled back and forth without scrutiny.'

Grimoire felt a rustle in one of his pockets.

'You got mice again?' said Ma Gwrach.

Grimoire slid his hand into several pockets before producing a piece of paper. 'Haven't had mice since I stopped carrying around your caraway seed biscuits,' he snarled, looking at the paper. 'Hmm ...'

'What's that there then?'

'It's a note from Gyffe.'

'What's it say?'

'Test.' Grimoire shoved the note back into a pocket. 'Rather an odd thing to write but then again squits are rather odd all-round.'

The boat surged forward as the current increased. It floated towards a narrow pass, barely squeezing through the opening, it dipped down a series of short cascades before being sucked through another opening. Grimoire had to hold onto his hat as the boat lunged forward. Once through the tunnel, it was more or less straight, stretching for about a mile and a half, its stony cavity slick with glinting shawls. Grimoire poked his nose over the boat's edge and could see several vessels of Annwyn passing beneath the water going the other way, their oars causing gentle ripples on the opposing surface. Ma Gwrach left the yoke to its course, and she took out a crystal ball from its pouch cradling it in her hands.

'I shall try and determine what lies ahead,' she closed her eyes.

'Shouldn't you be gazing into the crystal?'

'I have practised a technique which allows me to see within the ball using the eye of my mind.'

'And that works does it?'

'Hmm, I seem to be getting a lot of interference,' said Ma Gwrach.

'Is it dark magic?'

'No, it seems to be coming from directly opposite me.'

Grimoire bit down hard on the lip of his pipe before taking a long draw. As the boat drifted along, he eased himself back to observe Ma Gwrach taking in her visions. After some time he heard a curious noise emanating from her nostrils, it dawned on him that she had fallen fast asleep. He flicked his foot at hers to prompt a response. She stirred.

'Are we there yet?' she said, eyes still closed.

'There? Not at all, we are still very much here.'

Ma Gwrach's eyes barely opened. 'Hush now,' she said with an almost toothless yawn, 'we approach the Gate of Dreams.'

Grimoire turned to see two oblique faces on each gate. Their contorted mouths and lopsided eyes as if chiselled from a nightmare. He recalled passing through them many years ago when he was a younger, more capable mage in dealing with uncertain destinies. One door would lead them astray, the other would lead them directly to Annwyn.

'If I remember correctly,' said Grimoire, 'one gate when asked a question shall tell a lie and the other only the truth. A rather old chestnut, but one I successfully cracked at the time. Should be a doddle.'

The boat came to a bobbing halt just below the gates.

'Proceed no further. To pass onto Annwyn, you—'

Grimoire stood up at the bow of the boat.

'Yes, yes, I must ask you both a question. A question determining which one of you is lying and which one is telling the truth. I've done it before you know. All I need to do is just ask one of you if the other is—'

The eye of one gate opened just a little bit wider.

'We've changed the format.'

'Changed the format? Since when?' said Grimoire.

'Since we decided our answers only served to assert or deny what was being asked…' The gate on the right chewed over its words with its wooden lips.

'… Instead of actually being true or false …' The gate on the left gave a haughty sniff.

'… Completely countermanded the question.' The right gate spat out the statement with such pomposity it snapped Ma Gwrach out of her dreamy state. She wriggled upright.

'So what's it to be now? Noughts and crosses?' said Ma Gwrach.

The left gate ground its teeth with a heavy creak. 'Ask us a question, be it false or true, two answers we shall give, but only one shall let you through.'

Grimoire scratched his beard and found a biscuit crumb in it which he nibbled thoughtfully.

'One question, two answers. Only one answer will lead you to

Annwyn.' The gate on the right smirked with some effort.

'Yes, I get it,' Grimoire said irritably as he contemplated a question. 'Hmm, let me see.'

'Well,' said the left gate, 'we await your question.'

The boat bobbed silently in the water as Grimoire stood up to address the gates.

'Come on,' said the right gate, 'we're waiting.'

'Why can't you answer my question?' said Grimoire.

'What question?' snapped the gate on the left.

'You haven't asked it,' said the gate on the right.

'Right it is.' Grimoire grabbed the oars and pulled them through the waters. The boat surged forward, and Ma Gwrach slouched back again with a jolt. The gate on the right opened, letting them pass through.

'How can we be sure we've chosen the right gate?'

'One answer would lead us to Annwyn, only one gate provided an answer, the other asked a question. They've really let themselves go on the riddle front these days.'

The little boat drifted steadily down the river. The moist cavern walls curved about them, veering off around blinded bends. Onwards, they floated until finding themselves in a dim recess of an underground pool that stretched as far as the eye could see, and as it was so dark, that was not very far at all.

'There doesn't seem to be another way out,' Grimoire said waving his hand with a flourish and casting a lucency spell, but as soon as it was cast some darker magic extinguished it.

A gentle sloshing beyond the shadows, indicated that they were not alone.

'There's something in here with us, I can feel it,' said Ma Gwrach.

'Well, if something can get in surely it stands to reason it can get out. Therefore, so can we.' Grimoire peered into black nothingness. He could barely make out some shape at the water's edge. It was as if the rock itself had faces peering from the darkness.

Ma Gwrach reached into her bag, producing a handful of nuts, she snapped one open between her fingers and a little glowing sprite popped out. She popped another and, another, until the whole side of the cavern wall was lit with tiny bright sprites all whizzing about looking for a way out. 'I never travel without a pouch full of candela nuts.'

The lights cast shadows and the shadows cast faces. Faces locked in stone with bodies deformed into clumps of rock. Some hung from the ceiling and others sprouted from below the level of the water.

Grimoire peered at the faces, studying them as best he could in the dim light. 'Onlookers and bystanders, neither passing by nor looking on, trapped in a reflection of time.'

'Statues you mean?' Ma Gwrach said, 'it's a fairly typical character trait.'

It was possible for the boat to wend around the petrified forms as the sprites cast a path of light. Grimoire put his hand up to signal Ma Gwrach to halt her rowing.

'I recognise that one,' he said, looking at the figure which hung from the ceiling, its arms reaching for the water below. 'It's "Weirdly Bearded" Bardolph, the shaman who claimed to have beguiled the afanc into doing his will. Looks like he won't be at the meeting then.'

A small stone dropped into the boat, followed by another, and then another.

'It's pebbling pebbles,' said Ma Gwrach.

One by one, the little lights went out as the sprites turned to stone and dropped. Grimoire picked up one of the pebbles, its face like an owl in an ivy-bush. Grimoire skimmed it across the black waters.

'I consider this the first sign of trouble.'

He looked at Bardolph again, noticing that in one hand he held a hollowed-out stone.

'Get me a tad closer to Bardolph.'

Ma Gwrach inched the boat forwards. Grimoire stood up, trying to release the stone from Bardolph's grip. It was held fast. Ma Gwrach took out her wand.

'Need a hand?' she said, pointing the wand at the statue. Ma Gwrach spoke the word …

'ᛏᛚᚱᛜ'

A silver bolt shot out, it hit the wrist of Bardolph, shattering it from the arm.

'Well played,' said Grimoire catching the severed stem of rock. He held the stone aloft, it illuminated brightly, filling the entirety of the cave.

'What you got there?' asked Ma Gwrach, 'I wouldn't think this the time for a game of hurling.'

'This is an adder stone, the fossilised egg of a hydra. It is extremely rare as the ancient remains of pregnant hydras are not easy to come by, but it also happens to be an incredibly potent gorgon repellent. As we shall soon see.'

The statues were now visible in such detail that the presented scene was a gruesome diorama of paralysed imprisonment. Eyes affright, a dwarf with its hammer held high, a knight lifting his visor, a troll drooped with a daft stare, and a witch plucking her nose.

'I recognise that one,' cried Ma Gwrach, 'that's Nettle "Broom-Carver" the whittling witch of Dulwich. Thought she'd given up brooms for love spoons. I tasked her to fashion me a mop as I'm rather cloddish with me drink. More so after the fifth or si—'

'Shhhh,' Grimoire put a finger to his lips.

A deep shadow projected over the preening visage of Nettle. Grimoire held the stone directly towards the beast. 'The stone refracts light and casts a reflection. When the afanc can view its own reflection, it ceases to believe it exists and although we can see it, its own denial of existence is so powerful that our minds also cease to believe in its existence.'

Ma Gwrach invited Grimoire's words in one ear but quickly saw them out the other.

'So it's safe to look at it now?' she said.

'I wouldn't lean so readily on the word "safe". Let's just say it's less dangerous to view at this current moment.'

They both at once inched around and spied the dreadful mason nestled in the water. It had the eyes of an eel, the mouth of a rat, its slimy lump overhanging into the depths.

'It wants the adder stone,' said Ma Gwrach easing in the paddles and giving the boat some momentum.

The boat moved slowly around the statues until all that was present from the afanc was its dank breath heaving through the air.

'Do you think it still follows?' said Ma Gwrach easing the boat throughout the maze.

'Like all gorgons, the afanc is terribly persistent when it comes to the hunt.'

Ma Gwrach continued rowing until an embankment was in sight. They had landed at the mouth of a cave, the entrance enshrouded with ferns and liverwort, allowing only a modicum of light to enter.

Once ashore, Grimoire planted Bardolph's hand in the ground, pointing the adder stone towards the inside of the cave. 'That should do it.' From a protective leather wrap, he unbound his staff.

'You've still got Old Bollocks then?' Ma Gwrach squawked.

'Diabolical to you,' Grimoire growled as he rummaged through his bag, 'ah, here it is.' Grimoire took out a copper box. Opening it, he produced what looked like a knight's vambrace. He pushed it against the length of the staff, and it clicked into place.

'Ooooh, fancy, what does it do?'

Grimoire pressed his hand against it for a few seconds, and a screen lit up.

'He-he,' Grimoire held the staff in the palms of both hands as if to present it to Ma Gwrach. 'The question should be, what doesn't it do.'

'Er, okay,' said Ma Gwrach crinkling up her nose, 'what doesn't it do?'

'Well, err—' Grimoire appeared momentarily stumped.

'Can it brew a cup of tea?'

'It's not really designed for making tea, but it has been said that with the right spell it can move mountains.'

Ma Gwrach repeated the crinkling of her nose, placing one crooked finger on her chin. 'So it can move mountains, but can't make a cup of tea. Doesn't sound so all-powerful to me.'

Grimoire sighed and put the staff down. 'It was a gift to me from

Rasborah Pinkgill the notorious swynwyr of Musk.'

'Didn't want it then?'

'I have no idea, he gave it to me as a gift.'

'I wouldn't want one. Doesn't make tea. No use to me then is it?'

'No, it probably wouldn't be,' Grimoire grumbled, remembering how infuriating Ma Gwrach could be.

'I would have just settled for a kettle, something useful.'

Grimoire turned his attention back to the staff doing his best to ignore Ma Gwrach's remarks without being obvious.

'However, if a mountain stood between me and a cup of tea, it might have its uses,' said Ma Gwrach.

Grimoire touched his fingers over the screen, symbols appeared, he swiped and pressed the symbols before deactivating it with several firm taps. 'I thought our journey to Snowdonia might be across current time and place, but it seems we are being guided all the way through Annwyn. Right through elemental egresses no less.' Grimoire paused to observe Ma Gwrach, who had been heating some stones beneath her travelling cauldron. 'What may I ask are you doing?'

'All this talk of tea has made me want one. I'm making us a brew of red sage tea.'

'Tea? We've no time for tea.'

'We don't need time for tea, it's got a time of its own, tea time. Help us to feel better in the face of adversity.'

'Oh all right.' Grimoire sat down to wait for the cauldron to warm. 'I suppose we can afford ourselves a small reprieve.' A slithering noise in the darkness caused him to shift uneasily. 'Small, I must reiterate, as we are not entirely out of harm's way.'

Ma Gwrach produced two stoneware mugs from her bag.

'You've really packed quite a lot in that bag, haven't you?'

'I didn't know how long I'd be away for,' she said, dragging out of the bag a small Butler's basin. She took it to the lake and filled it with water. She rinsed out the mugs and then with a ladle, poured the tea. Together they sat for a while, despite their graceless slurping habits, in relative silence.

'Don't suppose you have a map of where we are supposed to be going,' said Grimoire draining the last of his mug.

'Map? To get to the Tree of Oracles from Annwyn? No, your guess is as good as mine.'

Grimoire looked down into his empty mug, and it dawned on him why Ma Gwrach had insisted on tea, apart from the fact that she always insisted on tea. 'Ah I see, red as in what's read, and sage as in what's sagacious. To read with wisdom. I should have known.'

'I'm not just a gnarled old hag you know.' Ma Gwrach cackled. 'Now observe the shapes they take.' Ma Gwrach plucked a small notebook from the bag, and with a charcoal stick, she sketched the remaining leaves. 'We must climb a mountain. Not sure which one but we'll know once we've climbed it.' Ma Gwrach scribbled stormy clouds in a squall. 'This must be the kingdom of Ysbaddaden, where the giants no longer look like giants because they are surrounded by giants.' She peered into the cup. 'This formation here must be the Rime of Unreason. The glacial belt of Annwyn where the Chwyfleian forever wanders the icy caps.'

'And what's this here,' Grimoire pointed to a cluster of leaves to the side of the mug.

'Ah, that is a clump of tea leaves.'

'Clearly, but what does it represent? A geyser of aquatic demons? A swamp of marsh things? A jungle of cannibals?'

'It is a dire sign and one of which is the only true certainty when reading the leaves.'

'Well, tell us then, what does it mean? Certain death? Imminent danger?'

'Far more terrifying, it represents the absence of tea, and in this case, the leaves are never wrong.'

'I see you've put exile to good use grinding that wit of yours, but remember the afanc will gradually move in on us if we dilly-dally.'

'I thought I'd make light of the situation,' said Ma Gwrach.

'What situation?'

'The er certain death or imminent danger situation,' Ma Gwrach said with a flush of unease over her face.

Grimoire turned his head away in exasperation, only to find that he was staring into an enormous eye. The eyeball was attached to a face peering into the cave. A sniffling sob emitted from the outside and the eye began to glaze over.

'Ah, that situation,' said Grimoire.

The eye blinked quizzically, as a tear formed, swelling up until it was a large globule of water suspended from its duct. Grimoire cautiously got to his feet and took hold of Diabolical. The tear swelled again doubling in size.

'All it needs to do is blink one more time.' Grimoire flicked through Diabolical's alphabetical spell selection, 'ABCD … HIJK … blast. Why water, why not air? Or maybe it's aqua. I'm sure I switched it from prompting the Latin to common.'

Ma Gwrach dived into her bag, trying to find the sections of her mop. 'Pole A connected to pole B2. At least I think that's right, can never remember, or is it B2 to D1?'

The tear finally burst sending a tidal wave of water in their direction.

Grimoire aimed his staff and spoke the magic word …

'ᛈᚪᚢᛁᚩ'

The waters slowed. Then Ma Gwrach, her mop finally assembled, pointed it at the current and called loudly …

As soon as the deluge touched the head of the mop, it began to absorb within the strands.

'Adddeerrrrrrrr ...' The afanc had been creeping nearer, although still repelled by the light of the stone.

'Pick a pickle, any pickle,' cawed Ma Gwrach over the gurgling din of water.

'Two birds, one stone,' Grimoire shouted, 'I read somewhere, that a salty tear can undo the afanc's hex. Let's try it shall we? As soon as I finish shouting at you, turn your mop on it.' Grimoire grabbed the adder stone and shone it at the eye, with a squirm and a squint, it vanished from the entrance. Daylight flooded into the cave. At the same moment, Ma Gwrach swung around and ejected the mop's contents towards the encroaching afanc. It was sent flooding back to its lair.

'Now run,' Grimoire shouted, as they both scooped up their belongings.

They headed for the cave entrance, from behind they could hear the swish and thrashing of the afanc writhing its way back through the waters. Followed by the bewildered pandemonium of the afanc's victims set free from their curse, especially one load cry of 'my hand, my hand, what's happened to my hand.'

Huddled behind a boulder was the giant, his hands overlapping his head, knees to his chin and the sound echoing through the hilly countryside was the unmistakable throb of sobbing.

'Reveal yourself,' shouted Grimoire who had by now regained his composure.

'Go away,' sobbed the giant.

'Oh, this is ridiculous,' snapped Ma Gwrach marching up to the heaving hunched giant.

As soon as the giant caught sight of her, he let out a wallowing scream and raising a foot attempted to bring it down on Ma Gwrach. Grimoire acted with speed, holding Diabolical aloft he aimed it at a cluster of nettles. The nettles began to increase in size thrusting up through the giant's toes. The giant clasped his leg in horror and hopped backwards, more tears streaming down his face.

'They sting, they sting the nasty beasties sting.' The giant hopped around in a circle before bending down, showing its fulsome face flushed red with great patches of orange freckle across his cheeks.

'It's just a boy,' squealed Ma Gwrach who although conclusively had no way with children what-so-ever, regarded her sex by default, motherly.

'A boy?' Grimoire roared, 'a foul tempted lout I should think.' Grimoire aimed his staff at a particularly nasty purple stemmed nettle and it shot up right into the giant's nostril.

The sound now issuing forth from the boy shook the heavens. The giant clutched his nose, wailing and kicking his dangerously large feet about. Then all of a sudden, the wailing stopped, the giant turned his back and took out something round with a long handle from one of its pockets. The ensuing sound that followed was more akin to a snicker than sob, he turned his head and grinned mischievously.

'What's he up to?' Ma Gwrach said, trying to get a better look at what the giant was holding.

'No good,' said Grimoire backing away.

The giant got onto its knees and held the implement so that a spherical glass was aligned to the sun. A sharp bright ray shot to the ground, the grass began to sizzle and blacken. The giant moved the beam towards Grimoire who managed to slide out of its way.

'What do little boys like?' Ma Gwrach said watching the direction of the ray intently.

'Little?' cried Grimoire side-stepping again, a corner of his cloak letting off a crackle of smoke.

Ma Gwrach reached into her bag and pulled out a small pot. She plucked out a lump of sugar and threw it at the ray. It sizzled, and although small, the slight strain of smoke that wafted up to the giant made him pause. The giant bent down closer and sniffed at its source. He licked his lips, stuck out his tongue and licked the ground.

'I think we need to make them a little bigger,' said Ma Gwrach.

'He's trying to burn us alive, and you're rewarding him sweets? What kind of message is that?' said Grimoire.

'Sometimes one must resort to bribery.' Ma Gwrach threw another one down. 'Go on, make it bigger.'

'Bribery? What he needs is extortion,' said Grimoire, 'pandering to him is just going to make matters worse.'

'Can you do it?' Ma Gwrach slumped her shoulders with stern a stamp of her foot.

'Do what? Extort?'

'No, multiply, make bigger, as you did with the nettles.'

Grimoire pointed Diabolical towards the sweet, holding the staff by the dongle he muttered a few words. Then it grew and grew until it was roughly the size of a boulder. The giant looked at it and then aimed his glass towards it. With glee, he sniffed at the aromas as it burnt. The giant then picked up the sticky mess and popped it into his mouth. He sat down cross-legged chewing with a benign expression all over his face, intently enjoying the experience. When he had finished, he looked down at his promising assailants.

'More?' said the giant with strands of toffee between his teeth.

'Only if you take us to the top of the mountain,' Ma Gwrach cradled the pot close to her.

The giant's eyes began to swell again.

'And then you can have as much as you can stomach,' added

Grimoire eagerly anticipating the promised effect with a degree of delight.

The giant put away his glass, placing his hand on the ground he offered the two a platform of fingers. They climbed up the arm and sat down on a shoulder each. Ma Gwrach rattled the pot of sugar to spur the boy onwards. They clambered up the rocky slope until reaching the summit. The giant bowed to the ground enabling Grimoire and Ma Gwrach to jump off with ease. He sat upright holding out his hand.

'Sweets,' he said, almost anxiously.

Ma Gwrach gave the giant the pot. He eyed the little container as it sat in the palm of his hand.

'Bigger, like me,' the giant looked pleadingly at Ma Gwrach.

'Ah,' said Ma Gwrach, 'first you must plant them to make them grow.'

'Plant?'

'Yes, put them in the soil and wait.'

'Wait? Want them bigger like before.'

'Well, that's not going to happen because we used magic and you don't have any magic, so you're going to just have to wait.'

'Don't want to wait, want to eat.'

'Oh I've had enough of this,' grumbled Grimoire as he powered up Diabolical. The magic word was uttered.

'⎁⌐⎁⎁⌐⎁⌐⌐'

The giant began to shrink, smaller and smaller until he stood in front of them nothing bigger than a regular-sized boy holding a pot. The once giant looked momentarily stunned before his face contorted as it turned a severe shade of pink, then the mouth opened and it began to wail but stopped abruptly. He plunged his hand into the pot and stuffed his face with sugar. He then turned his back and started to run down the mountain.

'He'll grow back again,' said Grimoire, 'the spell can only contain a giant's true size for so long, but at least the hideous thing has gone.'

'And he was only a small one too,' said Ma Gwrach.

On the summit was an umbilical pit, its rounded crevice grooved with gritty paths as if it had been dug on purpose. Clumps of silky moss clung to the stubs of splintered wood and scattered about was the occasional patch of gorse.

'Idris's seat,' said Grimoire.

'How do you know that?' said Ma Gwrach.

'I don't, but I can't determine any other reason for this crater other than that' said Grimoire,' this is where we are supposed to rest, and in doing so, we shall discover the way to the silver clouded plane.'

'We are to rest in the impression of Idris's prat?'

'Could be worse. We could be under it,' said Grimoire, 'at least we will have some opportunity for shelter.'

They snaked their way along the narrow paths and found a relatively sheltered alcove to set up camp. Grimoire wrapped his cloak about him and nestled into the ground. Ma Gwrach constructed a bed using leggings and a shawl she procured from her bag. She tied the leggings to several stiff shrubs and flopped into the hammock.

'Not too shabby,' she said, swinging from side to side, 'how much time do you think has now passed in the other world?'

'At a guess I would calculate about a thousand years,' said Grimoire taking the opportunity to light his pipe.

For a moment, the earth beneath them rumbled and, a thunderous growl resounded from a distance.

'The boy? Do you think that horrid child has returned? Or worse, grassed to his much more menacingly proportioned parents.'

Grimoire took a moment to release a swirl of smoke before answering Ma Gwrach's question. 'I should think it more likely he's been given a slap around the earhole and sent to bed for having scoffed sweets before supper. That's what I think. However, I do suspect there might be the off chance I am being followed.'

'Well, if you like I'll walk in front from now on,' said Ma Gwrach, 'I only lag a little cause me legs are shorter.'

'If only it were that innocuous, but I believe there is someone trying to get their hands on my book.'

'Still working on that tome aye?' Ma Gwrach tittered. 'Where is it then?'

'It's here.' Grimoire parted his cloak and lifted his shirt to reveal a battered notebook fastened to his waist by a belt. 'To throw whoever sought it, off the scent. I entrusted Gyffe with the safekeeping of one of my old student notebooks aptly headed with the same title.'

'I can imagine Gyffe is probably beginning to wonder the meaning behind the indecipherable shorthand of lewd limericks and angsty poems on the outbreak of spots,' said Ma Gwrach starting to doze.

'He would be unwise,' said Grimoire, 'to bury himself in books rather than taking the necessary precautions to ensure safeguarding the vulnerable residue of magic we have left scattered and fragmented behind.'

The stars stared at them as they lay lulling beneath the night sky. It couldn't be said whether or not they actually drifted off to sleep, as not long after, both were wide-eyed with the earth beneath them rumbling with a shaking fury and a thunderous growl bludgeoning their ears.

CHAPTER TWENTY

The first century in Crach's sunken abode passed by without much interference from the outside world. An enchanter was seeking dwarfish relics, a wyzen asking for directions to the Gate of Dreams, several healers collecting flasks of water from the river to Annwyn, and a door-to-door witch enquiring whether the inhabitants would like to be a representative of Crone Creams, Pomades and Bath Salts.

Gyffe kept himself busy reading, not only the books left to him by Grimoire but also the ones he found in Crach's vast library. The shelves were fixed at dwarf height and so Gyffe had to either squat or bend sideways to read the titles. This resulted in him cultivating a slight hunch. Most of the books were anthologies on the history of magic as reported by dwarf scribes. Some detailed complex alchemy. Others were technical logbooks on the methods of mining. He had read Dwarf and Peat, Lost Shovels and flicked through Grime and Sediment, all works by dwarfs of varying literary renown.

Patch had mastered the art of humming, having found a pile of sheet music, he was able to deftly hum Dunstaple's isorhythmic motets, all twelve of them, and could remarkably belt out Roy Henry's Sanctus without missing any of the three harmonies. Crinkum had, in contrast, spent most of its time trying to out-standstill several gargoyles, and whatever shrubby avocation Prunewick whiled away at was planted firmly in the field of guesswork.

It was clear that despite the confined space, they had all managed somehow to go their separate ways, but there was one visitation that would bring them all back to the fold, whether they wanted to or not. Patch had a frightful dream. In it, Gyffe had been spending the last century locked away in the library practising the dark arts. When he finally emerged, Patch saw that he was not the squit he used to be. His back was crooked, his hair down to his ankles, his eyes were colourless holes and his skin so pale that the blood beneath made him glow with a reddy flush. When he spoke no words were produced, only the clamour of knells. Patch lay frozen as the transformed squit dragged itself towards him. "Dong, dong, dong," moaned Gyffe. Patch tried to say something, but all that emitted from his mouth was, "Ding, ding, ding," still unable to move Patch found himself awake with the terrible squit looming over him, the mouth opened and an awful "Gong" rang out. Eventually, Patch woke up, he must have rolled off the sack of fleece he'd been using as a bed and face planted the floor.

'Dream. Had horrible dream,' Patch muffled into the rug fibres.

The bell at the front of the house clanged. Patch, somewhat relieved that the chime was not the stuff of nightmares, made his way down the wide staircase to the entry and stood by the door. As he did so, the thought rushed across his mind that, should he open it, he might expect to see the abominable squit on the other side.

'Who calls?'

'I've come to see Crach Ffinnant.'

'Know who dwarf is. Who wants dwarf?'

'I am Roger Bolingbroke. May I speak with Crach Ffinnant? This is his home, is it not?'

'Was,' said Patch, 'now not.'

'Ah,' came the voice from the other side, 'I see there is a much smaller door attached to this one. Am I supposed to enter it?'

'Not for humans. For dragoyles.' Patch remained silent for a moment, trying to gauge if the gentleman was in any way preparing to leave.

'I have travelled a great distance, I am tired, in want of food and my boots are wet.'

'Wet boots? Nasty things.' Patch wondered if this factor might just be the tipping point of letting him in, for there was one thing a hognome found more distressing than being left alone with a dwarf, and that was wet feet.

'Soggy socks,' said the man as if catching on to the sort of discomfort Patch found prevalent enough to garner his sympathy.

'Wrinkled toes …' Patch replied.

'Yes, yes, wrinkly feet, all damp and wrinkly … Do you think I might come in?'

Patch unbolted the latch. The man stood at the threshold bending slightly forward as if he had been resting his head on the door. He wore a puffy coat which finished its puffy descent at a pleated hem just above the knees, and a velveteen toque tapered to his receding hairline. His stature was at a bearable height for Patch, and the face which looked down on him was painted boyishly with unobtrusive features.

'Do I see another dwarf in residence?' Bolingbroke said.

Patch intuitively pushed the door shut.

'Sorry, did I speak out of turn?' Came the voice from the other side.

Patch felt a compulsion to elucidate on just how much out of turn. He opened the door again to see the man bending slightly backwards to deflect further assault.

'No dwarves here. Just hognomes. As should be.'

The man looked apologetic but said nothing. Patch accepted the look and stepped aside to let him through. Bolingbroke strode in, casting his gaze around the place.

'Still the same dwar … err … hognomish home. Why are the portraits reversed?' Bolingbroke looked at Patch who in turn looked the other way.

'Never mind,' said Bolingbroke extending his hand to be led somewhere else, 'I saw smoke billowing from a chimney stack, perchance you have a fire I may employ in drying off my clothes?'

Patch started ambling up the stairs with Bolingbroke behind him looking at the portraits lining the stairwell. These ones were not reversed but instead scribbled over with crude additions to their facial features.

'My, you really don't like them do you?'

Patch turned around and looked down on Bolingbroke, a privileged position from a few steps above. 'Do you?'

'I take every kind on their own merit,' replied Bolingbroke.

'Merits,' Patch scoffed, not quite knowing what the word meant but suspected it might be some sort of common lice attracted to the beards of dwarves and continued his ascent.

Soon enough they had reached the room which had become a collective living space for the encumbered quartet. Patch pushed open the door and ushered Bolingbroke inside.

'Sit. Fire,' said Patch brushing past him as he headed towards another door. 'Wait.'

Bolingbroke took off his coat, placed it on a chair and sat down with his feet pointed directly at the warming flames. Patch waited until he was settled before opening the door to the other room. Inside, a distant figure sat in near darkness, a single candle flickering against his form.

'Oi,' called out Patch.

'Busy,' snapped the figure at the other end.

'Got guest.'

'Guest?'

'Got wet.'

'Wet?'

'Socks.'

Patch could just make out an audible muttering from within the darkness.

'Got wet socks?' The figure jumped up from his chair. 'It can't be? Yet, can it? The prophecy …'

Patch waited for Gyffe to emerge from the dimness. At first, the horror of his dream momentarily returned. Gyffe looked tired, his skin paler than usual, a pair of spectacles pegged upon his sharpish nose which by now had a straggle of twisty hair poking out. The once sculpted waggle hung in dangly threads like a Chinese conjurer. The once lithe frame still thin as ever appeared more fragile and bony. And then Patch remembered it was just a dream and the fribbling feebleness presented before him called more for pity than fear.

'Why didn't you just say Bolingbroke was here?' said Gyffe.

Patch shrugged the kind of shrug as if to say that what he said was better than saying nothing at all.

'Not good,' said Patch.

'What's not good?' barked Gyffe nudging past him.

'That room. Not good for you. Not good for nobody.'

Gyffe paused as if wanting to give a response but instead just shook his head and strode towards Bolingbroke whose socks were now emitting steam.

'Bolingbroke?'

'I hear my name now mentioned several times, yet I am to believe I am not expected.'

Gyffe placed himself down on a large armchair and shifted it slightly to face the man. 'You were, and now you are here, as expected.'

Gyffe reclined into the chair with the look cast from his face which only he suspected was the best impression of fribbling smugness at having accomplished a neat bit of magic.

'I've never met you before, yet you know my name. Since you have mine, it is customary to give yours.'

'I am Gyffe. It was your socks. He who wears wet socks cannot be cursed, as wet socks cannot be burned.'

'Aye? Are you telling me, you foretold my arrival from the condition of my socks?'

'The Witch of Eye no less.'

'Oh, I should have guessed. Margery and her bogus magic socks, known for repelling evil spirits and midges.'

'Guessed? Bogus?' said Gyffe trying not to allow his astonishment to show.

'It seems, whereas, I foretell the future via the heavens, you on the other hand, foretell it from the linen. You've been in Crach's library, haven't you?'

Gyffe folded his arms in defence of the accusation despite having just emerged from that very room. He looked around the now ravished quarters. The tapestries now gone, used as either bedding, placemats or patches on the walls where roots beckoned from the soiled outer. He glanced at the broken furniture with parts fed into the fire. He then unfolded his arms.

'Too long,' said Patch, who was keeping himself busy by trying to look as if he was keeping himself busy.

'And what if I have?' said Gyffe, now feeling the dispirited edge of disillusionment creeping its way into his person.

'Ffinnant's library is rumoured to be abundant with many fine works, but it is also laden with misdirections and chimaera. When toyed with, this knowledge may produce nothing but ill effect.'

'In what way?' enquired Gyffe, preparing himself for the inevitable obstinance of which one can only resort to being confronted by another, whose very idea of what one has been doing, may be considered as folly.

'Judging by the unlikely coterie of my company I am to assume you are leftover familiars and servants of greater magic folk, abandoned to fend for yourselves while they remove themselves from a pickle by self-preservation.'

'What pickle?' asked Gyffe, now feeling his lengthy considerations into the conversation were themselves becoming obstinate.

'The pickle that the order of magi relishes in. The ensuing regulation of magic from within the order. Spiritual greed is what it is, but in their rush to covet what is sacred, there are many considerations left undone.'

'Such as?' Gyffe had not so much as heard the other side before, and it intrigued him.

'What they have not considered is the imperilment of leaving such vast amounts of knowledge in the hands of those whose prior understanding of such craft extends mostly to being able to beguile with bungling tricks.'

'Oh.' Gyffe was unimpressed with the answer. 'Why did you come here?'

Bolingbroke gritted his teeth and stood with his back to the fire. 'I was hoping Crach might join me in opposing this ludicrous decree of the magi, with their plan to repress the occult for fear of humankind sullying the ancient craft through science and religion. They believe cowering within stone and wood will protect them from Church and State. Thankfully among us, some do not share the same point of view.' Bolingbroke turned to admire the fire. 'Interesting didn't notice that scuttle there before.'

Crinkum, who had appeared as if out of nowhere, chomped down on the mouthful of coal it had scooped into its mouth leaving black crumbs at Bolingbroke's feet.

'Sherry?' said Patch, who had not been this entertained since at least fifty years ago when Gyffe attempted a spell to render him unseeable but ended up phosphorous for a week.

'Please,' said Bolingbroke breaking off the ascension of his passion, 'it has been a long journey.'

Patch went off to fetch a jar of fortified birch sap.

'And what about you, Gyffe? Have you not your own suspicions?'

Gyffe, although aged in wisdom through devouring Crach's varied collection on the art of magic, still retained the essential fribblingness about him expected of any squit no matter how learned. He secretly admitted to himself that there had been a degree of speculation concerning Margery's magic socks and the arrival of Bolingbroke. However, to call it mere guesswork was a little too belittling of the effort he'd put into such divinations. It also popped into his head that although Bolingbroke was a necromancer of some acclaim, his hot-headed sense of self-wizardry would perhaps someday see to it that his nose was cut off to spite his face, or worse.

'We were told by Grimoire that the magi, rebelling against the decision to lay rest to magic until the foreseeable future, would inevitably bring about their own destruction,' said Gyffe.

'Hogwash,' said Bolingbroke ignoring the scowl on Patch's face, 'I'm not at all surprised you think that, considering the kind of blind servitude that has led you here to your inevitable quietus.'

Gyffe rose to the occasion and cleared his throat as rather an ineffective launch to his defence. 'He was no more an overseer than we were underlings. His inequity was always equally apportioned, and yes, he was not at all times forthcoming with his knowledge but what mage ever is?'

'There are two types of mages,' said Bolingbroke taking a pronounced sip of his sherry, 'there are mages, and then there are mages like this Grimoire.'

'I don't understand what you mean,' said Gyffe.

'Look where he's left you. Of all the places, this is the last spot I'd want to be stranded,' said Bolingbroke. 'Have you not heard about this residence? They say there are no less than twenty-five dedicated apartments, two great halls, a large undercroft divided into four wings, six kitchens, ten storerooms, nine great chambers, and for some inexplicable particular dwarfish necessitate, fifty-three garderobes. Yet, it seems you have barely left this floor.'

'Knew an ogre once who lived in a sty,' said Gyffe, 'the size of the roof is not indicative of the size of the head.'

'Do you even know who, or rather, what Crach is? Do you know what kind of mage Grimoire is …?'

For some reason, Gyffe found himself drifting away from Bolingbroke's rant. His thoughts turned to what it was he did know, and what it was he didn't. Indeed, that very thought brought up a memory when he was all but chosen to apprentice under Grimoire. He knew of the mage because Grimoire would visit him to purchase his monthly sack of compost. At that time, Gyffe kept his keep by mixing and mulching a medley of muck heaps, each with a distinctive value for rare herbs and various plants useful in the pursuit of mixing potions. He had muck piles blended from comfrey, nettle, leaf mould, damson pulp, eggshells, fish emulsion, alfalfa, peat moss, and several blends of the more exotic stuff, such as dragon droppings and the vomit of Blodeuwedd the owl. During those visits, Grimoire would impress him with simple demonstrations of magic such as the convenience of a bottomless basket, how to seemingly vanish in a busy crowd, and shortchanging the payee. So at the end of each day when he counted his shortfall of earnings, he'd ponder on what it would be like to be able to practice such wizardry. The thought must have crossed Grimoire's mind also, as one day, he approached the stall behaving in a curiously contemplative manner. He sniffed at each bag of compost and commented on the fragrance and quality of each mix. The mage settled on two sacks of alfalfa and damson pulp before handing over some coins. Gyffe noticed before he pocketed the coins, that the amount Grimoire had handed over was exact.

'My retainer is reaching an age where assistance has become more of an insistence,' explained Grimoire, 'I require someone with vigour and enthusiasm to lighten the burden of practising the many fiddly and sometimes cumbersome magical tasks … as well as a few porridge pots that need particular attention after breakfast.'

He promptly offered his services and that night, the final night of tending his muck, he counted his earnings and noticed he was under. However, it wasn't Grimoire who came to collect him. It was Patch, hair combed up with such severity he looked like a teasel. He was dapperly dressed in a musty but smart suit with boots so enthusiastically polished that the toe caps reflected his nostrils. He recalled the questions he was asked. All of them probing and poking, about his past, his connections, and an amount of cross-examination into his personal habits of which he responded to with as much obliqueness that language would allow. As they reached the crooked stone building in the woods, he was asked one last question …

'Grimoire say, what happened to last apprentice?'

'Yes, he spoke quite highly of you.'

'Not I.'

'Well, then no, it was not mentioned.'

'Thought not,' was all Patch had said.

Bolingbroke spoke again but this time with the same edgy sternness he had displayed earlier and Gyffe shook the memory from his mind.

'Didn't think so.'

'Didn't think what?' said Gyffe now confused.

'Didn't think you actually knew what Crach is.'

'The afanc,' said Patch.

Gyffe suddenly found himself staring at the hognome, very much in the same way he had when he first met him.

'That's right,' said Bolingbroke.

Gyffe continued his bewildering stare as if the reverie was still playing out in his mind.

'Why didn't you mention this?' Gyffe said.

'Haven't seen you. Seen other things. Things seen by looking. Can't look from inside a book.'

'We have to leave then. We can't stay here, not with that thing about.'

'Exactly,' snapped Bolingbroke, 'you must come with me. Help me with my cause.'

'What cause?' said Gyffe.

'I plan to rid us of this King.'

'Who is the King anyway?' Gyffe asked.

'The King is the ruling monarch decreed as such by men, who call themselves the representatives of God.'

'I know what a king is, but who is he? What is his name?'

'King Henry.'

'Well, I never,' said Gyffe.

'The sixth,' said Bolingbroke.

'Oh, so what is your plan?'

'I shall chart his demise by way of the stars.'

'And how will that rid England of its monarch?'

'If a man encounters death at the top of a cliff,' said Bolingbroke, 'does it not stand to reason that the man would jump off the cliff to escape his destiny and therefore fulfil it?'

'Wouldn't it be much more practical to hire an assassin, put poison in his drink or just push him off a turret?'

Bolingbroke went to the fire and stood in such a way as if to address an audience. 'Do you think Guff—'

'Gyffe.'

'Err, Gyffe. That I would be so foolish as to see my days out as Ortgis the magician did, in blatant cannibalism of my scruples?' Bolingbroke posed along the mantlepiece.

'So your plan is, by showing the King how he will die, he will somehow fulfil the prophecy on his own, thus leaving your hands free from blood?'

'As Pliny, the Elder once remarked, in a nutshell, yes.'

'Nuts,' said Patch.

'So what's it to be?' Bolingbroke threw his arms up. 'Bury the occult forever or join me and expel the naysayers.'

Gyffe felt that between a rock and a hard place was on the whole not such an uncomfortable predicament, considering the options. 'So you truly believe that Grimoire wished us ill will?'

Bolingbroke scrunched up his boyish face. 'I saw it as an augury from the celestial body. I knew there was a reason for me to be here other than tracking down Ffinnant, and now he's gone, and here you are.'

'Well, I can do better than that.' Gyffe got up and plucked Prunewick from the mantel. 'This sprig grew from the same source that put forth the

Tree of Oracles, I shall ask it what it thinks we should do. Go with you or stay put and await our fate. Whether it be at the mercy of the afanc, the resurrection of magic or by the ruin of ennui.'

Gyffe held Prunewick towards the flames, for an instant, he thought it winced but decided it was a trick of the firelight. 'Answer this, oh clustered bud of yore, should we egress? If need be, then I command you to confess. If not, then hold your tongue and save your breath.' Gyffe continued to hold Prunewick to the light. All ears were pricked for a reply, but none arrived.

'And?' said Bolingbroke.

'There's your answer,' said Gyffe putting Prunewick back, and for an instant thought it looked relieved but once again suspected it a trick of the firelight. 'You're on your own.'

'Don't say I didn't warn you,' said Bolingbroke.

'If it comes to that, I won't have the opportunity.' Gyffe smiled, feeling at least for the moment in charge.

Bolingbroke grabbed his coat and wrapped himself in it. 'Before I leave you to rot in this dankness, let me give you some parting advice. The longer you await the afanc, the less time it waits for you.' Bolingbroke then stomped out of the room.

Gyffe and Patch were silent.

'I realise I've been neglecting my duties,' Gyffe finally said.

'Don't think it.'

'Oh but I must,' said Gyffe 'I should have been more wary about the potential dangers of this place instead of shutting myself away in that library day and night.'

'Was peaceful,' said Patch gathering up the sherry glasses.

'I've learned my lesson, we can't live here with the threat of the afanc looming over us.'

'Go where?' said Patch.

'Go? I'm not saying we go anywhere. We must slay it.'

CHAPTER TWENTY-ONE

Grimoire staggered out of the pit. He held onto his hat as a warm wind blew across the alcove. The rather pungent scent of the breeze forced Grimoire to try and pinpoint its direction. Looking down, he saw a mottled face pockmarked with stone and grass looking up.

'Fiddle-diddle-diddy-dee, who is sitting on top of me?'

'Oh no,' said Grimoire.

Ma Gwrach clambered up to join him, 'I smell ramsons and crab apple breath.'

'Why do giants always have to rhyme with such nonsense?' Grimoire said, scowling at the enormous features now clearly visible as that of an extremely ugly giant.

'Because it's easier to remember the words,' said Ma Gwrach.

Grimoire cupped his hands around his mouth and shouted. 'Terribly sorry, didn't know you were below.'

'Speak louder little man,' said the giant.

Grimoire tried again. 'Didn't know you were below.'

'You want to blow my nose?' shouted the giant.

Ma Gwrach took off her hat and through a hole in the tip shouted out. 'We thought your belly was a hill.'

'Dee-dee-dum, dee-dum, dee-dum, your bed instead was a giant's tum.'

'More rhymes' groaned Grimoire.

'We want to reach Ysbaddaden,' shouted Ma Gwrach, 'can you help us get there or at the very least, point the way?'

The giant sat upright sending Grimoire and Ma Gwrach toppling backwards but they landed safely in the palm of the giant's hand. He raised them to his face. Creepers and ivy dangled from his enormous nostrils. The corners of his eyes encrusted with downy ferns. With a sonorous voice, he spoke as gently as he could so as to avoid a gale.

'You have arrived,' said the giant, 'the only way to reach Ysbaddaden is to fall asleep on the girth of a resting giant. Everybody knows that. The difficulty is finding the right giant, but luckily my name is Sualda. I am son of Idris, and I shall take you the rest of the way.'

Sualda placed them either side of his head so that they sat reasonably secure on each shoulder. The giant got to his feet and stood just above the canopy of clouds stretching far into the horizon.

With his staff Grimoire tapped the giant on the earlobe. 'Before we head off, I must inform you that, we, your passengers, are powerful in the way of magic. If this is a ploy or means of giant trickery, beware. We will not hesitate to conjure one of our particularly nasty spells if the need arises.'

'Dee-da boo, I do dutifully move you through to … Ysbaddaden …' said the giant. The giant climbed up onto a podgy cluster of clouds and proceeded to leap from one cluster to another across the clouded plane.

His giant steps elevating them from a world of white swirls and mist, and into a world that began to take a soldier shape. They moved steadily upwards, creeping into the whites and the grey temper of burgeoning storms until the unbroken starkness of ebony mountain peaks crept into view.

'It will get a little rough,' the giant boomed.

Both Grimoire and Ma Gwrach held onto their hats as heavy winds lashed about. The giant's shoulders were broad and, despite the lumbering ascension, they both managed to keep a steady seating on the way up. Finally, they had reached a plane stretching for miles beyond and before them was a fortress the likes they had never seen before. Its garrisons were built entirely from the remnants of fallen knights. Armour affixed to skeletal remains hooked on bloodied swords and shattered lances. Halberds, like lattice work, locked into bent shields rising up the walls like slated tiles. Greaves and gauntlets piped together to form uneven eaves where turrets of battered helms were pointed with crushed bone marrow for mortar.

'Who were they?' asked Grimoire.

'Giant slayers,' said Sualda wiping his brow 'although, in name only as through those doors, you will meet the giants who slew them.'

'Looking forward to it,' said Grimoire gruffly.

'Don't suppose they've got the kettle on?' shouted Ma Gwrach.

The giant headed towards the fortress and with a mighty pull, managed to open a solid door moulded from pummelled breastplates. Once they were inside the fortress, it was too gloomy and large an area to make out any real detail. Grimoire thought he heard the sound of snoring coming from somewhere within or if it was the rumble of distant thunder, he couldn't be sure.

'In there,' said Sualda pinching the backs of Grimoire and Ma Gwrach. He flicked them into a small cell, closing the door and bolting it. 'Wait.' Sualda stormed off into the shadows, his wicker clogs petering out with each clomp against the stone slab floor.

'I warned you about giants,' said Grimoire tapping the cage with his staff, 'this cage is enchanted. We'll never get out.'

'You never warned me about giants,' said Ma Gwrach, 'you have warned me about black cats, broken mirrors and the perils of using your privy but you have never mentioned giants.'

'Well, I should have. Completely untrustworthy and far too big for their boots.'

'Not all giants surely?' Ma gwrach said, 'what about Freckled Blewit, the towering giant of Squat? He was trustworthy.'

'He wasn't a giant. He was a nutter,' said Grimoire.

'What do you mean he wasn't a giant? He had all the qualities of a giant.'

'He was shorter than me,' said Grimoire.

'But he was taller me.'

'That doesn't make him a giant per se. He was a giant by name but not by stature. He used to stand at the top of a hill and shout "I'm coming to get you little man, or I'm coming to get you little woman" and when he finally stormed down to the bottom, it was apparent the only thing the person he was coming for would get was a crick in the neck from having to look down at him.'

'But he was still trustworthy.'

Grimoire ignored the remark and turned his thoughts to escape. It wasn't long before those thoughts were dashed by a furious roar.

'Who dares intrudes on our afternoon nap?' a voice boomed.

'It is I Sualda,' said Sualda.

It was difficult for Grimoire to judge just how far away the voices were as the echo bounced around the enormous fortress. He resigned himself to sitting on the floor and watching Ma Gwrach curiously adjusting her hat at different angles.

'Sualda, what brings you to the castle of Ysbaddaden?' said a giant with a gruff voice.

'I have an offering that will please you.'

'Not another cartload of equine, those beasts are but hors d' oeuvres on a toothpick. Bring us something substantial,' said a third giant whose voice was pinched with the nasally whine found from those afflicted by a head cold, 'perhaps, a few of those African elephants we keep hearing about.'

'Or those, what are they called? Rorquals? Perfectly suited to being sliced and served on toast,' said the other giant.

'I'm afraid, I've brought no such exotic delights. I've brought wee folk,' said Sualda.

'Oh no,' said the gruff giant, 'we've long gone off eating tiny humans.'

'Especially children, one might as well feast on fleas,' said the other, 'remember that Frankish village we threatened to sit on unless they fed us? They sent us all their worst brats which we spent hours grinding into sausages?'

'I do. Might as well have had grilled maggots.'

'These are not to eat,' interrupted Sualda 'but for the board.'

'Ah, for the board,' said the nasally voiced giant 'now that may be just the thing to stave off our appetite.'

'Missing pieces?' said the other giant.

'A wizard and a witch,' said Sualda.

'But we needed two wizards or two witches,' said the gruff giant.

'What's the difference?' said the other giant.

'They won't match up.'

'What do you mean they won't match up? They both perform magic, don't they?' said the other giant showing a glimmer of irritation in his voice.

'They will look different. It will make the whole board look irregular.'

'Oh, I don't know about that,' said the giant with the nasally voice 'they both will be wearing pointy hats, ridiculous boots and a fair share of warts.'

'Both of them are ugly,' said Sualda.

'One will have a beard and the other not,' said one of the giants.

'The witch has kind of a beard,' said Sualda.

'She does?' said the gruff giant.

'Yes, a few strands on her chin. There is certainly, in time, the potential for one.'

'Really?' said the nasally giant sounding pleased.

'Really,' said Sualda.

'In that case,' said the giant whose particular want for symmetry was the fundamental essential to a good game 'let us play a game today.'

'Ahem, my prize?' said Sualda.

'Prize? What prize?'

'My prize for bringing the missing pieces.'

'Should there be one?' said the gruff giant.

'Usually, there is some kind of prize, a reward for loyalty,' said Sualda.

'We never mentioned a reward. Did you mention a reward?' said the nasally giant.

'No, didn't mention such a thing,' replied the other.

Sualda must have squirmed in his wicker clogs, and they creaked annoyingly as he did so.

'Can I have one?'

'Have one of what?' said the gruff giant irritably.

'A reward?'

'For what?' snapped the other giant.

'For bringing the missing pieces,' shouted Sualda who then gulped the outburst.

'No,' said the gruff giant.

'Not today,' said the other giant 'come back with an African elephant and we'll see.'

The wicker clogs creaked in the darkness and it was clear that Sualda was leaving, the breast-plated door closed, and as they did, the faint sound of sobbing was heard from outside.

'Son of Idris,' scoffed the gruff giant.

'Idiot,' chuckled the other.

Grimoire had been listening to the whole conversation with a lump of dread in his throat. He put his hand to it and realised it was only his Adam's apple but the dread remained. It was not the impressive size and strength of giants he really feared but their estranged sense of reason which he felt was intrinsically linked to some sort of imbalance between the capacity of the brain and the overall capability of the mind to fill such a vast space. Tiny brains could fill their quota satisfactorily due to the limitations of organic matter housing it, but giant brains meant that an enormous allowance of logic would inevitably be lost and unaccountable. It was this sheer unused capacity for intelligence that made giants so unpredictable in their behaviour. Grimoire turned to Ma Gwrach to see if she had picked up on his thoughts. She seemed to be examining her shadow.

'I thought me scraggy chin sprouts gave me an air of learnedness.'

The gate swung open, but whoever had opened it could at not first be seen. Grimoire then noticed a wafer-thin woman, almost concealed by the frame of the gate, holding it open.

'You are free to leave,' she said.

'Free to leave?' said Grimoire.

'Free to leave, oh that's good. Ma Gwrach shot a look at Grimoire. 'Untrustworthy, indeed.'

'Free to leave the cell,' uttered the woman stepping back to allow Grimoire the opportunity to exit.

'Who are you that bids the giant's will so easily?' said Grimoire.

'I am Maelor Gawr's mother,' said the woman.

'Maelor, the giant?' exclaimed Ma Gwrach 'who'd have thought.'

'I wouldn't even attempt it,' said Grimoire.

'Follow me, Maelor and Bran are waiting for you.'

Grimoire and Ma Gwrach followed the woman closely. The hall was mostly enshrouded in darkness. An occasional torch illuminated the grim carvings of wild giant faces before the Arthurian crusades eradicated their earthly presence. That's when Ysbaddaden, king of the giants, founded a kingdom in a world inside the otherworld, a kind of netherworld. Grimoire eyed the crazed faces and shuddered at the memory of times when giants raided villages during the winter and the forests resonated with infantile rhymes. Finally, after what felt like an eternity to get there, light poured into the farthest end of the hall. It was brightly lit by a candelabrum, the candles were propped in knight's gauntlets and the frame made up of twisted pikes. There was much clutter about, great weapons that either needed repair or were on display as evidence of giant ferocity. Nasty looking triple-headed axes, barbed mallets and spiked clubs sat side-by-side more mundane implements like enormous toenail clippers and earbuds made from silage attached to poles. Two thrones, each cut from a single stump of a great oak were either side of a vast chessboard covering the floor.

'We don't propose to stay long as we are just passing through,' Grimoire said, stepping into the light.

The giants roared with laughter.

'Passing through what? My digestive tract?' said the nasally giant, laughing so hard he nearly slid off his throne.

'I am Bran the Blessed,' said the other giant with the gruff voice, 'and that giggling lump is Maelor Gawr, he's also got a cold, so careful he doesn't sneeze on you.'

'Watch your tongue,' said the lithe woman.

'Sorry, Ma Gawr,' said Bran looking shamefaced.

'You are in the kingdom of Ysbaddaden. There is no passing through, you have reached your final destination,' said Maelor Gawr wiping the tears from his eyes.

Grimoire felt at his throat again. It was still his Adam's apple, but this time it felt more like a bramley than a pippin. Grimoire felt uncomfortable, trying to rationalise with pig-headed giants was like trying to convince dwarves that the more they mined, the fewer resources they'd have to dig.

'Can we go now?' said Ma Gwrach, who didn't seem to be taking in anything the giants were saying.

'Um, yes,' said the giant, whose name was Maelor Gawr.

Ma Gwrach shot Grimoire another "told you so" look. 'See, untrustworthy, indeed.'

'What a relief,' said Grimoire 'let's go then.' Ma Gwrach's distracted composure and inability to divine the seriousness of the situation was starting to annoy him.

Grimoire began to turn when Maelor Gawr's mother promptly spun him back around. Her wiry assemblage disguising underneath what proved to be the strength of a giant.

'Not that way,' shouted Bran 'you must go to the board.'

'Just as I feared,' mumbled Grimoire, he turned to Ma Gwrach and raised an eyebrow so high it almost looked as if it might creep away into his hair. 'Trustworthy, you say?' Grimoire sullenly made his way onto the chess board with Ma Gwrach tiptoeing slightly behind him. Bran pointed to Grimoire.

'You, there,' he said, moving his finger towards a white square.

Grimoire took his position upon a square resting his staff down upon it.

'You,' shouted Maelor Gwar.

'Me?' said Ma Gwrach with a shrill.

'Yes, you,' shouted back Maelor Gwar, 'over there.'

He pointed to a black square parallel to Grimoire. Ma Gwrach this time shuffled onto her spot, resting her mop on it.

'Now what?' said Grimoire to Ma Gwrach glumly.

'At least we're on the same side.' Ma Gwrach made a face she made when contemplating the words but not the meaning.

A thunder clap echoed from above. 'Bring on the other pieces,' bellowed Bran rubbing his hands on his knees after having brought them together with such might.

Maelor Gwar's mother quickly disappeared, and soon the creak and clang of gates could be heard swinging open from the recesses of the great hall. Figures wearily appeared out of the darkness and headed towards the remaining empty squares on the board. Grisly ogres were slobbering and dragging their feet, fidgety goblins nervously seeking their spots, solemn centaurs with a slow jog-trot positioned themselves, a group of dwarves dispersed side by side on the second row, and many more posted themselves on the board. Next to Grimoire stood a man who represented the king. His hair bedraggled, his beard frayed, both as white as the square he stood on. His eyes though, warm, dark and aged.

'Arthur?' said Grimoire beneath his breath.

'Aye,' said Arthur in his faded raiments.

'Pendragon?'

'Aye,' said Arthur, 'what be it to you?'

'What cursed you to end up at Ysbaddaden?'

Arthur turned and frowned. 'Curse? I was all but dead wizard.'

'Mage,' said Grimoire under his breath.

'Mage, wizard, king, subject, a difference only by name. Without, it would be tall, short, fat, thin, you, me, those, we—'

'Yes, I get your point,' said Grimoire, 'but I thought you were bound for Avalon?'

'Bound? Like Bladud over there?' Arthur nodded to the opposing king, a man with scarred skin and a scruffy-looking boar by his side. 'He was bound to fly off on his demon wings, but look where it landed him.' Arthur leaned a little closer to Grimoire. 'Look at his neck,' said Arthur nodding to Bran.

Grimoire peered up at the giant. What he previously mistook as a necklace of some intricate design, now became clear that the skin was stitched all the way around.

'The ferryman,' continued Arthur, 'was not the expected Charon but a disguised sorcerer called Megodawful Phew, or something like that. I didn't quite catch the full extent of his name as I was not entirely compos mentis. He forced me to lead him to where Bran's head lay buried and with magic only known to the undead, he stitched it back on and handed me to Bran as an offering.'

Grimoire scratched his head. 'Megodawful Phew? Sounds familiar, and to have such magic as that would signify a sorcerer with quite a lot of skill.'

Arthur placed both hands on the pommel of his sword, legs astride, and poised for combat. 'Anyway, what's done is done,' he said with a sigh.

'What happens next?' Grimoire said, 'we don't actually need to hurt each other do we? It's but a game.'

'Put it this way,' replied Arthur, 'at the very least you will die trying not to hurt each other.'

'Let the maiming begin,' shouted Maelor Gwar, 'oh sorry, did I just say that? I meant, let the gaming begin.' Maelor Gwar laughed so loud that every one-legged dwarf on the board toppled sideways.

CHAPTER TWENTY-TWO

The year was 1565. Many moons had passed since Gyffe duly locked the library door and gave the key to Patch to conceal. Instead of pouring over books, he had set about devising and rigging ingenious traps about the place. However, the lure of the library was never far away and Patch frequently found himself probed by Gyffe to as where the key might have been put.

'Where did you end up hiding it?' Gyffe said, following Patch's gaze for any recognition to its hiding spot.

'It?'

'I didn't want to put you in the position of having to answer, but the thought crossed my mind.'

'Crossed?' said Patch.

'Yes, laying in wait to trap the afanc night after night got me thinking. I ought to have some reference to it. Some sort of knowledge that might aid in its capture.'

'Ah, thinking,' said Patch returning to the page of an opened book.

'I see you are still helping yourself to the library.'

'Learning to read, not magic.' Patch returned once more to the page.

Gyffe counted in his head how long Patch could hold his attention to the page before looking back up. 'And the key?' said Gyffe after counting to five.

'Inside cushion,' replied Patch, who had recently just finished fluffing all thirty-six of them.

'A cushion, you say?' replied Gyffe eyeing off each one.

'Cushion,' said Patch,' or neath rug.'

'Oh, could be a cushion or under a rug?'

Crach was quite a rug enthusiast. In fact, Gyffe couldn't help but acknowledge that covering the floor were at least fifty if not a hundred rugs of all sizes and designs.

'Or none,' said Patch abruptly.

'In any case, no more library for me.'

'No.' Smiled Patch.

'Where is Crinkum then?' said Gyffe casually fluffing up a few cushions before taking a seat.

'Stand-off with gargoyle.'

This was a game dragoyles could play for weeks, years even. Although the dragoyle would inevitably have to forfeit it was within dragoyle reasoning that because they could move and the gargoyle couldn't that it showed much more skill on the dragoyle's behalf.

'How long has that been going on for?'

'Since man left.'

'You mean Bolingbroke?'

'Who else?' Patch licked his finger and pompously flicked over a page.

'Just Bolingbroke,' said Gyffe airily.

'Then that's him,' said Patch turning away with the book now closer to his face.

Gyffe jumped up and strolled around the room giving a few rugs a little lift with his foot. He paused to peer at Prunewick who despite the years, seemed as perennial as ever.

'I wonder if you're missing Ma Gwrach?' Gyffe said to the idling tree. 'I know I am missing Grimoire. I even miss scrubbing out his porridge pot.'

Patch grunted.

As Gyffe watched Prunewick for some sign of movement, a howl echoed from beyond the walls.

'The afanc,' said Gyffe turning quickly to Patch, 'it must be ensnared in my trap.'

Patch lost his composure. He dropped the book and crouched forward cupping his hand to his ear.

'At last,' said Gyffe, 'the afanc. If indeed it and Crach Ffinnant are one and the same we shall soon find out.'

'Afanc, dangerous,' said Patch straining his ears for further indication of the beast's presence.

There was none.

'A little danger won't do us any harm. We've had almost two centuries of absolutely nothing menacing happening at all. The closest we've had to any real threat was when you put fool's parsley in the soup instead of wild chervil.'

'Seem alike, was tired. Needed rest.'

'Well, you were close to resting in peace.'

'You go,' said Patch, making a sound of hesitation which Gyffe caught as something between a moan and a sigh.

'That's the spirit,' said Gyffe 'I've the wand Grimoire gave me and have spent enough nights practising using it to aid us, should the beast turn hostile.'

'Turn?'

'In case it attacks,' said Gyffe.

Another caterwaul was heard from outside.

'We must be brave,' added Gyffe, 'the longer we allay, the more likely it will have a chance to escape. If it truly knows this place as well as we suspect, it will have no trouble finding us first.'

Gyffe and Patch crept out of the room, down the narrow corridor towards the entrance steps. They tiptoed to the bottom and Gyffe, as quiet as could be, pried open the door. They both peered out of the crack to where Gyffe had set up his trap. Gyffe opened the door some more. They could see something thrashing about in the pit.

'Help,' called a voice.

'It must have transformed back into Crach,' whispered Gyffe.

Whatever was trapped was at least as long as the pit itself. Its head seemed to be poking out of the hole with two beady-eyes looking through the gaps of the net.

'Tall for dwarf,' said Patch.

'Maybe it is standing on its toes,' whispered Gyffe who had his wand at the ready.

As they approached, it was clear that whatever it was, it wasn't a monster nor a dwarf.

'Who goes there?' said Gyffe.

'Quite the contrary, I can't go anywhere, I'm stuck.'

'Give us a name to put to the voice.'

'My name is Thomas Charnock.'

'What brings you to this place, Thomas?' Gyffe slid the wand back in his belt.

'I was on my way to Crach Ffinnant's house.'

'This was his place, he is no longer the resident.' Gyffe peered in closer to get a better look at the man who had fallen for his trap. 'Where have you come from?'

'I've come from France, where I was conscripted to fight a war,' said Thomas trying to wriggle free from the net.

'So you're a soldier then?'

'I have no bent for camaraderie and no interest in the war. These traits, it seems, disappointed my commanding chief more than my inability to wield a sword.'

'So you're a deserter then?'

'Not really, look, would it be too much to ask if we could carry on this discussion somewhere else?'

Gyffe turned to Patch who was already on his way to free the man.

Once inside, all three of them settled down before the fire. Thomas went to sit down on a wooden chair, but Gyffe stopped him and motioned to a more enticing armchair.

'That's very kind of you,' said Thomas, sitting comfortably.

'Pardon me,' grunted Gyffe, he picked up the wooden chair and swung it against the mantle. It splintered into pieces and Gyffe fed them to the flames.

'Our wood situation,' said Gyffe coyly, 'or lack thereof, has become very dire indeed. I fear for the books.'

Patch looked away and coughed into his sleeve.

'And how to do you come to know Ffinnant? Through sorcery?'

'Oh no nothing like that,' said Thomas, accepting a mug of ground elder wine and taking a roasted pilewort from a bowl put in front of him. 'I dare say, for a tag-rag crew like yourselves in an abandoned sunken keep, you're not doing too badly on the supper front.'

'We get by,' said Gyffe.

'I knew of Crach,' continued Thomas, 'but personally no. I came across his name through the Old Book of Hergest which was leant to me by a friend who knew Hopeyn ap Tomas.'

'Ah, now he was a sorcerer.'

'Much so,' said Thomas popping another pilewort which disappeared into his bearded mouth as if by magic. 'As for sorcery I have dabbled in the arcane, but for the most part, it is alchemy I have come to know well.'

'And what is Ffinnant's connection in all this?' enquired Gyffe.

'Now then, here's the interesting bit. In the book, there were several loose leaves. Undoubtedly, these were penned by Hopeyn but destined to not be included. Those pages detailed this property and the dwarf who resided in it. A dwarf, who was said to be an alchemist and may have been the owner of the wordless book. Heard of it?'

'The wordless book? I think Grimoire had a copy.'

'I have been searching all my life for this book. That is why I snuck away from that tedious battle and managed to get myself here.' Thomas suddenly looked very alert. 'Grimoire? A friend of yours? Has a copy you say?'

'My old master, alas departed,' replied Gyffe.

'Departed? Oh, I'm sorry to learn of your loss. I am imbued by the enigma of mortality, it is my holy grail, thus my interest in the book, as it provides the recipe for producing the elixir of life.'

'Not lost, left,' butted in Patch who despite finding visitations a welcome break from the monotony of isolation, also tired quickly of the company. 'Swapped book. Book gone.'

'Swapped? For what?'

'Scarf,' said Patch.

'A scarf?' Thomas did a double-take. 'Tell me who was this person who accepted such sacrosanct secrets in exchange for a scarf?'

Gyffe took a moment to remember if Grimoire actually did at one time possess the book. He remembered Grimoire bartering with a doddery wizard at the Knucker's Knest over some such codex. 'Yes, he did, I seem to remember he traded it with a wizard.'

'Do you remember the wizard's name?' Thomas seemed to almost be hovering over his seat.

Gyffe turned his head away, trying to think. 'Spindle Tarcrust, I think, something like that. It was a long time ago, and Grimoire didn't make much ado about it. He did, however, mention a few days later that the scarf was slightly shorter in length than he would have liked it to be and the fabric gave him hives.'

'A scarf,' repeated Thomas, disheartened. 'Hives? What on earth was this Grimoire thinking?'

'Cold,' said Patch. 'Got stiff neck from drafts.'

Gyffe pressed his fingers together as if about to postulate.

'Well, that's that then, isn't it?' said Thomas curling himself in the opposite direction of everyone in the room. 'Can't imagine there are two wordless books. Unless it was a copy.'

'We could,' began Gyffe.

'Could what?' jumped in Thomas.

'We could,' Gyffe hovered over the sentiment for a few seconds, 'take a look in Crach Ffinnant's library.'

'Could we?' Thomas glanced at Patch whose distinctly distasteful expression caused him to glance away.

'No.' Patch drilled himself down in a cushion.

Gyffe went to the library door. 'It's only through here. With the two of us, we could easily break down the door.'

Thomas took from the folds of his coat several sheets of paper. 'That's not it,' said Thomas examining one of the papers. 'You see, it seems there's a second library, probably concealed as I see no description of its whereabouts on this document other than the words "Hidden Library".'

'A second library?' baulked Gyffe. 'You mean I've spent hundreds of years pouring over book after book in Crach's general repository, when all along there's been a secret archive under my very nose in this very house?'

'Afraid so,' said Thomas. 'It seems that your mage friend didn't want you to know about it.'

'It must be found,' said Gyffe, his eyes gleaming at the thought, 'but there is also the threat of danger.'

'Danger?'

'Foolhardiness,' mumbled Patch.

'Well,' said Gyffe placing his hands on his hips in the most patronising of manners, 'that's the longest word if ever I heard you mutter. May I ask where you got it?'

'Book,' groaned Patch, 'chapter on fribbling squits and inquisit ...' Patch appeared to internally squeeze himself together. 'Nosiness,' he finally said in a gasp.

'Never trust dwarfish ethnology, it's always completely prejudiced.' Gyffe huffed and spun back around to Thomas. 'Yes, it would be hazardous, we've never so much as set foot in any of the other rooms below. You see, we can't be sure the rest of the place isn't inhabited by something ... well ... something that might be waiting for us to find it.'

'A what? A dwarf? Come, come.' Thomas leapt to his feet. 'But needs must when the devil drives. Access to the archives will equip us with the puissance needed to repel any demon or monster in residence.'

'Good thinking,' said Gyffe, trying to reel in his enthusiasm.

'Or bats,' said Patch as he settled back into his chair and pulled a blanket over his knees.

'Bats?' Gyffe gave the hognome one of his "oh really" looks.

'In belfry, either good thoughts or bats.'

Gyffe waited for the hognome to clarify but then decided that he might be waiting for quite some time. 'You're not coming with us?'

Patch wiggled further into his seat, making it completely clear that he had no intention of getting back up. 'Must stay. Keep Prunewick safe.'

'Leave him,' said Thomas, 'he obviously has no appetite for adventure. Besides, we'll need someone up here should our hunt go awry.' Thomas examined the sheet from Hopeyn ap Thomas's book. 'Unfortunately, these room annotations are terribly convoluted, for instance, not only are there ten storerooms, but there are also ten rooms for storing each storeroom.'

Gyffe fetched his wand and pointed it towards the sheet. He fiddled with the panel on the dongle until a cloudy haze fumed. Thomas stepped back, letting go of the paper and watched it hang in the air until, with a swoosh, the cloud around it drew back into the wand.

'What on earth was that?' said Thomas snatching the paper before it fell to the floor.

'A simple dowse spell,' said Gyffe, 'now if I've coded this correctly, it will lead us to the archive. Grimoire preloaded the wand with a few rudimentary spells, some more useful than others.'

'Such as?' said Thomas attentively examining the magical instrument.

'It can levitate objects, you can set it to imitate the sound of a cockerel at dawn, it can seal a tear in almost any fabric, suck up cobwebs and dust, and the pungent pot spell removes odours from the privy.'

'I see,' said Thomas, 'does it only come in one colour?'

'It's pre-set to match any witching or wizarding garb. It also has a handy carry—'

'Go,' resounded the hognome in such a boom that Gyffe and Thomas hastened out the room without another word.

They made their way down to the entrance hall. A crescent of wooden panels lined the far wall, each looking remarkably like a door. Gyffe waved the wand at each one until he felt a tingle shoot through his hand.

'Aha.' Gyffe pushed the panel, but it didn't budge. 'Maybe it's stuck.'

Thomas went to lend a hand, and together they pressed all their weight against it. The panel remained obstinately fixed.

'Give it a kick,' said Thomas.

Gyffe thrust his foot against it. Still nothing.

'You kick it,' said Gyffe.

'We'll take it in turns,' suggested Thomas.

Both proceeded to kick at the panel until they were so worn out that relief came only after collapsing on the floor in a panting slump. Then, as soon as they caught their breath, the adjacent panel creaked open.

'It should be noted, the dowsing spell isn't a hundred per cent accurate,' said Gyffe getting to his feet and prying open the panel. Thomas followed behind him into a dwarf-sized passageway built of stone. They followed the passage until they came to a dead end.

'Now what?' said Gyffe, 'I'm not sensing anything from the wand.'

'Wave it around a bit more.'

'I am,' said Gyffe giving it a sound wave.

'No, like this,' said Thomas making a grab for it.

'Hands off.' Gyffe shielded the wand behind his back.

The two of them, poised at an impasse, glared at each other.

'Let's go back,' Gyffe finally said.

'You're right,' conceded Thomas, 'this behaviour is childish and getting us nowhere.'

Bent double they marched back up the tunnel, but when they stepped through the open panel, they found themselves in an entirely different room. The surround consisted of a wrought iron buttress pegged against a stone, and at the far end, a gate spun with gold. Gyffe and Thomas, arm in arm, danced with each other trumpeting with excitement. They wiggled their bottoms and teetered their arms, sharing shrill giggles while kicking their legs. Eventually, once again, finding each other slumped on the ground in a panting fit.

'It must be through there.' Gyffe directed the wand towards the gate. He felt the tingle run up his arm, but when they tried the gate, it refused to open.

'Does not the wand enable an opening spell of some sort?' said Thomas.

'Grimoire neglected to program one in. When I asked him why he mumbled something about cats.'

'Oh,' said Thomas giving the gate another yank, 'there must be a lock somewhere.'

As they felt along the golden threads, the gate gave a jerk clockwise.

'The whole thing is a revolving lock,' said Gyffe, 'look around the circumference for symbols or numbers.'

They both peered around the periphery of the gate, but no stone revealed any indication of a code.

'Interesting,' said Thomas, 'all of these stones are cut from different rocks.'

'They all look the same to me,' said Gyffe.

'Years of alchemy has provided me with a solid grounding in mineral identification. And I can tell you right now that this stone is cut from diorite, and this stone is cut from gneiss.' Thomas gripped the gate with both hands. 'Now if I turn it counterclockwise to this stone.'

Thomas turned the gate another five times until with a click it swung open.

'You did it,' said Gyffe.

'Indeed, I did. From unakite to norite, limestone to obsidian and from chert to kimberlite, the beginning letters of which spell unlock. Not very imaginative dwarfs, you see.'

Through the gate there was a concourse floored with a canal brimming with an unsightly black liquid. Each side of the canal was adorned with stone statues, dwarfish knights holding battle axes or wielding maces. The air, dank and clotted, smelt like the festering carcasses of rotting fish. Hardly a sound came from within except the heaving anxiety being pushed from the lungs of Gyffe and Thomas.

'Look,' said Thomas, 'there's some sort of door at the end of the canal.'

'And there's a boat.' Gyffe pointed to the small coracle tied to a mooring stone. Thomas and Gyffe climbed into it and cast themselves along the viscous water.

CHAPTER TWENTY-THREE

Grimoire observed the living pieces shuffling at speed across the board as the giants commanded each one in accordance to algebraic notation. The key motivation to move, and move swiftly, seemed to be the gruesome hammer held by Bran which threatened to swiftly pulverise any would be disruptor to the play of the game.

'King's wizard to queen's faun seven' shouted Bran.

'I think I've been summoned,' said Grimoire, turning around to Arthur.

Arthur didn't look at him, he held his head down and breathed slowly. 'Move,' said Arthur.

Grimoire hesitated. 'How long have you been playing?' he said before taking his first step onto a black square.

This time Arthur raised his head and seemed to look through Grimoire rather than at him. 'Long enough,' he said, 'now make your move otherwise you'll end up a coal-roasted sorcerer.'

'Mage,' grumbled Grimoire under his breath, 'and I don't roast well,' he said, moving towards the waiting faun.

'Queen's ogre to king's goblin,' shouted Maelor Gwar.

A burly ogre crashed its way across the board, for a moment the goblin appeared to try and run, but something held it to the spot while the ogre raised its blockish fist bringing it down hard upon the pointy green head of the goblin. Each thwack caused the goblin to become shorter and shorter until nothing much was left except for a knobbly and wet green-lump framed within a white chess square. After a few minutes, the frail woman, who called herself Maelor Gwar's mother, came onto the board carrying a shovel. She scooped up the remains and shuffled off again. Grimoire winced and turned to Ma Gwrach who oddly enough was not paying any attention to the game whatsoever.

'King's ... er ... witch to faun,' bellowed Bran.

'Your move,' nudged the tall queen standing beside Ma Gwrach.

'Mine?'

'Yes, off you go,' said the queen.

Ma Gwrach trotted away, not in the direction of the faun, but the other way.

Bran slapped a hand to his forehead. 'Wrong way, hag!'

Ma Gwrach just kept on walking until she reached a square which aligned herself directly with Maelor's King.

'Checkmate,' she cackled, clapping her hands together in delight.

'What?' Maelor roared.

Bran looked closer. 'She's got a point,' he said with a grin 'it does seem to be checkmate. I win.'

'Never!' Maelor stomped his feet and was about to cast all the pieces off the board when Bran reached out and held his arm tightly. Grimoire was about an inch away from being sent flying towards the wall.

'I demand a rematch,' snarled Maelor 'you cheated. The witch should never have had free will. Free will is against the rules. The ogre may scratch its behind and lick its runny nose, but that's about the sum of it.'

'All right, we'll play again tomorrow after I've had my supper and drunk my mead.' Bran heaved himself out of the throne and stomped off into the darkness.

Maelor leaned in close to Ma Gwrach, his face red with anger. 'Next time you cheat,' he growled 'I will pickle you in my witch pickling jar.'

Ma Gwrach, for the first time, appeared unnerved at the suggestion there was actually such a thing as a witch pickling jar.

'Now all of you,' roared Maelor' back into your cells before I change my mind on chess and settle tomorrow for checkers with flat round pieces.'

Everyone sloped off into their cells, followed by Maelor's mother, who firmly bolted each cell to the chorus of moans and groans.

'Well, that was a surprise,' chortled Grimoire 'all the while I thought you were away with the fairies. How did you do it? I never took you for a chess master.'

'I'm not, and I was away with the fairies,' smiled Ma Gwrach 'I've got fairies in my hat.' She lifted her hat and revealed a circle of wee folk sitting on her mat of hair. Grimoire peered closely at them.

'Ah, that makes perfect sense.'

'These fairies also happen to be remarkably skilled at the game of chess, a result of having nested a fairy-ring under me witch's hat. Frankly, there's not a lot else to do but play games. Occasionally, they do get up and dance, but it itches me scalp so.'

'How though did you crack the enchantment of the giant's chessboard? I attempted some subtle magic and failed miserably to break the spell.'

'Fairies are free will, they cannot be held by such magic. Especially by the oafish magic of giants.'

Grimoire packed his pipe and lit it thoughtfully. 'The question is, tylwyth teg or no, how do we get out of here?'

'Out of here ...' echoed Ma Gwrach going to scratch her head but realising fairies were on it.

'You know I met Arthur on that board. We had all wondered where he had gotten. Now it's clear, the prophecy, once and future king. That future may very well as easily become us too.'

Ma Gwrach sat down cross-legged in the corner of the cage and took from her pocket two small sticks. She touched them together and inhaled deeply.

'Divining rods?' said Grimoire.

'No, these are defining rods,' Ma Gwrach took another pint of air, twisting her head as she did so as if about to enter a trance 'they determine a definition to the problem at hand.'

'Ah outstanding,' said Grimoire with enthusiasm 'if we define the problem, we can then apply the appropriate solution … err … but I would think the problem is quite clear.'

'Not clear enough …' spoke Ma Gwrach her eyes tightly shut.

Grimoire waited a few minutes as Ma Gwrach fiddled with her sticks.

'Well? Anything?'

'Not a peep,' said Ma Gwrach stretching her eyes open, 'must be defying rods.'

'That's useful then,' humphed Grimoire, 'how about we then use one of them to pick this lock here?' Grimoire snatched a rod and wriggled it around the lock. The gate swung open.

'Interesting, someone wants us to escape.'

'Of course, they do,' said Ma Gwrach getting to her feet and striding out the gate, 'your shadow probably.'

'You're really starting to get on my nerves,' mumbled Grimoire under his breath.

Without a second thought, Grimoire followed Ma Gwrach. That was mainly because he was lingering on his first thought which was that, although Ma Gwrach was capable if not certifiably sure of such behaviour, this oblique way of tackling the current circumstances of being trapped in the lair of two nasty giants was simply, almost, irresponsible.

'Where do we go now?' said Grimoire.

'To the chessboard,' said Ma Gwrach scuttling off into the darkness.

The enormous chessboard, illuminated under fragments of moonlight radiating from the fortress windows, looked more sinister than it had when it was populated by the unwilling pieces. To Grimoire's surprise, standing on e1, was Arthur with his hands firmly clasped together and the long robe he wore covering his whole body, even his head which was cloaked by a hood.

Ma Gwrach reached the king first and taking off her hat, she bowed forward in respect. As Grimoire approached, he noticed that Arthur held out his hand and the wee folk in Ma Gwrach's hair scampered along Arthur's arm and disappeared in the folds of his garment. Ma Gwrach screwed her hat tightly back on.

'That's better,' she said, 'no more itching.'

Grimoire finally joined them, bowing he also took off his hat and, balancing without so much of a jiggle, was an overripe apple which Arthur took.

'I'll take this as well,' he said making it disappear beneath his robe, 'the food here is quite miserable as you could expect from giants whose only culinary achievement is smashed potato.'

Grimoire corrected himself and put his hat back on. He had forgotten about the apple, a rosemary russet. He had plucked and stashed it with the intention of savouring at a later date. Arthur reached into his robe and

Grimoire sensing that perhaps he had noted the chagrin, thought that Arthur might return the apple, but it was not to be so. Arthur took out a key which he handed to Ma Gwrach. She slipped it in her bag. Then grabbing Grimoire's arm hastily led him across the chessboard.

'What's going on,' whispered Grimoire.

'Shhhh,' Ma Gwrach stopped suddenly.

The sound of someone crunching an apple echoed in the darkness.

'This way,' hissed Ma Gwrach pulling Grimoire with a fair bit of force for one with such a bony frame.

They had nearly completed all the squares when a terrible sound bellowed from within. A growling so fierce it could only come from the jaws of a hellhound. In the darkness they could just make out the shape of a rather large dog and next to it, the enormous outline of its owner. Next, came a noise that made the hellhound's growl as comforting as the purr of a pussycat.

'Gwg gog ydy, I spy the wizard and the witchy.'

They both skidded to a halt.

'All the time, rhyming this and rhyming that, it's enough to make you have a spat,' snapped Grimoire.

It was Maelor who was standing at the centre of the chessboard. His muscular frame swaying from side to side as he held aloft a club formed from what could only be an entire tree.

'We need to get to that door,' whispered Ma Gwrach pointing at a smaller door carved into the large giant-sized one.

'King's giant to d5,' shouted Grimoire, 'king's dog you're on f3.'

Maelor paused, he looked at the board, trying to work out the directive. Grimoire and Ma Gwrach seized the opportunity to flee as fast as they could towards the small door. As Maelor went one way, his dog went the other, causing a tug-o-war between the two.

'Quick thinking,' said Ma Gwrach inserting the key and, with a twist, the door flung open.

Once outside on the clouded terrain, Grimoire turned to Ma Gwrach, she placed one hand on her hip and grinned at him. 'Don't you want to know how I did it?'

'I am wound up in excruciating curiosity, but there is the pressing matter of being squashed to avoid, once whatever crumb of intelligence catches up he'll be after us, cussing and rhyming all the while.'

Ma Gwrach was about to speak when a hot wind caught her face.

'Could it be?' said Grimoire feeling the same warm flow of air.

Buried in a cluster of thick white clouds was a form that stretched almost thirty metres long. It was hardly visible in its foggy blanket, but Grimoire could just make out the lazy glimmer of an eye peering ever so faintly in the mist.

'A white dragon,' he gasped, 'haven't seen one of those since the fall of Owen Lawgoch. No doubt, enchained by Maelor and Bran for their own amusement.'

Grimoire followed the iron links up to the fortress wall and saw that they were fastened in the fashion of a lead. From inside the lumbering footsteps of Maelor could be heard along with some ditty about popping lice between his fingernails. Grimoire prepared himself for a spell to break the chains, but something stronger was blocking his efforts.

'Won't work here, dear,' said Ma Gwrach, 'giants may be daft, but if there is one thing they excel at, it's the stubbornness of their enchantments. We'll need to outwit them. Tell you what, take off your hat and cloak and climb aboard the dragon. I'll do the rest.'

'Take off my what?'

'Hat and cloak, won't hurt a bit, be like a tiny pinprick, trust me.'

Maelor had reached the doors and was pushing them open. Grimoire handed over his cloak and hat to Ma Gwrach. He then mounted the dragon and held on to its neck, he was in an instant joined by Ma Gwrach who hopped on behind him.

'All sorted,' she said.

Maelor burst through the door and surveyed the cloudy peak with beady eyes. His dog sniffed through the fog and began snarling in the direction of Grimoire's discarded clothes. The giant raised the tree and shouted. 'I see you behind that chain wizard!'

The tree came crashing down, breaking the links as it did so. The dragon, feeling the release, bucked into the sky. Its wings gushing down a hurricane of force towards Maelor who swayed backwards and nearly toppled over. As the dragon surged fiercely into the air, Ma Gwrach screeched at Grimoire.

'Don't worry, we'll get you some new rags. About time methinks.'

CHAPTER TWENTY-FOUR

Gyffe noticed that as they drifted towards the doors at the end of the canal, Thomas's eyes looked as if he was a newt about to consider an inattentive ant for its next meal. He was scratching the nail of his thumb against that of his index finger. The sound began to resonate an uncomfortable rhythm.

'Is that necessary?' said Gyffe in a lowered voice.

'Necessary? What?' said Thomas pulling his gaze away from the doors.

'The noise you are making with your fingers.'

Thomas immediately stopped. 'How do you suppose we get the doors open? There's no handle, no lever, nothing.'

Gyffe looked them over, surveying each one for a way through. 'I suppose we knock three times or something like that.'

'Three times?' said Thomas.

'Yes, three, that is what it usually is, three or some such number divisible by nine.'

'Three is an odd number, isn't it?'

'I'm not sure I understand your meaning?' said Gyffe.

'Well, three, it is odder than four, don't you think?'

'Why do you say that? It is no more odd than seven.'

'One might mistake it for a pair of buttocks ...' began Thomas.

'Are you feeling all right?' Gyffe eyed his companion.

'Or on the other hand a bosom,' mused Thomas, circling his hands in the air.

'What are you doing?' said Gyffe.

'I'm making rude gestures with my hands,' said Thomas as if it were the most natural response in the world.

Gyffe was becoming astutely aware that his companion was in the grip of some mania. Thomas settled his twitches with a sudden rigidness and began a contemplative wringing of his hands.

'Anyway, this knocking business suggests there is something behind the doors which should answer.'

'There may very well be,' said Gyffe.

'And it stands to reason that, whatever is behind those doors wants us to know that it is there?' said Thomas pointing to his temple as if he'd located the very spot of reason.

Gyffe started to feel as if this line of questioning did not really fit into the ethos of curiosity, which had its benefit mostly in consideration of the unknown possibility of danger, rather than the gradual realisation that the perceived threat was actually imminent.

'Or rather only wants you to know,' said Gyffe feeling adrift with a potential madman.

Thomas ignored the remark and proceeded to scratch his tongue in the most uncouth manner. They held tight as the coracle was brought bobbing against the doors. Gyffe stood up, steadying himself on the wobbling craft, he knocked three times. They both then sat silently, waiting, but after a few minutes, it was clear nothing was going to happen.

'Try seven times,' suggested Thomas

'Why seven?'

'Because it seems to be a number prominently featured in numerical collations of the divine.'

'And what does the number seven remind you?' said Gyffe.

'What ... Do ... You ... Mean?' Thomas stammered.

'A beak? An upside down leg? An armpit?'

'I have no idea what you're getting at. Seven is, as it appears to be, seven,' said Thomas soberly.

Gyffe knocked seven times giving each tap at the door the emphasised wrap that Thomas expected and still ... nothing.

'Bother,' said Thomas slumping back into the boat. 'What could it be? Perhaps we should try rubbing the door as if a lamp.'

Gyffe sensed that the lunacy was returning. The stench in the air combined with the mania of his companion was proving too much. As curious as a squit may be, the thought that behind those doors may lay the actual afanc proved unbearable. They sat in silence for a moment. The deathly water lay relatively still like a mirror into oblivion. The brooding doors stubbornly fastened against each other were testament that whatever was to be found behind demanded a trial of faculty which Gyffe, despite his heroics, deferred all decisions to his legs.

'Let's go.' Gyffe took hold of the paddles.

'Wait,' growled Thomas scrunching up his face, his eyes darkening.

Gyffe witnessed for a second Thomas crank his neck with a crack. 'Whatever is the matter?'

'Go? But we're so close,' pleaded Thomas.

'No, you're so close, I'm stuck on a coracle with someone who by degrees is steadily coming undone.'

Thomas rose up like a snake ready to strike. 'Listen to me squid, your scarf trading days are over, this time the wordless book is mine, do you hear me?'

It was only a heartbeat, he felt Thomas's hands around his throat, the coracle rocked violently. Gyffe's head faced the murky waters as it was plunged in and then pulled back out with a swift yank.

'Are you mad?' spluttered Gyffe, spraying out foul-tasting liquid.

'Mad? Me? Is Thomas Charnock mad? Renowned occultist, distinguished alchemist, nephew of Thomas Charnock, confessor to Henry VII, mad?'

'I was being rhet—' Gyffe's head was thrust back under the water and then quickly pulled out again, '—orical.' Gyffe fumbled with his fists but failed to make an impact with anything other than air.

'Oracles, you want oracles? Let's see what Pisces has to say about squids.' Thomas thrust Gyffe's head back into the water.

'Mad?' Thomas's hands tightened. 'Had not nought about it until thou.' He allowed Gyffe's head to resurface.

'You're choking me,' croaked Gyffe, spluttering the foul liquid from his mouth.

'Am I? Terribly sorry, I intend to drown you,' said Thomas, 'however, I'm open to suggestions.'

Gyffe tried to think if there was such a thing as an "expel the grip of an enraged looney and shatter him to pieces" spell. Nothing came to mind. He was dragged out again for another gasp of air.

'We're not leaving here until I have the frilly loafers tone, tone, tone …' his voice bouncing against the walls and whirling around Gyffe's head.

Gyffe gargled the vile liquid, his legs buckled under the weight of Thomas. Just as he was resigned to his fate, the sound of winching chains rattled across the waters.

'It's the doors, the doors. They open.' Thomas loosened his grip enough for Gyffe to be able to crawl to the other end of the coracle, which was no great distance, but far enough for him to feel proportionally safer on the spectrum of unsafe.

'Oh,' cooed Thomas, his eyes widening, 'they do indeed open. The key was throttling you. I shall do it again should we encounter further doors,' he snapped.

The doors churned the waters as they swung to reveal a cavern illuminated with the glint of gold gilded books. Books of all thickness and size stacked on top of each other. The tomes surrounded a raised rock where sat a ring of puny faeries, naked except for tatty rags fastened in modesty. They lay in repose, feasting on slimy raw fish. Gyffe noted that Thomas's face now held the expression halfway between pleasure and disgust. He thought about silently slipping into the water and making his way back across the canal while Thomas was fixated on the wee folk, but his initial thought was dashed by the second thought that he had never learned to swim.

'Tylwyth teg,' groaned Gyffe, 'I should have thought as much.'

'The secret library,' said Thomas, 'it exists. Perhaps these wee librarians can help me.'

'Help?' said Gyffe, 'I hope you're using help in the loosest sense of the word.'

Thomas held himself steady on the coracle, throwing one foot out opposite the other to keep his balance.

'Ahem, I seek the elixir of life.'

The faeries looked at Thomas blankly before erupting in a spasm of croaky unfaery-like giggles.

'He seeks,' said a faery sucking up a fibrous intestine.

'He quests,' piped up another.

'He thirsts,' chimed in a third.

'He's wasting his time,' grunted one chewing on the tail of a fish.

Gyffe remained silent. He knew that these were not the kind of faeries to meddle with. Generally, it had to be said that faeries were, on the whole, a friendly race and although it was well known that there was not actually anything like a bad tylwyth teg, it was also generally accepted that there were some who were just not up to the standard of goodness as their kin.

'I was told,' resumed Thomas, clearing his throat to avoid the squeak of disappointment, 'that Crach Ffinnant, the alchemist may have possessed such a thing.'

The faeries chuckled and nibbled at their fish bits.

'Oh maybe he did,' said one. 'Maybe he didn't. Why ask us?'

'Did you have a look?' said another mimicking the act of looking. 'Did you have a rummage?'

'Did you check beneath his pillows and overturn his bed?' said another.

'Yes, yes, did you have a nosey about the place? Did you put to use your human nostrils in sniffing out the prize?'

'Truffles,' said one.

'Perfume,' said another.

'Flatus,' said the one crunching down the last of the fishtail.

The faeries led by their noses bobbled their heads. Gyffe thought it all rather rude, but considering they were being offensive to a potential maniac sharing a small craft with him, the rudeness was an acceptable diversion.

'I just thought ...' squeaked Thomas.

'Did you hear that?' squealed one of the faeries. 'He just thought!'

The faeries cupped their ears.

'I didn't hear it,' shouted one faery.

'He never said, excuse me,' said another.

'He who thought it sought it,' mumbled yet another.

One faery scooped out a fish eyeball and popped it into its mouth. It stood up and chewing loudly went to the edge of the rock. 'What did you think?' it said. 'What exactly did your human brain just do right now?'

Thomas was getting agitated, it was clear that his lifelong search, the obstinance of the faeries to cooperate and the helplessness of the situation was becoming overbearing. Gyffe watched as Thomas clasped his hands together and squeezed them until red before thrusting out his arms, trembling.

'Please, I have begged Her Majesty to confine me to the tower in order to manifest this substance. I have forgone all worldly possessions, and to my shame, I have even traded my soul to the Lord of Darkness.'

'Queen?' Gyffe said.

'The Lord of Darkness?' the Tylwyth teg said in unison.

'The Lord of Darkness,' Thomas cried exasperated, 'the very devil himself.'

The head faery looked back at the other faeries, they all glanced off in different directions as if the words were no more meaningful than if he had said he had traded his horse for a slow-worm.

'Perhaps we can help you,' said the faery.

'Really? Help? Me? You can?' Thomas's neck stuck out, and a weakened grin spread across his face.

The faery crossed its arms and nodded. It looked back at the other faeries who quickly nodded before launching into a fit of sniggers. Gyffe started to nod too, but for what reason other than wanting the faeries to help him get rid of Thomas, he knew not.

'Do you see?' Thomas said, turning to Gyffe, who was not expecting to be noticed at that point, 'these faery folk are more than willing to aid me in my quest.'

Gyffe forced his mouth into a toothy smile and held it there as long as it took for Thomas to return his attention to the faeries.

'See?' repeated Thomas turning back again to Gyffe.

Gyffe propped up the toothy smile again, but this time it was accompanied by an involuntary frown. Thomas finally turned back to the faeries who by this time, had stopped nodding.

'Help me then,' said Thomas.

'First,' said the faery, 'remove anything made of metal from your person.'

Thomas removed his coat which had metal buttons, his boots which had metal buckles, and his rings. Finally, he stood in his shirt and stockings. The faeries cupped their mouths to suppress the snickers and giggles behind their hands.

'Now, Thomas Charnock, climb the rock, and you may choose the book you seek.' The faeries got up and formed a circle. Thomas climbed the rock one foot at a time until he reached the top.

The faery who had been directing him stood back. 'Enter the ring, and have a browse.'

Thomas stepped over the faeries who were now all holding hands and dancing an awkward jig.

Gyffe watched as Thomas without hesitation, joined in with the dancing. 'Thomas,' called Gyffe, 'don't forget the book.'

'Who?' Thomas cried cantering like a horse, 'what book?' He pranced in a fit, kicking his legs up and bobbing up and down like a pigeon. Until, gradually with each crazed movement he began to fade away until finally the faeries broke the circle and he was gone.

One of the faeries came to the edge of the rock and pointed to Gyffe. 'And you?'

Gyffe thought for a moment he had been conveniently forgotten and had started to make his way to the middle of the coracle, quietly taking the paddles in hand.

'Me?' said Gyffe. He pulled at the paddles, but no matter how much force he could muster pulling the oars through the water, the boat remained motionless. He let go and stretched his arms out.

'Ah, nothing like a bit of upper arm strengthening, feel better now, I really should be getting along. It was nice to meet you.'

'Do you also seek a book?' said the faery.

'The only thing I seek right now is a hot bath and a mug of burdock mead.'

'Did you also trade your soul with this Lord of Darkness?'

'What? For a hot bath and a mug of burdock mead? Lucky day for Lucifer if I did.'

'Are you sure that's all you seek?' said the faery swiftly checking in on its fellow faeries who were all paying keen attention.

'We've heard whispers,' said another faery.

'Whispers?' squeaked Gyffe.

'We've seen traps and tricks.'

'Traps?' Gyffe's knees, which had no reason to announce their presence, began to knock.

'We know what you seek.'

'The afanc, the afanc, that is what you seek,' the faeries chanted.

Gyffe felt himself tighten-up at the word. He considered for a moment that the dreaded beast might make an appearance then and there. That these faeries perhaps were subjects of the creature and bidding its will.

'Where did Thomas go?' Gyffe asked changing the subject, albeit not a very nice one, in an attempt to buy more time.

The faery at the front smirked.

'We sent him home, back to his hovel and heart's desire.'

'You said his yearnings would end?'

'All human yearnings end,' snapped the faery with a smirk.

The faeries congregated at the edge of the rock and, raising their hands limply, swayed back and forth in a trance. Gyffe felt the boat move backwards. The vision of the faeries became fainter.

'We shall help you put an end to your yearnings,' called the faeries as Gyffe watched the stone doors closing in on them, 'all yearnings end, even those of squits.'

CHAPTER TWENTY-FIVE

The white dragon dived down towards a landscape thick with snow. Down the dragon soared into an icy fog, its wings lashing out against the bitterly cold wind. Deeper and deeper it went into the indistinguishable whiteness, picking up speed with urgency as if to break an invisible barrier. Gradually, it cast its wings and finally glided towards a cave grooved into the abyss of a black mountain.

Grimoire and Ma Gwrach cowered upon the back of the beast. The dragon prepared for entry, its claws extended, scraped against the glacial floor, shattering the ice and churning snow. They held on tight as the descent to land rattled their bones and popped their ears. Through the turmoil, Ma Gwrach managed to pass Grimoire a lump of birch sap.

'S-s-sap? Ch-ch-chew it, it he-he-helps,' said Ma Gwrach trying to get the words out as the juddering beast skidded for half a mile along the cave floor.

When the dragon finally came to a halt, Grimoire and Ma Gwrach unclamped their frozen hands from the dragon's hide and slid to the ground.

'Well, I must say, quite a ride.' Grimoire was unusually animated at the afterthought of just having dismounted a dragon.

'Do you think it now wants to eat us?'

Grimoire stopped to consider Ma Gwrach's suggestion that instead of having been rescued by the dragon, they were, in fact, some kind of meal ticket.

'Eat us? White dragons,' began Grimoire, 'are notoriously friendlier … err … well, not friendlier … but more even-tempered than their red counterparts.'

'I'm very aware of the personality distinctions between dragons, but this one hasn't eaten properly in a long time, it's emaciated, it's all scales and bones, I'm surprised it even got us this far.'

The dragon expelled a cold blast of air from its nostrils as if affronted at the derision at its appearance. Grimoire worried that Ma Gwrach's observations might persuade the dragon to eat them whether it was hungry or not. She was always one to speak her mind. Unfortunately, thought Grimoire, it is not the act of speaking one's mind that had the potential for disaster, it was the sort of mind that did the speaking.

'Is it mute? Can you speak, my dear?' Ma Gwrach put her hand on the creature affectionately, but Grimoire thought it came across as patronising. The dragon snorted.

'There's your answer,' said Grimoire.

'What do you think it means by that?' Ma Gwrach said, 'the indigenous dragon language has around a hundred different snorts and huffs, I wonder what that one meant?'

'I presume it translates to "leave me alone," and in short, it is not an indication of a vernacular but rather an indication of indignation.'

'Well, that's a bit rude, isn't it?'

Grimoire refused to argue the finer points about dragon decorum but felt he had to at least explain if not defend the dragon's taciturnity. 'Generally, dragons can't speak unless they have at some time served a sorcerer or wizard. This one has obviously had the fortune not to.'

The dragon placed its head down on the ground. It closed its eyes and let out a snore.

'Or it's choosing to ignore us,' said Ma Gwrach.

'I've always proclaimed that in the interest of one's personal well-being, it is much better to be ignored by a dragon.'

'We ought to at least wake it up and ask for directions,' said Ma Gwrach.

Grimoire went to bite his tongue, knowing full well that although most of the time Ma Gwrach thought she knew best, but didn't know best, it was best not to show he knew it. However, on this occasion, not knowing best when it came to dragons was a sure-fire way of coming to know nothing at all. Grimoire untwisted the thought from his mind. 'I think we should count what blessings we have and leave the beast to its slumber.'

'Perhaps you are right,' said Ma Gwrach in such a way that Grimoire suspected she was saying it only to make him feel like he knew best in such a situation.

He took Ma Gwrach by the shoulder and started to steer her towards the entrance when he felt a wriggle underfoot. Looking down, Grimoire saw that his boot had just landed on the curled tip of the dragon's tail. 'Oh, dear ...'

'You've done it now,' raved Ma Gwrach, we could have been having a friendly little chat, but no, instead you've gone and trod on the tail of a great big–'

The next few minutes were but a blur to Grimoire, who could only recount the following stages of their ejection from the cave in regrettable flashes of horror.

First of all, Ma Gwrach's face had turned from the imposition of being ignored to the consternation of having a tail lash across her body. Like a scorned cat, except it being a dragon which made its scornfulness much more ferocious than mere cattiness, it spun around baring its jagged teeth.

As Ma Gwrach was sent hurling through the air. The dragon snapped at Grimoire. He toppled backwards as it raised its serpentine neck, ready to strike down on the mage.

His ears were numb from the banshee screech which tore throughout the cavern. It had been Ma Gwrach on her mop. In her hand, she held the bone of some poor unfortunate, which she connected forcibly between the dragon's eyes.

Grimoire painfully recalled the dragon's claw swatting at her and sending her spinning. He had gotten to his feet and powered-up Diabolical just as a blast of frost erupted from the dragon's mouth. The staff blossomed an umbrella of thermal energy, shielding Grimoire from the deathly chill.

By that time, the dragon had risen to its full height. The banshee screech resumed as Ma Gwrach, still spinning out of control, careered towards the beast which at that stage was hell-bent on mauling her out of existence or at the very least, out of earshot.

Grimoire pressed the reverse function on Diabolical's dongle which upturned an umbrella of energy and shot it towards the dragon. There was a tremendous pummelling of ice and rock as the beast flung itself against the cavern wall.

What happened next, would forever impress its caricature upon his mind. Ma Gwrach had by then gyrated to a halt, she slumped on the ground, giddily pivoting her head as the cavern around her ceased to rotate. Meanwhile, the dragon heaved itself onto all fours. Grimoire readied Diabolical for the second strike, but the creature seemed reticent to retaliate. It arched forward awkwardly, its neck extended, an indignant face, and with bulging eyes, it stared vacantly into space. Its mouth gaped and flopped out the tip of a limp tongue. Its body began to convulse and heave. Grimoire stepped away, pulling Ma Gwrach with him as they backed towards the entrance.

'Snowball.' At least that was what he thought she had said.

Finally, he remembered the dragon retching a glob of sleet. They had rolled and tumbled about the wet blizzard until compacted in a bundle of ice particles which avalanched down the mountain and broke free by the bank of a frozen lake.

'Well, I never,' rasped Ma Gwrach, her face dislodged from the snow.

'Well, did we ever,' murmured Grimoire, his face still absorbing the soothing effect snow had on the bruises he incurred.

'Thought you said they were even-tempered?'

'More even-tempered, I said.' Grimoire began to groan, his body was catching up increasingly with the impact.

'Lost all me stuff now,' whimpered Ma Gwrach, 'dress is in tatters, cauldron's missing, how do I brew me tea now?'

'We'll face that hurdle when we get to it,' said Grimoire turning his attention to the vast spread of thick snow that surrounded them. 'First I suggest we think about the immediate task of getting away from that dragon.' As he said it, a gust of chilling air thrust itself upon them. Up above, a lash of white dragons brightened the sky, with thundering wings beating down in time with their murmuration.

'Or perhaps rather, those dragons,' said Ma Gwrach.

'Stay still and try not to look like a grub,' said Grimoire.

Ma Gwrach froze, which by all accounts, seemed counter-intuitive considering under the circumstances. Grimoire watched the parade flyover. He'd never seen white dragons in such a formation and in such numbers. They were typically solitary, like their red counterparts, but white dragons on rare occasions were known to form pacts. This was usually due to having a leader dragon amongst them. One, which perhaps had served before a sorcerer or mage. This thought sent a shiver down Grimoire's spine which only exacerbated the chills already running up it.

'They appear to be fledgelings. They must be heading to the lair. We should follow them,' said Grimoire.

Ma Gwrach gave him a cocked-eyebrow look she administered when assessing the state of his sanity. 'Into a dragon's lair? We've only just escaped from one.'

'Where else is there to go? If I'm correct, there should be a leader amongst them. Someone we can reason with, beyond dangling ourselves as live bait.'

They both momentarily scanned the landscape as if wishing for the other to spot an alternative plan and route, but the long stretch of snow beckoned before them as the only way forward.

'Come on then.' Grimoire dug his staff into the snow, leveraged his body to a standing position and propelled himself forward. Without his cape and hat, the chill was unbearably cold but with gritted teeth he managed to surge forward.

They clumped their way up the slope of a snowpack, an ice fog obscuring any visibility beyond a few yards. Clambering to the top, they both leaned on their respective sticks to take rest before traversing the next stretch.

'It is even foggier across there,' said Ma Gwrach, the snow buried up to her ankles as she gradually sunk in a few inches.

'That's not fog, that's smoke, and where there's smoke —'

Ma Gwrach sniffed at the air. 'There's chimneys.' She pointed to the arbitrarily aligned stacks poking out from the blanket of white. The wind beat about their ears, the squad of dragons long gone, the chimney stacks gushed out a foam of greyish cloud. Ma Gwrach started marching towards them.

'Let's see if we can find a doooooooooooooooooooor ...' cried Grimoire.

She stopped when she noticed the distinct lack of moaning and groaning beside her.

'Grim?' she called.

From somewhere within the thick set snow, she heard the faint groaning noise all too familiar when she used his pet name. Ma Gwrach smiled to herself and staggered back up to the spot where they had just been. She noticed a sizeable hole and pricked her ear to it, listening intently for any further grumbling below.

'Grimoire?'

'Down here. It's the door. I've found it.'

'Oh, delightful,' screeched Ma Gwrach, 'how do I get down it? Is there a ladder?'

'Unfortunately, I neglected the use of the ladder, but yes, there does appear to be one.'

Ma Gwrach dangled her foot until it came into contact with a rung. She made her way steadily down the hole. Eventually, after some time, she stood side by side with Grimoire, who was covered head to foot in dirt. He was intently reading etchings around a small alcove.

'Presumably, a sort of unused visitor's centre,' whispered Grimoire, 'to do with goblems.'

'You can read that can you?' Ma Gwrach screwed up her nose and eyed off the text quizzically. 'Looks like drivel to me.'

'No, it's gobbledegook, that's the translation for the language goblems speak. They call it boobledeggok.'

'Is it really? How do you know so much about goblems?'

'When I was a young mage studying the fine art of magic, our school employed goblems to …' Grimoire cleared his throat, 'Well … clean the chimneys. They have bristly features see, that when directed up a narrow space tend to loosen the grit.'

Ma Gwrach eye-balled Grimoire intensely.

Grimoire coughed heavily into his hand. 'Fortunately, the school changed its code of conduct. Not long after I left mind you, and subsequently, they hired chimney sweeps with actual sweeps. Something to do with non-normative ethics …' Grimoire returned his attention to the plaque.

'What's it say then?'

'It seems to be a short history on goblems,' said Grimoire.

Goblems had the unfortunate circumstance of being distantly related to goblins, and what made matters worse, goblems were considered the poorer cousin of the two. Whereas goblins left the colder climes to seek greener pastures, goblems stayed behind and made extensive warrens below the great blankets of snow.

'Sounds similar to that of the neanderthal and homo sapiens.'

'Quite so, but you see goblems never became extinct, although, their numbers never thrived,' said Grimoire.

Before, what they called The Spark Age, the goblems made their homes in the many natural caves carved within the highlands. These caves provided shelter, but alas, they also offered a convenient feeding vessel for hungry dragons, who like an oystercatcher plucking a gastropod from its shell, foraged daily on the helpless goblems huddling in their conclaves.

'Well, after today, I can certainly empathise with that,' said Ma Gwrach.

Goblems are herbivores. It is customary for them to not only eat vegetables but also to hunt, enslave and sometimes even torture plants for the benefit of feasting. A band of goblems laying in wait, ready to seize a patch of common sorrel, is a frequent sight. A particular favourite is the tuber. When tubers are ripe, goblems harvest them from the ceilings of tunnels exclusively dug for this purpose. During the harvest, a festival is held called the Beating of the Root where serpentine flutes are played, and a distilled drink made from fermented parsnips called Nip of the Passed is drunk in almost catastrophic quantities.

'Well, we can safely say, we are not top on their menu' said Grimoire.

Physically, goblems share, on the most part, similarities with goblins. They are wiry with dark olive green skin, large feet and hands, with oversized pointy ears. Goblems, however, have heads burred with stiff bristles mapped out across the length and breadth of their spiny heads. This makes them look both fierce and ridiculous at the same time.

'You are not frightened by the goblems I take it?'

'Frightened? I consider them to appear fiercely ridiculous in a ridiculously fierce kind of way.' Grimoire pulled his collar in tight and puffed out his chest. 'Frightened? No.'

'Then why are you still here reading all this?' said Ma Gwrach.

'But one does wonder,' said Grimoire, 'if some kind of atonement lies in the wake of past misdemeanours committed, I might add, solely through the actions of my forebears.'

'What does that mean?' asked Ma Gwrach.

'It means …' said Grimoire clearing his throat, '… it means that wizards may not be the most welcomed guests here and we are about to encounter a rather large hoard of possibly dissonant goblems.'

'Then let's get it over with and by all accounts don't mention where you studied.'

Ma Gwrach pushed open the door leading to a corridor which fanned out into a large dug out space. The ceiling was brimming with sweet potatoes, parsnips, swedes beetroot and earth apples. Grimoire and Ma Gwrach found themselves knocking heads against these knobbly roots as they almost had to feel their way through the dim dug-out. At the other end was a small round hatch which Grimoire reached to open, but upon feeling for a handle realised that the latch must be on the other side. Grimoire stood back and pointed his staff toward the door as he chanted.

'ᛢᚤᚢᚤ'

The door bowed before splintering from its hinges with a mighty snap. The way forward was brightly illuminated, and the two stood motionless as the sight that greeted them sunk in. A long table occupied by rows of goblems holding cutlery, as if posing for the benefit of an artist. They were clearly stunned at the sudden intrusion. Not a blink nor a sniff was to be seen or heard.

'Lehol, ew rea leasped ot emet uyo.' Grimoire's intermediate attempt at gobbledegook failed to impress.

A long way down the table, a particularly grisly goblem, broke the diorama by dropping his knife and fork. They clanked on the table, ringing throughout the room until the vibrations came to a shimmering standstill.

'Thaw,' he bellowed, allowing every lung full of breath to complete the word, 'rea uyo dongi heer?'.

'Ah,' replied Grimoire scratching his head and shuffling about as if to avert the attention he was getting, 'we could easily have asked ourselves the same question, funnily enough.' He battered his eyes at Ma Gwrach, who held her mop in such a way as to cover her face.

'Not helpful at all,' mumbled Grimoire to Ma Gwrach, 'anything you want to add to our predicament or should I just carry on?'

Ma Gwrach shook her mop as she responded, 'No, fine, you just carry on.'

'Right,' huffed Grimoire, he returned his attention to the goblems and raising his voice boomed, 'we are but modest travellers spent by the strenuous undertaking of our journ—'

A potato found its way to Grimoire's nose, giving it a good belting thwack as it made an impact.

'Rudertins!' shouted the head goblem.

The rest of the goblems dropped their utensils and picked up whatever cannonball shaped comestible was to be found on their plate. They proceeded to hurl the missiles, shouting 'Rudertins! Rudertins!'. Grimoire and Ma Gwrach quickly ducked and swerved to avoid the ferociously fast incoming baked vegetables. Finally, Grimoire raised his staff.

'About time,' squealed Ma Gwrach taking a turnip in the eye.

But instead of casting a spell, he swung it towards a hurling beet knocking it back at the goblems.

'Are you mad?' cried Ma Gwrach, but it was to no avail. Grimoire was well and truly in the swing of things. He potted the tubers back at speed while knocking goblems off chairs and clonking heads with spiralling spuds.

'Gotcha!' he bellowed as Ma Gwrach edged her way behind him, figuring this was the only safe spot to be.

One well-aimed, rather sizeable sweet potato managed to avoid Grimoire's frenzied batting, only to clout him right between the eyes which in turn knocked him out cold. At this moment Ma Gwrach, suddenly unshielded, attempted a calming toothless smile at the aggressors, but before she could widen her mouth enough, another sweet potato met its mark and Ma Gwrach fell to the floor.

CHAPTER TWENTY-SIX

Waking up, throbbing throughout every temple and a bombardment of pain coursing through them, Grimoire and Ma Gwrach gradually regained consciousness. They found themselves slumped in a corner watching the fingers of a fire waving at them from the hearth. A sitting goblem, bent double on a stool, was sipping from a clay pot. By the wafting aroma, Grimoire ascertained it was some kind of mushroom soup. Grimoire turned to Ma Gwrach. He tried to open both his eyes, but one refused to do so in harmony with the other.

'My goodness,' was all he could say as he examined the puffy bruised visage of Ma Gwrach, who was also attempting to open one of her eyes.

'Knocked me tooth out they did. I've only got four left but luckily.' She held the mottled brown kernel in her fingers, 'I found it.'

Grimoire watched with a slight pang of disgust as Ma Gwrach forced the molar back into the gum.

'What do you think?' She bared her fangs ungraciously.

'I think you've put it in the wrong spot.' Grimoire turned away and looked around for his staff. 'Excuse me?'

The goblem drained the contents of the pot in one satisfying slurp.

'Have you seen a long stick, about yay big?' Grimoire attempted to outstretch his arms, but the painful motion kept them slightly bowed.

'Uyo anme shit?' said the goblem licking the inside of the bowl before putting it down. The goblem then pulled from the fire Grimoire's staff which it had obviously been using as a fire iron. 'Sode ont nurb.'

'What's it saying?' Ma Gwrach said.

'It's telling me that my staff refuses to burn.'

'And I thought goblins were irksome,' blabbered Ma Gwrach through swollen lips.

The sight of this ill-mannered goblem holding Diabolical to the flames gave Grimoire the impetuous to rise to his feet. He wobbled a bit and caught his hip which steadied him but spasmed unbearably. 'Hand it over.'

The goblem looked at Grimoire, then looked at the staff, then looked back at Grimoire before he finally spoke.

'On,' it said.

'Right.' Grimoire thrust his arm towards the goblem, his arm began to tremble with the strain of holding it elevated, but he was determined to retrieve what was his. One painful syllable at a time, the words trawled from his lips with a burbled effort, but soon the magic was released. Biting and callous, the flames leapt at the goblem, pricking its skin and making it jump into the air. It backed away from the fire, but the fire continued to stab and swipe, the goblem screeched in pain, its skin seared as if lashed by a burning whip.

'Cryme, Cyrme,' it wept.

Grimoire lowered his arm, keeping the flames at bay.

'Now, hand Diabolical to me.'

'Dia— thaw?'

'My staff, give me the staff.'

The goblem frantically picked up the staff and tossed it to Grimoire. It floated through the air, gently placing itself within Grimoire's grip.

'Now goblem, explain yourself, what were you planning on doing with us?'

'Gnonthi,' whimpered the goblem.

'And enough with the gobbledegook, I know you can understand me well enough and therefore be able to speak our tongue.'

'Nothing, nothing,' cried the goblem, 'we won't eat you, we don't crave meat.'

Grimoire raised his hand, and a flame shot off from the fire sizzling a patch of the goblem's hair.

'Lobod dan ebon,' cowered the goblem.

'Blood and bone?' said Grimoire.

'For the soil, feeds the soil, grows the plants.'

Grimoire pursed his lips together and hummed in a low disapproving tone. 'What have you done with Ma Gwrach's mop?'

'Ma thaw?' whimpered the goblem glancing at the fire, then at Grimoire and lastly at the door, presumably calculating a means of escape.

Grimoire puffed himself up to his full height despite the aches that creaked across his body as he did so. 'Listen, we plan to get out of here, and we plan to do it with your help.'

Ma Gwrach hobbled over to the frightened creature and weaved a gnarly finger towards it. 'And if you don't help us, we won't help you from us.'

She smiled a wicked smile and as she did so, the tooth she had recently inserted popped out. She spat it into the fire and snarled for effect.

'We can be very callous,' snarled Grimoire.

'And careless,' added Ma Gwrach.

'Careless?' said the goblem.

Ma Gwrach prodded the goblem fair in the eye. 'Oops.'

'How careless of you,' said Grimoire kicking the goblem square in the shin.

'Butter foot,' said Ma Gwrach elbowing Grimoire in the side.

'Ouch,' Grimoire shouted, 'what was that for?'

'Sorry,' Ma Gwrach cooed, 'I really can be careless.'

'Enough,' cried the goblem, 'I will show you the way out.'

'Oh no,' said Grimoire raising his staff, 'not show but take us and not only that, you will take us to the white dragon's lair ... personally'

'Oh I can't do that,' said the goblem.

Grimoire and Ma Gwrach began circling the goblem thrusting out their feet and hands in a threatening jig until the goblem collapsed on the floor, huddling in a weeping mess of sobs and grizzles.

'Stop, stop, with the weird dancing. I'll do it, I'll do it.'

'So just to be clear, what exactly will you do?'

'I'll show you ... take you ...,' it heaved in a sob, 'personally ... to the dragon's lair,' it heaved in another sob.

Grimoire visibly relaxed. 'And who are we addressing?'

The goblem looked perplexed.

'What is your name, dear?' added Ma Gwrach.

'I am Bugle, the garlic presser.' Bugle held up his left hand, displaying an unusually large and flat thumb.

'Well, Bugle, let us not linger any longer. The first thing we must do is locate Ma Gwrach's mop. It's a shaggy bur on the end of a stick if that helps.'

'It can be found in the eating hall. I can take you. All will be sleeping, we must watch our step.'

Bugle opened the door, and as they moved out into the dark corridor, Grimoire noticed a sea of shadows on the floor. Some twitched, others let out a snuffling sound, but on the whole, there was stillness.

'Have you not beds?' Grimoire whispered.

'No, we sleep when and where tired.'

The three of them stepped around the slumped goblems, carefully placing their feet between spread arms and curled bodies. Eventually, they made it to the hall. The hall fire had become dimly burning embers, but it shone enough light throughout, Ma Gwrach eagerly surveyed the room expecting her mop to perhaps have been put to use similarly as Diabolical. However, she was relieved to see that across a sea of snoozing goblems it was to be found, head first in a bucket. She whispered its secret name, and the mop plucked itself from the bucket. It hovered over the sleeping mass before gently landing in Ma Gwrach's grip. They crept out of the hall, following Bugle, through a maze of tunnels. The garlic presser finally stopped at a door.

'This is where I leave you. Through this door is the cellar of shining shallots. We planted them hundreds of years ago but dare not eat them. It will lead you straight to the stairs going up into the mountain of the white dragons. It is where we once lived, our old kingdom before the dragons came. Before our race was divided.'

'Well, goodbye then.' Grimoire stuck out his hand. The goblem looked at it quizzically.

'No more fire, please.'

Grimoire gave the warmest smile he could muster. 'A tactile treaty satisfied by the signature of a shake.'

Bugle went to take Grimoire's hand in its own but pulled away at the last minute. 'No, can't do it. Won't.'

Grimoire beamed an even warmer smile. 'We owe you our lives. Never were two lives in gratitude to one, such as yourself. We are indeed indebted to you, you have shown yourself to be above and beyond.'

Ma Gwrach extended her foot. 'Here, if a hand doesn't suit you, would it be better to shake a foot?'

'No,' uttered Bugle, 'must go. Doog cluk.' Bugle smiled at them both before disappearing into the darkness.

Grimoire glared at Ma Gwrach.

'I don't know their customs do I?' said Ma Gwrach.

'I'm sure we will be all right from here,' called Grimoire.

'What was that all about,' said Ma Gwrach, 'all that smiling and such?'

'We shall soon see.' Grimoire opened the door, and they entered the cellar. It was a large dug out hollow aglow with phosphorous shallots hanging from the ceiling. The glow from the shallots revealed a mass of hairy outlines fidgeting in the room. At a quick count, there were at least fifty goblems all wielding objects that became apparent as trowels, forks and hoes.

One goblem stepped to the front. 'You didn't think it would be that easy to persuade Bugle to betray his own, did you?'

Grimoire blindly searched for the speaker. 'Indeed, I did think he would betray you.'

'What? That's not what I said.'

'That's not what I said,' replied Grimoire.

If a dark shadow could ever be criticised of looking confused, it was this one. Grimoire's words seemed to waft in its direction before being swatted away like an obnoxious fly.

'What did you say then?'

'I said that he would betray you, not that it would be easy.'

'And what do you mean by that?' said another shadow a little less uncertain than the first.

Grimoire cleared his throat. 'Well, to put it mildly, he stinks. Bugle permeates garlic wherever he goes. What a poor fellow to have to endure such an odour every waking day of his life. In cooking, garlic is luscious …'

'Is there a point to this? Or should I take refuge behind you any moment now?' Ma Gwrach peered into the dimly lit room, trying to calculate their chances of escape.

Grimoire continued. 'But garlic upon the person and upon the breath, permeating permanently, must inevitably drive a poor goblem to act irrationally.'

'Like do what?' spat the first goblem.

'Like to have the organised ambush waiting in a room full of syncopal foxfire,' said Grimoire pushing Ma Gwrach back through the door and slamming it with such force it shook the very foundations of the cavern.

'Well,' said Ma Gwrach, 'you might have sai–' But before Ma Gwrach could finish, from the other side of the door a ruckus of wheezing and coughing could be heard followed by slumping thuds, satisfyingly dropping one after the other. Grimoire opened the door again. The cellar was littered with passed out goblems and deflated onions.

'They won't feel a thing,' said Grimoire, pushing Ma Gwrach into the crowded heap.

Ma Gwrach was the first to test the theory. She planted her foot on a goblem's chest. She pushed down a little harder. It produced a wheeze, but the goblem didn't budge. Grimoire did the same, and together they proceeded to climb over the collapsed wreckage of goblems in a cacophony of wheezing and spluttering until they reached the steps ascending to the peak of the mountain. Behind them, the room lay silent.

'What about Bugle? I feel somewhat responsible for his … fate.'

'It is a repercussion he must mull over, not us. He may have shared a brief moment in our past, but we do not share his future. Nor must we.'

'In any case, I'll charm a good luck spell for him.'

'Yes, yes, why not, you do exactly that.'

The climb was long and confined. The steps narrow and steep. Grimoire could hear Ma Gwrach well enough as her voice travelled past him but because he couldn't turn his head all that he said was lost on her. For the first time since sipping tea in the afanc's cave, both of them fell silent. Finally, the last step broke their silence, a glorious ice cave twinkled and glistened in front of them, with denticulate frozen crystals giving the feeling of having walked into the mouth of a white dragon itself.

'Glad to be out of the frying pan then?' said Ma Gwrach to Grimoire who was looking particularly perturbed.

Before them, two frosty stone pillars framed a ripened white dragon curled up on a gleaming black rock. Upon its head was a crown cast from either stone or pig iron. Its long jowls finished off with a tousled moustache draped over its mouth. When it saw them standing at the entranceway, its cerulean blue eyes froze Grimoire and Ma Gwrach to the spot.

'Ah,' it said, its voice deep, gentle, yet with hints of threat and malice, 'I see we have guests.'

'We?' Grimoire took his eyes off the beast and with an unnerving chill sweeping across his body, he took in the view around him. As if almost transparent in the vast whiteness of the cave, outlines of wings, tails and then specks of eyes became suddenly a very present and terrifying announcement that they were not alone with the great white dragon. In fact, they were very much in the company of a nest of white dragons.

'Yes, we are guests,' offered Ma Gwrach as a means of pronouncing the idea of being guests over having guests, which may for white dragons all too well mean, that to have may lead to having had.

'Come closer,' snarled the white dragon, 'though my eyes may shine brightly, they don't take in the light as well as they used to.'

'Witches first,' muttered Grimoire nudging Ma Gwrach towards the dragon.

They shuffled closer, as close as they dared.

'What brings you here to the farthest plain of Annwyn?'

Grimoire knew that there was no hoodwinking even a partially sighted dragon of this sort. 'We are on our way to the Tree of Oracles. No doubt you have heard of the meeting of the high order of magi?'

'I have heard, but what makes you think that I agree with the high order? What makes you think that I won't feed you both here to one of my hungry children?'

There was a fluttering of wings and a sliding from tails as the white dragon king spoke these last words.

'Well,' said Ma Gwrach, 'you know how there are some plants that are perfectly tasty but look similar to other plants that are not, in fact, sometimes lookalikes can be fatal. We are a bit like that, we look like a completely tasty mage and witch but are in actuality quite disg—'

Grimoire subtly pressed his foot down on Ma Gwrach's toes to silence her, but the white dragon interrupted.

'To be honest, you both do look disgusting, and under the circumstances of your predicament, you may take that in any complementary way that relieves you.'

'Whether you agree or not with the gathering,' said Grimoire, 'we must be there, we must be there to represent all magic folk.'

'You don't represent me.'

'Not individuals, we must represent magic itself.' Grimoire reached into one of his pockets and pulled out a small piece of paper, quill and ink bottle. 'Let us leave, and I will give you this?'

The white dragon craned its neck closer to see the goods. 'What is it?'

'It's a quill made from the feather of a Tattle-tale tit and a bottle of Think, thought-provoking ink.'

The white dragon grinned at the objects. 'What does it do?'

'It transfers thoughts from one parchment to another.'

The white dragon accepted the gift, and as it held the paper in its claws, it squinted at some writing that was upon it. 'Help? What does that mean?'

'I'm not too sure,' said Grimoire, 'shake the parchment, and the words will be gone.'

The white dragon gave the paper a quick shake, and sure enough, the word disappeared. It pointed a claw to an arched opening to the side of the cave. 'The ice steps will take you to the ice bridge. Be careful as the bridge is only safe during the coldest season when it is frozen completely, otherwise it will surely crack, even with the lightest step, and you both will fall to your death.'

Many eyes watched as Grimoire and Ma Gwrach made their way

towards the ice steps.

'Nice enough fellow,' said Ma Gwrach.

Grimoire shook his head and mumbled something about recompense.

The first step upon the top step of the ice stairwell was easy enough. However, the second step brought them both hard down on their buttocks. The proceeding steps served to provide their buttocks with several hundred bruises as they jounced their way down. Legs were extended and feet strategically placed to avoid the descent as it was, but no matter what, they both pranced on their behinds until reaching the very last step which allowed some form of stance. Holding their rumps with somewhat coy abashment, they saw before them the ice bridge, its length reaching out over a deep craggy ravine.

'Do you think it's set?'

Grimoire turned to Ma Gwrach, ice follicles forming on his beard. 'Yes,' was all he managed to say between chattering teeth.

'I could use me mop to take us to the other side.'

'No ...'

'It would get us there faster,' said Ma Gwrach.

'... Magic,' Grimoire chattered.

The balustrade was too icy to provide support, so Grimoire punted himself along using his staff and, Ma Gwrach did the same using her mop. Slide by slide, they made their way across. At the end of the bridge, they entered a deep tunnel. It led them to an opening of wilderness blanketed in snow. Large conifers bent with the weight of snowy shawls provided a smack of greenery across the whiteness. For days on end, they trudged until finally, they came to the Gap of Knowledge, the deep ravine of the unknown, and where the second bridge led to the Tree of Oracles.

CHAPTER TWENTY-SEVEN

Gyffe stared at the ox. The ox stared back. Patch stared at Gyffe. Crinkum stared at the ox. Prunewick stared.

'Tell me again how did all this happened?' Gyffe finally said to their latest unannounced visitor.

'Well,' said Iolo, 'it's funny, strange see. I was contacted by some wee faery folk who told me the most outlandish of tales, so outlandish I figured it could only be true. A sunken house, a water spirit, and a weedy squit looking to get rid of the afanc. The only way they said was using an ox and since I'm no farmer, it seems, this one has been idle for far too long, so I thought I'd bring it to you, fit for purpose.'

Gyffe sighed the sigh of having weathered yet another uneventful century only to be gifted a white bovine by a tribe of cavern dwelling faeries, delivered no less by a bearded druid.

The ox, looking completely complacent in its regal surrounds, emptied its bowels on the carpet.

'Can't stay here,' retorted Patch grabbing the coal shovel and scooping up the mess which he promptly tossed into an ash bucket, 'no heap.'

'No heap?' said Iolo raising an eyebrow.

'No heap, no muck, no ox.'

With his foot, Patch steered the bucket forward until it was positioned strategically below the ox's rear end.

'What do we do with it?' Gyffe said.

'The ox?' Iolo gave it a scratch behind the ear. It flicked its tail and lowered its head sniffing at the floral patterned carpet but seemed unimpressed with the lack of real foliage. 'It seems that we should lead the animal straight to the water spirit, lasso the watery devil and let the ox do the rest.'

'Have you ever lassoed a demon before?' asked Gyffe, trying to ascertain the success of the project over a fate worse than death.

'Well, er, ...' Iolo twinkled his brow.

'To an ox?' added Gyffe elaborating on the degree of worst to which such a fate might occur.

'I can't say all those particulars have been available to me at any one time. However, I can say that an ox, a rope and water without the addition of a demon, has at one time or another been familiar to me.'

'The afanc,' said Gyffe getting to his feet, 'is a petrifying beast whose powers can overcome even the most experienced of wizards and the ox is ... well, the ox is an ox.'

'A cow,' muttered Patch scratching his head.

'A cow indeed,' said Iolo, 'but this is a speckled long-horned ox, a faery cow, from Annwyn. Remember, these beasts are capable of banishing evil spirits. Their milk, so I'm told, is rather delicious.'

Gyffe turned to the others. 'So, what shall it be? An attempt to defeat the afanc or an evening of delicious fresh milk?'

Patch furrowed his brow. 'Grimoire told us to wait, not capture creatures.'

Prunewick gaped vacantly in silence, and Crinkum took flight, disappeared for a moment and returned with a rope.

'Where did he get that?'

'Bell tower,' said Patch.

'There we are, two against one.'

Patch deepened the furrow in his brow. 'Tree did not speak.'

'Quietude is assent as far as this matter is concerned. If Prunewick really objected, I'm sure it would creak or drop a leaf or something like that. So let us not delay. Iolo will tie the rope around the neck of the ox so we can lead it to the river.'

Iolo fastened the rope around the ox's neck, but the sudden call to action was muted as the ox stood its ground.

'How do we get it to move?'

'It will follow me,' said Iolo stepping in front of it, pulling at the rein. The animal stayed put. Iolo was, as he said, not the farmer.

'Maybe a push,' suggested Gyffe.

Gyffe, Patch and Crinkum all got behind and tried to heave the beast forward. Gyffe noticed that the ox kept glancing at Prunewick. He realised that it was eying off what little greenery Prunewick bore.

'Aha,' said Gyffe removing one of the curtain rods. He fastened

Prunewick to the end of it with a curtain tieback and dangled the cloche in front of the ox. It started to move, hungrily following the small tree. Prunewick may have been mortified, but at least he didn't show it.

Once outside, they were able to steer the ox towards the river bank. Following along its length, they approached the Gate of Dreams where many centuries earlier Grimoire and Ma Gwrach had passed.

'We can't go through it,' said Gyffe, 'we must bait the end of this rope with something that will attract the afanc.'

Iolo folded his arms and limply relaxed to one side. 'Recalling my misspent youth reading about the many creatures of Annwyn, this water spirit can turn any mortal who catches its gaze into stone. Since, this winged pet here is already made up of the same substance, it serves me well to think that this creature is best to bait the beast.'

Crinkum recoiled. Patch knew that it wasn't that Crinkum was petrified of such a task, as he was already kind of petrified anyway, it was the use of the word "pet" that had taken him aback.

'Not pet,' said Patch.

'Yes,' joined in Gyffe, 'not pet, one doesn't choose a dragoyle, it chooses you,' he said, trying to be helpful.

'Well, then,' Iolo hurrahed, 'let us not stand in the way of our winged friend here, let it show the way.'

It had to be said that by Crinkum's expression, it was much more satisfied with this description and taking the end of the rope, it flew towards Gate of Dreams.

Gyffe, his curiosity although somewhat dulled by the centuries, still teetered on overbearing excitement. He excitedly watched as Crinkum approached the gates. 'Will they open?'

At that point, as if in answer to Gyffe's question, the gates slowly pushed through the waters until they were wide enough to let Crinkum through.

'From what I have read, if a creature does not speak, if a creature does not dream, the gates will open,' said Iolo.

'Now what?' said Gyffe.

'We wait,' said Iolo.

'To hook fish,' prompted Patch.

'Ah yes,' said Iolo catching Patch's drift, 'we wait until the rope tugs, and when it does we have caught ... the afanc.' Iolo rolled his head and eyes at the same time inducing a pronounced sense of the dramatic.

They waited in anticipation, except the ox, which seemed more interested in nibbling at some seaweed. A deep low rumble echoed throughout the cavern. Gyffe and Iolo both looked at each other in fear.

'What was that?'

'Stomach,' said Patch half considering joining in with the seaweed, 'hungry.'

Eventually, there was the inevitable yank which startled them all. Shooting through the darkness screeched Crinkum, its eyes frightfully wide, it dived onto the stones and rolled for several yards before falling

flat on its stomach. In shock, the others braced themselves. The ox felt

the strain of the tightening rope, its eyes bulged as it reared backwards.

'It's a big one,' cried Iolo stepping back as the ox bowed its head in

determination.

'Must run away but at the same time stay and watch,' murmured

Gyffe, stepping this way and that.

Patch, who over the centuries had become almost painstakingly slow,

had somehow managed to appear at the door of the house before anyone

else had realised what was happening. The ox shunted backwards, its

enormous strength now becoming translucently clear by the rippling

muscles formed on its hindquarters. It pulled itself across the pebbles as

they flew underfoot from its powerful kicks. Bursting through the Gate

of Dreams, a terrible sight became apparent, the afanc, writhing and

tossing its weight against the waters.

'Don't look at it,' shouted Iolo, not knowing that this was possibly

the worst thing you could say when a fribbling squit was present.

Gyffe shielded his eyes, but parting his fingers a crack, caught the

horrific beast's eye as it thrashed towards them. Everything went blank,

he couldn't see, he couldn't hear, he couldn't draw a breath nor swallow

but disturbingly he was able to think of all the things he couldn't do.

This is somewhat uncomfortable, he thought, I wonder what is going

on? How are Grimoire and Ma Gwrach getting on? What has happened to Patch? Am I dead?

The thoughts trailed through his mind.

Is this what it is like to be dead? I could do with taking a breath, can I take one? Did I take one? Or imagine it? Am I dead? Did all that just happen? Did anything happen? When will I stop asking myself questions?

Something inside him was still ticking, although clearly, it was not his heart. He couldn't feel a thing. He could think of a thing. Thinking of a thing was easy.

My heart, he thought, but the thought of a heart and feeling the actual thing beating was very much disconnected.

This is magic, perhaps? Any moment now the spell is going to wear off.

CHAPTER TWENTY-EIGHT

The Tree of Oracles loomed ahead, its vast trunk, vermiculated, twisted over time. The many needles of its canopy pricking at the sky to let flecks of sunlight through. Grimoire and Ma Gwrach walked along the imposing stone bridge, the wind at times threatening to cast them off like specks of dust. They reached the end of the bridge, the entrance to the tree was flooded with the amber glow from hundreds of candles burning within.

'There's no door upon which to knock, no bell or chime to announce our arrival.' Grimoire hesitated on the threshold.

'Mages first,' said Ma Gwrach offering Grimoire the opportunity to be the first to step into the light. He entered the tree, laying his foot on an ancient weave that stretched all the way down to a circular engraving.

'It appears we are the first to arrive.'

As they approached the circle, a hum of murmuring started to fill the space, figures began to appear. At first as wisps and shadows and then a throng. The entire space was gradually cast with a mass of nattering magic folk.

'Or the last,' said Ma Gwrach scanning the room for any familiar witches.

From above, the tree had formed a brocade of galleries where shamans glared brandishing sticks of wild herbs and sacred bones tied to knotted ivy. Wyzens in Arabian regalia sat cross-legged resting their chins on ornate silver rods. The visendakona mingled wearing their symbol inscribed hangerocks, their braided hair as bright as the glare of the sun on sand. Around the circular engraving stood a circle of sorcerers, wizards and witches. Just beyond the ring was a throne shared by two dragons, one red and the other familiar to both Grimoire and Ma Gwrach, it was the white dragon they had met in the ice cave.

'Daroganwry,' said Grimoire, 'I should have known.'

One place in the circle was empty.

'Here come the stragglers,' said the white dragon, 'take your place Grimoire.'

Grimoire looked about him as if at any moment another Grimoire might be found lurking amongst the throng. Then he thought the dragon must have called for another, like Grinwort or some such similar sounding name.

'Yes, you Grimoire,' said the dragon, licking its tongue with each syllable as if pasting it to Grimoire's person to make absolutely clear it was indeed Grimoire it desired.

'But …' Grimoire hesitated, however, no sooner had he began his rebuttal, a firm finger nudged him gently in the back.

'Off you go,' said Ma Gwrach, 'I'll just be over there with some witches I've spotted, catching up on all the witchy gossip I've missed for several thousand years.'

Grimoire shuffled towards the circle, for a moment he felt all eyes upon him. He lowered his head and on catching sight of his person understood why he was being made a spectacle. His clothing, torn and muddy, with one boot showing a row of naked toes. With no hat or cape and in such a state, Grimoire realised he looked more like a vagabond than a mage.

'Let the meeting begin,' roared the red dragon.

There was a fading murmur as the room crept into silence.

'As you are all well aware since the first official covenant was signed in Persia, we have had a more or less mutual and somewhat agreeable relationship between the quotidians and the order. However, the quotidians are now intent on taking the premise of magic and mimicking it with their own science.'

The dragon coughed out a spark or two before turning to the white dragon. 'Pass me the blood of the banshee.'

The white dragon took a large phial containing an almost black crimson liquid and the red dragon gulped down half its contents before continuing. 'Much better. Where was I? Ah, yes, as the naysayers of the occult take hold, humankind will at the same time forget the principles of its design. They will speak through input, they will see through output, they will live and think through their devices. They will become the apparatus as will the apparatus become them.'

The dragon took another gulp from the phial and cleared its throat.

'As a consequence, there are many of us who believe that magic must be put to rest until the foreseeable future.'

The soothsayers appeared recognisably puzzled at this last sentiment. There was a general murmur from the crowd. One wizened practitioner spoke by the light of a candle. 'Surely you don't think that those who practice the dark arts are going to just hang up their cloaks and take up pottery or some other such paltry past-time on account of us?'

'A daroganwry believes only in the lore, there is no dark to us, there is no magic of light, it is all just as it is and we have sought to uphold the tenet whether its use is wise or otherwise. Some of you amongst us have no doubt cast for reasons that are perhaps cruel or unjust, others have cautioned themselves against such actions, that is not of our concern. Nor are the uncooperative who wish to keep on practising in the face of adversity.' The red dragon smugly adjusted itself looking at the congregation to gauge the effect of its words.

The white dragon huffed a frosty snort from its nostrils. Grimoire neatly coughed under his breath. 'And this ...' said the white dragon, clutching in its claw the paper Grimoire had gifted it, '... is not the way to go about upholding that tenet.'

Grimoire shuffled back a little, nervously looking around at the others.

'Is it? Grimoire,' the white dragon bellowed, 'because if this type of technology gets passed around willy-nilly to whomever one comes across, who knows what accursed hell awaits the future of all worlds put together.'

The white dragon dangled the paper in the air while the red dragon spat out a projectile of fire burning the document to a crisp.

'Technology?' muttered Grimoire.

'Yes, technology,' roared the white dragon, 'Tattle-tale tit and thought provoking ink, you must think I'm a fool. Do you think I don't know a capacitive circuit polymer when I see one?'

Grimoire chewed at his lip uncomfortably but was thankful the reprimand finished abruptly. The white dragon turned its attention once more to the crowd before changing the subject. 'Before I continue, does anyone here have any beckoning thoughts on the matter of which we are about to proceed?'

'I do,' shouted a rotund mage wearing checked trousers and an oversized woollen top. 'What exactly is the risk of letting the quotidians develop their imitation sorcery alongside our own faithful art? We've managed to do this for centuries, why now must we exile ourselves?'

'There are some who would have it that way. They have made their thoughts clear on the matter and have refused to join us. Humankind will not thank them for it. Listen, when I was a lecturer at the daroganwry House of Hax Pax Max Deus Adimax, it was clear that this technology humanity is so keen to develop would one day fulfil a purpose of which magic does not. It was all very academic in those days, and the daroganwry stance is predominantly geared towards the practical rather than the pedagogical.' The white dragon held its position as if expecting a rah from the crowd, but the only sound was a honk from the rotund mage's familiar who happened to be a goose.

'We have never been safe,' called out a warlock.

'They will find excuses to destroy us,' called back an onmyoji decorated in her elegant silk robe.

'Wat snatted cod tots,' growled one of the shamans bearing his yellowed teeth.

The fellow shamans chorused with a snarling, 'yer, yer, yer.'

'Hmmm,' the red dragon squinted at the group of shamans.

'Many will perish,' grimaced the white dragon, 'but in time magic will be treated with indifference and the many faiths will have their own distortions aggrandised by those engineering the content of advanced technology.'

'We must not let them get the better of us,' shouted an enchanter, eyes as white as chalk, blackened long nails flailing as he spoke.

'Let them have their illusions, and we shall have ours,' cried a conjurer, his voice appearing to come from a completely different part of the room from where he was standing.

'Grandee sodded grits,' grunted a shaman, the deep-set clay crackling on her face.

The fellow shamans chorused with a snarling, 'yer, yer, yer.'

'Quite,' replied the red dragon tickling its chin with a claw before turning to the white dragon and shrugging its shoulders.

The white dragon leaned towards the crowd. 'In time, their technology will become their medium, they will become entirely dependant on it. Their infrastructures will be immense, their manipulation of the natural world inveterately linked to their very existence, but once their fallibilities begin to unfold, for humankind the greatest challenge will not be going forward, it will be the curse of having to go backwards. Then and only then must magic return, to serve its purpose and fulfil its place amongst the order and chaos of all living and all dead things.'

'We understand that four wizards shall be encased in stone but how will we all know when the time has come for us to return to our homes and continue our practice?' said the rotund mage in the oversized woollen top.

'At some point, quotidians will have run their race, they will know everything yet understand nothing. Furthermore, the technology will get the better of them. It has been predicted that this advance will take place in a brief period, of which humankind will not have advanced enough as a people to use it wisely, civilly or ethically.'

'Aren't we being premature in our judgement?' said a sorcerer waving a hand with nails curled in yellowing spirals, 'I have had many of them place their name on my list, despite their sometimes unpredictable behaviour, shouldn't we give them some benefit of the doubt considering through my own divinations, I've witnessed some incredible acuity amongst their kind.'

The red dragon turned to the sorcerer, its nostrils panting with a deep grey fog as if at any time a spark may erupt from the billows causing a ferocious wheeze of magma. 'Sorcerer,' it hissed, 'we know of your list. It is of no importance to the order of magic and therefore it is of no relevance to our decision.'

'That voice is familiar,' muttered Grimoire to himself, he peered through the throng but the sorcerer inched back into the shadows while the white dragon turned to the congregation. He patted his waist and realised his book was missing. He recalled having it as they crossed the bridge, so someone here must have pilfered it. Grimoire gleaned the crowd to determine a potential thief.

'Now,' said the white dragon, 'before us stands the circle of elements of which gathered about are the wizards we have chosen to be voted to the dolmens.'

Grimoire gave a startled jolt. He cleared his throat and raised his hand. 'Excuse me?'

'What is it now Grimoire?' The white dragon puffed a cloud of frosty mist in Grimoire's direction.

'I need to go.'

'Well, you should have gone before you got here, there is no time for such things, you will just have to hold on.'

Grimoire kept his hand raised. 'No, I mean, I need to leave the circle. I am not a wizard, I am a mage, and mages cannot be elemental as we all know.'

'Stuff and nonsense,' scowled the red dragon, 'we have a record of you as a wizard of the element of earth.'

'Then the records are incorrect,' said Grimoire finally lowering his hand.

'Desertion,' roared the white dragon, 'it was not us who chose. A higher order of magic made the decision of who should take to the circle. Therefore, it is not our decision whether or not you can leave. You must stay and stay you will or suffer the consequences.'

At this point, Grimoire turned to Ma Gwrach, but he could not see her.

Oh, dear, thought Grimoire, something is terribly wrong with all this.

His thought was brutally interrupted by the white dragon.

'Grimoire? What is it to be?'

Grimoire turned to the white dragon and frowned. 'Do I have a choice?' he uttered miserably.

'No, not really,' was all the dragon had to say.

CHAPTER TWENTY-NINE

Gyffe gradually felt movement. The movement was coming from his eyes, his eyelids to be exact. They fluttered, he felt them twitch as a blink of light flared for a second and then it was gone.

I can think about something I have seen, this is progress.

Then he felt the soles of his feet against a surface, the ground possibly.

I feel planted, some kind of bracing that is grounding.

All across his body, physical feeling was beginning to return.

I have elbows, they feel connected between two things, arms probably.

He then felt weighted.

I feel sunk down on something. Is it my bottom? I've got a bottom, I can feel it, sitting on a chair maybe?

Inch by inch, limb by limb, the slight movement of reawakened nerve endings tickled his entire body.

It seems I'm not just thinking these things, these things are actually happening.

Finally, his eyes opened. A face looked back at him. It was not an attractive face. It's flaky skin crimped with deep-set lines of oily black scum. An untidy mass of coarse hair dropped around the cheeks joined by a bristly thick set beard and moustache of which two bloated lips protruded. The lips parted as the face gave a somewhat lecherous leer, tawny bricked teeth dropped into view as the mouth spoke.

'Who'd have thought I could turn a tear for a squit. But I did it, had to hit my thumb with a hammer, but it worked. You see, we're not very giving of our emotions, if indeed we even have any. You'd be much better off trying to make us cry with laughter than sorrow.'

Gyffe took a moment to focus on what was happening and realised it wasn't the monster he had first laid eyes on, it was another monster, a much stumpier, haggard, fiendish one, it was Crach Ffinnant.

'I can tell by the look in your face that you have recognised the reluctant rescuer.'

'I can see it, but I can't quite believe it.' Gyffe gave a few hardy blinks as if stretching his eyes could make the scenario clearer.

'It is no illusion, trust me. If it weren't for your friends here, you might have remained an ornament for my house. A fountain, maybe?'

'Where is Patch? Crinkum? Where are they?'

'I have sent them above to fetch food. It is mostly what hognomes are good at, fetching stuff.' Crach hobbled over to the fire. 'As for this little one,' he peered at Prunewick, 'lucky escape for it. I was tempted to use its limbs as kindling. You've managed to burn all but a few pieces of my furniture.'

'It is true then,' said Gyffe, 'you are the afanc.'

'It was not my choice, Hopeyn ap Tomas, he was my mentor when I gave up the bardic pursuits for other interests, and it was he who cursed me. Turned me into this thing, forever craving the depths and the darkness.' Crach crept around, almost as if he expected the very creature to be lurking somewhere about the room, which was an altogether pointless affectation as he was the very creature he spoke of. 'And it was Grimoire who sentenced you to this place.'

'That is unlikely,' said Gyffe, 'this place was meant as a refuge.'

'Do you think so?' Crach laughed, his head bobbed with each guffaw. 'Did he tell you to stay down here, not to meddle in the affairs of men, to bide your time in a dank grave of a cursed dwarf?'

'I have no reason to distrust him, and Patch even more so.'

'Patch,' Crach spat the word, 'the ability to reason is not a trait commonly associated with hognomes.'

Gyffe ignored the remark. 'Grimoire left hastily, there was little he could explain, but I am still in touch with him.' Gyffe pulled out the parchment. Unfolding it, he saw written upon were two words, "No connection".

'Did you not notice,' said Crach, 'that this place attracts magic folk like flies, some leave, others don't?'

'Are you implying that Grimoire betrayed us?' Gyffe rose from his chair. His legs were a bit wobbly, but he let the gravity of his voice steady his resolve to put Crach in his place. 'Grimoire has been nothing but ...' Gyffe searched quickly for the word, '...supportive.'

'You mean he patted your back when you carried his tomes, he praised you when you endured all weathers to gather his ingredients, he kindly offered his leftovers when you had no meal?'

'I have known him for hundreds of years, he is like a ...' Once again Gyffe raced through suitable expressions, '... an uncle.'

Crach sniggered at the analogy. 'I had an uncle once, he'd pilfer my alchemy flasks and get drunk at magic ceremonies, he'd borrow my gold and never pay it back.'

'If there is one thing I know Grimoire would never do and that would be to ...' Gyffe couldn't help but check in his mind as to whether the words that were about to come out of his mouth would be entirely accurate, '... betray us.'

Crach's face once again took a turn for the worse. It scrunched up into such a tight-fisted ball that Gyffe, for a moment, expected it to pop.

'As of yet,' Crach spluttered, letting his face snap back as the words splattered across the room, 'your time will come. You think squids, and frogroans, and dragboils and that weirdo bouquet garni will be spared? Once the majority of the magic order take leave to their warrens, all bunked up with books and pots swilling with prophecies and the like, you lot will be the first on the pyre. You think Myrddin, the great prophet, was condemned to exile under duress?' Crach thrusted his finger towards the fire. 'Look into the flames fumbling git and see your future.'

Gyffe couldn't but help turn to the burning fire. The dancing flames flickered rapidly casting shadows within that became apparent as people. People in terror, more succinctly witches and wizards being tortured. Screaming in agony with nothing to abate the fury of the mob.

'What you see and what I see bears nothing on what will be. The future is not in your fire.' Gyffe backed away.

'The future has already happened. Step outside and see for yourself. I'm not here to convince you of the virtues of your wayward master, sooner or later you will rot in this place. There will be no great reprisal of the old order of magic, there will be no ...' Crach had stopped speaking, suddenly Gyffe was much closer, holding his wand directly at the dwarf. Gyffe fiddled with the controls using only a few fingers, a task much harder when attempting to look like he knew what he was doing.

'Save your speech Crach, I learned a great deal in your library despite the prolific amount of tiresome dwarfish history and crude wood engravings. One particular spell of interest was found in the book The Three, who are Afraid of one Another.'

'What three are they?' Crach said with a grimace.

'You, myself and the elephant in the room,' said Gyffe aiming the wand while chanting the spell.

'What elephant?'

'It's just a little expression I came up with to describe our shared impediment ... the afanc.'

Crach appeared to understand what was about to happen. He slowly backed away from Gyffe and then suddenly pointed to the other side of the room.

'Lookout,' he shouted, 'the afanc.'

Gyffe didn't know quite why he did it, perhaps Grimoire was right in that someday curiosity would indeed get the better of him. He turned his head to see. As he did so, Crach leapt upon the wand. Gyffe tried to hold it steady, but it flipped upwards releasing a wave of energy which shook the foundations of the house. Gyffe kicked at Crach, sending him rolling across the floor.

'Off button. Off button …' Gyffe frantically fiddled with the dongle, but the intensity of the waves increased. At that moment, in walked Patch carrying a basket of ceps, borage and bittercress. Seeing Gyffe wrestling with the wand, he dropped his gatherings and hobbled as quickly as he could to where Gyffe stood.

'Give here.'

Patch tried to snatch the wand, but it had other ideas. It sprung from Gyffe's grasp and darted about the room like a trapped bat. The walls began to rupture. Crach was once more on his feet, prancing through the air as he attempted to catch the wayward stick. Crinkum flew in through the door but was propelled backwards. Gyffe turned to Patch, he lifted the hognome up by the collar. A mighty stone from the ceiling dropped onto the floor where Patch had just been standing.

'Why did you try and take it off me?' Gyffe snapped.

For a moment Patch hung with his foot back as if he was contemplating kicking Gyffe in the shins. Nevertheless, the foot didn't meet its mark. Instead, Gyffe released him and Patch backed away slipping outside the door, closing it, and with the clank, bolted it.

'What did I tell you?' Crach huffed and puffed, 'you've been betrayed.'

Gyffe thought fast. 'Fetch the wand Crinkum.'

Crinkum leapt into the air and with a spiralling dance intercepted the wand between its teeth. Crach raced towards it.

'Give it here, gargoyle,' said Crach.

Dragoyles, on the whole, are reasonably benign creatures, but there are several things they really don't like. The first is the cold, the second are gargoyles, and the third is when someone calls them a gargoyle.

'I said give it here gargoyle.'

Crinkum dropped the wand and dived at the dwarf. Gyffe crawled over to where it fell. As it danced on the ground, it sent out fractures across the entire surface. Gyffe managed to catch it but not before parts of the floor started to cave in.

'Got it.'

A great hole opened up, dragging Crinkum and Crach down it as they grappled with each other.

'No,' shouted Gyffe but it was too late, they had disappeared into the blackness.

Gyffe made straight for the door, he gave it a push, it remained shut. Patch had locked him in. He looked around the collapsing room for another exit, but the only way out was down into the crumbling abyss. He clung to what was left of the floorboards desperately trying to think of a spell he could cast to elevate or pass him through the other side. He remembered a spell he had never tried before, and if it succeeded, it would allow him to pass through solid matter. Heavy stones crashed from above. Gyffe tried the spell.

'⟨И◊⟨'

Nothing happened. The fireplace gave way, as it fell, smoke poured from its dismantled hearth, filling the room and Gyffe began to feel dizzy. He made one last attempt at the spell, muttering it with as much conviction he could muster.

'⟨И◊⟨'

As his consciousness wore thin, he felt himself sliding into the corridor. Then sliding along the corridor, then up the narrow stairs that led outside. As he resurfaced and was being pulled away, he caught a glimpse of Grimoire's house collapsing into the ravished pit. Wet grass brushed against his body as he slid across the ground, finally coming to a resting halt against a tree.

'I did it,' he said to himself throwing his head back with a chuckle against the trunk.

'You most certainly did,' said a voice.

Gyffe looked towards it to see a man hovering over him. A flash of white hair and matching beard, as bright as snow. The man had his hands planted in the pockets of a shabby brown overcoat, parted in the middle, revealing a green thick woollen buttoned-up waistcoat.

'What a mess,' he said eying the rubble that now made up part of a crater where both houses once stood, 'lucky I came when I did then. Otherwise, you'd have been left under that lot.'

Gyffe groaned but then sprang up quickly. 'My wand?'

'You mean this thing?' The man passed him the rather battered rod.

'A wand is it?'

Gyffe took the wand and slipped it into his boot. 'Yes, and something I perhaps ought not to use again. Who are you?'

'I'm Gerald, Gerald Gardner.' The man extended his hand. 'I was just passing through when I saw a great disturbance ahead, I was told there was a wizard in these parts, thought I might try and find him. Have a chat with him, learn about the ways of magic from an expert.'

'Mage,' said Gyffe, 'and he's long gone. That was his house. It was also my house.'

'Oh, dear.' Gerald knitted his brow, looking very serious indeed. 'Got anywhere else to go?'

'Go? No, nowhere, I've been betrayed.'

'Blimey, you really have had the worst of it. Well, you are welcome to come with me.'

'With you? Where are you going?'

'I plan to get in my car and drive back to Bricket Wood,' said Gerald.

'Your what? Cart? Bricket Wood? Where's that then?'

'A village in England. I intend to hold a coven there, I'm gathering disciples of a group I call Wicca, we plan to keep magic alive.'

'Is it dead?'

'It's not dead, it's just ignored or ridiculed. In some circles it's considered demonic or disturbed. You are welcome to come with. I could always do with someone like you to advise us on the arcane arts,' said Gerald.

'If it means I can somehow get back to Grimoire, then let us not waste another second, it has been a long few centuries.'

'What's your name?'

'Gyffe.'

'And, Gyffe, you also dropped this.' Gerald held up a pocket-sized black-bound book. 'What is it? Some kind of book of shadows?'

Gyffe took the black dragon-hide bound book and slipped it into his tunic. 'Oh, just a book, the black book of Gyffe the Fribbling Squit.'

Printed in Great Britain
by Amazon